UNDINE

BY

OLIVE SCHREINER

WITH AN INTRODUCTION BY
S.C. CRONWRIGHT-SCHREINER

British Library Cataloguing-in-Publication Data
A catalogue record for this book is available from the
British Library

Contents

Olive Schreiner

Olive Schreiner was born on Wittebergen Reserve, Cape Colony (present-day Lesotho) in 1855. After finishing school, she found work as a governess and a schoolteacher, and during her free time began to work on a novel about her experiences in South Africa. When Schreiner had saved enough money, she travelled to Britain, hoping to become a doctor. She lived in London where she began attending lectures at the Medical School, as well as attending socialist meetings. Schreiner met the publisher George Meredith, who in 1883 published her best-known novel, *Story of an African Farm*. A commercial and critical success, it is now seen as a defining work of early feminism – as is her later work, *Women and Labour* (1911).

Over the rest of her life, Schreiner made the acquaintance of a number of figures in London society, including future Prime Minister William Gladstone. In 1889, she returned to South Africa to be with her family. Her brother, William Schreiner, later became prime minister of Cape Colony. Over the next few years she published two collections of short stories, *Dreams* (1891) and *Dream Life and Real Life* (1893). She also became heavily involved in politics, and was a fierce opponent of racism and imperialism. Her 1897 work

Trooper Peter Halkett of Mashonaland (1897) was a strong attack on British rule in South Africa.

At the outbreak of the First World War, Schreiner moved back to Britain. Over the next four years she was active in the peace movement and worked closely with organizations such as the Union of Democratic Control and the Non-Conscription Fellowship. She returned to South Africa in of August 1920, and dying following a heart attack later that year.

INTRODUCTION

HERE, in this novel, which precedes *The Story of an African Farm* and has some curious and interesting facts associated with it, we have Olive Schreiner "Mewing her mighty youth."

Some years before her death Olive Schreiner said to me that, if ever a biography of her were to be written, she would like me to write it, or, failing me, her "oldest and best friend," Havelock Ellis.

I was in London when she died, and wrote to Ellis as soon as possible. Telling him of her wish, I asked him if he would write the biography. This he found himself unable to do, but offered to place at my service all the information he had if I would undertake it. Without delay I engaged quarters near him and got to work. At our first "business" meeting, he brought up the subject of an unfinished novel of Olive's, much to my surprise, for I had never even heard of it. This was *Undine*, the manuscript of which she had placed in his hands in 1884, shortly after they met. I had the manuscript typed and left the original and a carbon copy with him.

But the novel was not complete; the concluding part was missing. On my return to South Africa in March, 1921, I found the missing section among my wife's papers.

It consisted of twenty-two foolscap sheets in two separate lots which connected up unbrokenly with what preceded it. The handwriting is in Olive's large, strong, rapid style, an approximate specimen of which is given on page 228 of her *Letters*. The paper is faded and the matter is clearly a final revision. At some time this manuscript had been posted to "Miss O. Schreiner, c/o Advocate Schreiner, Cape Town," by her mother, whose handwriting is unmistakable. From the official cancellation of the postage stamps I cannot now make out when or where it was posted. The stamps are Cape Colony stamps, long out of date. Well weighing all the facts within my knowledge, I think, however, that the novel was completed in South Africa before she left for England in 1881, that the now-recovered missing section consists of the two parts mentioned in Olive's letter to Ellis of the 20th November, 1884 (given later), that it was taken by her to her mother at Seymour at the end of 1876 (as mentioned in her Ratel Hoek journal later), and left there, or that she left it with her mother in Grahamstown as she passed through on her way to England in February, 1881, and finally that her mother posted it to Advocate Schreiner from Grahamstown after Olive's return to South Africa (which was in November, 1889). There is another interesting fact in connection with this manuscript: on a wrapper tied round the roll I found Olive's description of its contents, written in ink in her own handwriting, "Bit of early novel when I was about 16 years."

We now come to the actual writing of the novel.

The Kimberley Diamond Mine was discovered in July, 1871. The great rush that at once set in towards it soon caused it to be called New Rush, a name it retained until the Camp at the Diamond Fields was proclaimed as Kimberley in July, 1873.

Olive's brother Theo (later a Senator) was one of the early diggers who joined the Camp at New Rush. He was followed by his sister Ettie (later the temperance orator), while their youngest brother, Will (later Prime Minister of Cape Colony), used to travel up from Cape Colony to spend his school holidays working with Theo on his claims. Like other diggers, the Schreiners lived in tents near the edge of the mine, where Kaffir "boys," under an overseer, worked the claims. Theo himself supervised the "washing" and personally did the "sorting."

In 1872 Olive went to visit her brother and sister. Setting out from the little village of Hertzog where her parents lived, not far from Grahamstown, and travelling by passenger coach the hundreds of miles to the Diamond Fields, she arrived at New Rush early in December. During her stay she lived in tents as the others did. There was no other shelter; and a "pretty time" they had of it in the dust, the heat, the violent thunderstorms and the myriad fleas of the Camp.

The first mention of *Undine* appears in her New Rush journal on the 18th June, 1873: "I have finished the first Chapter of *Undine Bock* this morning." [1] At the time she was eighteen years and three months old.

[1] This is her only use of the title *Undine Bock*; thereafter she omitted the *Bock*.

It must not, however, be inferred from this entry that she had only then begun the novel. Among her papers I found (and still have) a small, cheap, paper-covered child's exercise book, part of which she had used for doing her juvenile sums. The colour and condition of the paper, the writing, spelling, and other factors about this little book of sixteen pages indicate, in my opinion, that its contents considerably antedate the manuscript of the book we now have. But they are without doubt part of the novel; for practically the whole of the little one's "scribble" is included in *Undine* as we now have it.

After this entry of the 18th June the next reference to the novel is in her Hertzog journal of the 3rd November, 1873. She "has not yet finished the first chapter of *A Queer Little Girl.*"

From May, 1874, to the end of February, 1875, she was acting as governess at Colesberg. Her journal of this period contains no reference to *Undine*. However, as will presently be seen, she was just about finishing the first draft of it.

In March, 1875, we find her employed at the farm Ganna Hoek (that portion styled Klein Ganna Hoek in the *Life*), teaching the children of Mr. and Mrs. Stoffel Fouché, Dutch farmers. This farm lies in the Karoo mountain-veld of Cradock (Cape Colony) about twenty-five miles southwest of the village and at that time some two hundred miles from the nearest railway. Here, possibly, Olive wrote the whole of the second draft of *Undine*, except for the revision of parts of Ratel Hoek, a farm about sixty miles away, near Tarkastad, in 1876.

A full description of the whole of Ganna Hoek, belonging mainly to the Fouchés and the Cawoods (Olive's intimate friends), is given in the *Life* (pages 103-120). From these pages I now give an extract with photograph, describing the room in which she lived and wrote while engaged on this novel:

"It is the little room under the flat roof of the lean-to the window of which may be seen between the aloe and the ladder; to the right of the ladder is the baking-oven with the kitchen chimmey above it. The door of the oven is through the kitchen wall; the oven is built of brick and has no chimney; a huge fire is made in it, the 'live' coals are then scraped out, the bread is put in and the door closed; in competent hands, this style of oven (universal in the old days) is most excellent, especially for bread, in which the Boer women excel. It will be seen that there was a wall between Olive's room and the kitchen and that these two rooms as well as some other out-rooms were not in the main part of the house but in a flat-roofed lean-to, the roof of which has some stones on it to strengthen its edges against the wind. The front of the house is where the tree stands over the left of the lean-to. In the gable may be seen the door of the loft. Olive's window faces almost north and looks straight up a kloof on the steep side of the mountain, which begins within a few yards. The room was mud-floored and ceilingless. It leaked badly; when the rain was heavy Olive used to put an umbrella over herself and lead the water out of the room by making a small furrow in its mud floor. The room contained a primitive bedstead, a box to hold her clothes, and nothing else (except Mill's *Logic* to read); she used to wash in the little stream in the kloof near by until she secured a basin. Such was the room in which the greater part of *Undine*, the forerunner of *The Story of an African Farm*, was written, and almost certainly part of *An African Farm* itself too. A little way up the kloof, on which her window looked, were great rocks and a pool of water from which the garden was irrigated.... Here large wild trees grew, and here she often saw what she always called 'the long-tailed monkeys,' of which she was very fond, as well as many other untamed veld creatures."

The first reference to *Undine* in her Ganna Hoek journal is in June, 1875: "I mean to try and finish the first copy by the end of July and to have it written out [i.e. id est , revised] by the end of August." Then in July she writes: "Have got *Undine* on board ship" (on her way from England to South Africa). In September: "I am at Mrs. Snappercap's" (a character of the novel).... "Mean to try and finish *Undine* by the end of this month, and write it out next." In October: "*Undine* is at New Rush. Hope to get it done by the end of the year." At the end of December she has "nearly finished *Undine*." On the 26th January, 1876: "Afternoon, I have finished *Undine*; I must read out or correct and new-write if I can and get it done before I leave." Her last entry at Ganna Hoek is in April, 1876: "I have made up my mind not to have *Undine* published, not yet at least."

She left Ganna Hoek at the end of April, 1876, and went as governess at Ratel Hoek. Soon after this she is writing *Thorn Kloof*, the first title given to the novel afterwards to be known as *The Story of an African Farm*. In July, 1876, she enters in her journal that she has not yet decided whether to finish *Undine* or *Thorn Kloof* first, and adds (apropos of *Undine*): "I have just finished reading over as far as I have written her out (a very wicked woman) and I am not disgusted," and she hopes to take the completed novel to her mother at the end of the year. On the 23rd September, 1876, we have her last reference to *Undine*: "I think I shall finish and read over *Undine* tomorrow. Then to the new work [*Thorn Kloof*]." [1]

Olive first met Havelock Ellis in March, 1884.

[1] The extracts from her journals do not comprise all her references to *Undine*.

They soon became great friends and before long she had placed the manuscript of *Undine* in his hands. A month or two later he wrote to her about it. She answered on the 24th November: "I quite forget about Aunt Margaret. I don't know what her relation to Frank was. I know that Ettie was in my mind when I drew her and Ettie's love for Theo. Not the woman of talent and eloquent lecturer, but my soft-hearted sister Ettie who used to stroke my hair. I had quite forgotten that there was such a character in the book. It's not finished either; I left off in the middle of the last chapter and tore up the half I had written. I ought to have burnt it long ago, but the biographical element in it made me soft to it."

With reference to the last sentence of this letter, it may be added that, as her journals show, she, alas, wrote and destroyed many of her writings. She told me she was so weary of *The Story of an African Farm* when it was finished (about the end of 1880) that she nearly threw it into the large dam at Lelie Kloof, where she was then employed as a governess.

This novel, the first book she ever wrote, is the last of her writings I have to publish. It has been a privilege to complete my work and give to the world since her death *The Life of Olive Schreiner*, *The Letters of Olive Schreiner*, *Thoughts on South Africa*, *Stories, Dreams and Allegories*, *From Man to Man*, and now *Undine*—the last five being, of course, by herself. During her lifetime she published *The Story of an African Farm*, *Dreams*, *Dream Life and Real Life*, *Woman and Labour* and *Trooper Peter Halket of Mashonaland.*

S. C. CRONWRIGHT-SCHREINER.

THE STRAND, CAPE PROVINCE, SOUTH AFRICA, 13th September, 1928.

I.
A QUEER LITTLE CHILD

KAROO, red sand, great mounds of round iron stones, and bushes never very beautiful to look at and now almost burned into the ground by the blazing summer's sun. An old Dutch farmhouse built of the brightest red brick to match the ground and stones; an old stone wall broken down here and there at irregular intervals, as if to allow for the ready ingress and egress of the hundred enterprising goats, whose delight it is daily to regale themselves on the deformed peach trees and leafless cabbage stalks which the enclosure contains; an old tent-waggon, whose tent and floor have long gone the way of all flesh—wood flesh—into the fire; an ancient willow tree, which stands vainly trying to reflect itself in a small pond of thick red fluid, and under which may at all times be seen a couple of dirty and benighted ducks, who there disport themselves under the happy delusion of its being water.

All these parts compose a picture in which, when looked at by daylight, it were hard work to find the slightest trace of beauty; but tonight, penetrated in every nook and corner by the cold white light of an almost full moon, there is a strange weird beauty, a beauty which the veriest sheep-souled Boer that ever smoked pipe or wore vel-skoen, might feel if he had but one ray of light left in him.

It was a silent night. Even the great dogs had crept to sleep under the old tent-waggon, and nothing living or moving was to be seen except a small child and a smaller ape who were perched in one of the gaps of the stone wall.

There they had sat for the last hour, never moving but very busy cogitating, if one might judge from the grave expression of both faces. Likely the smaller pondered on the dire injustice of tying him up all day and giving him orange peel in place of orange pulp, and uncracked almonds, which all the world knew he could not break. His thoughts might have been the most profoundly philosophical, however, if judged by the appearance of his small black countenance—abstruse inquiries into the nature, origin, and destiny of the moon, whose course he was following with eyes hardly less grave and earnest than the large brown pair above him.

He was wrapped up in the end of the small blue pinafore which the child had on, the only parts visible being the small wizard-like face and a small black hand, with which he held his chin and every now and then raised for a soft sympathetic pat of the little white hand that served as chin-rest to the white, dark-eyed face above him. The child might have been ten years old, but she looked much less as she sat there, perched on the top of a large round stone with her thin little legs drawn up under her in a queer little fashion of her own.

"Socrates," she said, presently. The monkey turned his soft brown eyes and fixed them full on hers.

"I wish we knew," said the child.

Socrates gave a long sigh in answer and turned the gaze of his great sad eyes back to the slowly moving moon.

"Come to prayers, come to prayers," shouted a stentorian voice from one of the back windows, and Socrates' reflections for that night were ended. He was tied up to his stand; and with a kiss on the crown of his little grey head the owner of the blue pinafore left him and went into the house.

The house, as we have said, was Dutch, built in the true Dutch style, with one large front room, from which opened six or eight cabin-like apartments to serve as bedrooms; and with that indispensable of all Dutch farmhouses overhead—a great loft.

In the front room were two large glass cupboards let into the wall, which in the days of their old Dutch proprietor had been wont to contain dolls, earthenware, and all the wealth and glory of the household, and which even now, in spite of their being filled with books, had an uncomfortably Dutch appearance. The room was well furnished, and lighted by a great lamp standing on the centre-table. Before it, with an open Bible and Prayer Book, sat the farmer: an English Africander with nothing worthy of remark about him, if it were not the unusually fine development of his tall muscular figure and the unusually large amount of yellow hair upon his face. There were five others in the room—his wife, a delicate, refined, fair little woman who reclined on the sofa—his son, handsome and bright-eyed, and now home for the holidays—and two little Dutch girls, grey-eyed, yellow-haired, pudding-faced, who were here to share with his step-daughter the instruction of the very stiff and upright individual who sat on a chair near the door. This individual wore three curls on each side of her head and carried a large wart on the tip of her chin.

"Late for prayers again, Undine," she said, as the owner of the little blue pinafore slipped in at the door and took her way to the nearest seat.

No one else took any notice of her entrance, and the chapter being finished they kneeled down to pray. Undine did not listen to the prayer but to the great red clock overhead, that was ticking away such solemn words, the child thought, as she bent below it:

"Another week gone, another day gone. What have you done? We never come back, we moments; we fly, but we never return, never, never, tick, tick. What have you done with us? If you do the best you can with all the rest of us, you can never bring one of us back, never, never, tick, tick."

Undine tried to listen to the prayer, but the old clock's voice was louder.

"Tick, tick," cried the inexorable old clock, "what good have you ever done? How are you better able to die now than you were last week? You are nearer death, but are you ready, ready, ready, tick, tick, tick?"

Undine tried to listen to the prayer again, and she caught these words: "Thousands, O Lord, are going to destruction every moment."

"Yes, yes, yes," said the clock, "tick, tick, hell, hell, going, going, going, thousands, thousands, thousands, tick, tick, tick, tick."

She could kneel there while the old clock told only of her own sins and fate, but now—when every tick talked of half the world, for whom there was no help, no hope, who were going, going, going—she felt as though she were being suffocated and the walls and roof were throbbing and coming down on her. She leaped up from her knees, and was recalled to a sense of things present only by being very sharply pulled onto them again. Fortunately the prayer was almost ended, and when they rose there were at once so many human voices trying to make themselves heard that the voice of the old wooden prophet was quickly drowned.

"Undine, my dear, I really must report your conduct to your mamma; it really is most reprehensible," said the stiff and upright individual. "You surely have time enough in which to run about; you might forget your play and worship

God, when you come *here*. Your mamma thinks so. Do you not?"

The lady thus appealed to not only fully endorsed the opinion, but also, on hearing the nature of the offence, ordained that henceforth the offender's seat should be in the centre of the room, beside her stepfather, and so to speak under the eye of the assembly. This was intended as a direful chastisement, but the child's thoughts were still occupied with the ominous tickings of the old clock, and she would have cared nothing just then if they had sentenced her to sit next some savage king of Timbuctoo who makes his meals off little girls. She stood there before them, with the end of the blue pinafore twisted round one small arm which the other was nursing and patting as tenderly as if it had been Socrates.

"Really, Undine, you are the hardest child to manage. There is no need to put on that look of proud indifference; go to bed at once and let me see no more of you tonight," said her mother; and the child took up her light and went. Soon she had put it out and crept into bed, but she could not forget the old clock; and how dark the room was! Perfect, boundless, endless darkness it might be, for anything she could see; like that silent darkness which surrounds poor lost souls and is all the answer they get when they cry aloud to God. She pulled the cover over her head and buried it under the pillows; but whoever has tried these means of dodging disagreeable thoughts knows how signally they always fail. She found this out; for by and by a small white face showed itself above the blankets and a pair of troubled eyes looked out into the surrounding darkness.

"Dear God! great God!" cried the little child, covering her face with both hands, "You who are so very happy and great and strong, who can do all things, O dear God! save them. They are going, going, forever, forever, O God! God!"

She lay still for some minutes and then burst forth again, this time in a perfect agony:

"O God! great God! save just one soul tonight because I pray. I know that I am wicked and will never be saved, but I pray with faith; save, oh save one soul, for my prayer. Great God! God! God!"

She sat up and buried her face in both her trembling hands. What was the use of her praying—she who did not love God, who could not believe, who could never be saved? How easy it was to understand how the great Son of God could come down to die for souls. The child felt that night as though she, too, could have died to save only a few, a few souls from the great company of the God-hated who were passing over the edge to darkness. How many had gone since she came into that room tonight! How many through the long dim ages of the past! The old Greeks and Romans, and the wild millions of Asia; and how many would pass over long after she had taken her place in the great company and vanished into sin and woe forever! Before and behind her seemed to stretch a chain of endless pain and anguish.

After a time she lay down and tried to close her eyes and drop asleep; but now it seemed as if already she had passed into that unknown land, prepared by God for the souls at whom he laughs. In Dante's hell there were fire and fellowship, earth and pain, but in hers there was nothing so merciful or so material. She seemed in a wide void in which there was only endless space and blackness, and she had not even two hands, the one of which might touch the other and in touching find fellowship; and when she cried aloud her voice fell dead upon the air. There was only emptiness, and black space, above, around, below, and she was one alone. Oh, how the silence ached! One throb of pain, one touch, one sound, how blessed they would be.

An indescribable terror seized the child. Such must be death, eternal death, the death of the wicked, changeless and everlasting as the throne of the God who made it. She crept out of bed trem- trembling bling and lay down on the cold mud floor; that at least was hard and solid, and it seemed to calm her. She pressed her face onto it, and a few burning tears fell on it; then she lay as still as though she were asleep. How comforting it was, that solid earth; but it was dead and cold, and she would like the touch of something warmer; so after a time she got up and, noiselessly opening the door, stood in the large front room. It was dark and quite still but for the ticking of the old clock and the sound of her own breath. She stood for a minute listening; then she crept on till her fingers touched a door at the far end of the room. After a little pressure it opened, and she went in. There were two beds in the room, both occupied, and she kneeled down at the foot of the nearest and stretched out her hand. It came in contact with what she was in search of—a small foot, soft and warm and full of life. She held it for some moments in both hands, and then, afraid of waking the sleeper, rose to go, noiselessly and softly as she had come.

How the owner of the foot—one of the grey-eyed, cheese-faced little Dutch girls—would have wondered and been mystified, could she have watched the proceedings of her little white-nightgowned visitor, who, feeling her way softly by chairs and tables, soon found herself again in her own room.

She was comforted, but not sufficiently; so she drew from between the mattresses on her bed a small brown New Testament. Pressing it close to her side with one little arm, with the other she dragged a large wooden chair to the window; and with its aid, and that of a stool, climbed up into the window seat. Pushing her hand through a broken pane, she sent the heavy wooden shutter flying back on its hinges. A flood of white moonlight fell into the room, and the face of the moon herself looked in—on the little tumbled bed and the whitewashed walls and the mite of a thing, with its little white nightgown and bare feet, perched up in the window.

The mite of a thing closed her eyes tight and opened her book, turning the leaves over and over again, and at last brought down a small finger upon one of them. She opened her eyes and stooped down to read by the moonlight the words on which it had alighted; they were these—"Which was the son of Melchi, which was the son of Addi, which was the son of Cosam, which was the son of Elmodam, which was the son of Er."

She closed the book and sat looking at the cover in silence, with very much the expression of Socrates when lost in the contemplation of a nut he had vainly endeavoured to crack. Faith is strong, however, and reason weak, at ten years; so the brown comforter was opened again; and, after the fashion of the Apostles and good men of old, Providence was appealed to.

This time the words were these—"Strive to enter in at the straight gate, for many I say unto you shall seek to enter in, and shall not be able."

She did not close the book this time but sat looking at its open pages with her eyebrows slightly bent; then she caught the book up tightly in one hand and flung it from her with such force that it left the story of its journey written in a large brown dent on the whitewashed wall opposite. She threw her head down on the window seat and cried long and bitterly; but by and by, when she grew quieter, she sat up and pressed her little burning cheek against the window pane. How calm and still the outside world was; so far removed from all passion and strife, damnation, fire and brimstone; so strong, so self-contained. How peacefully the great round stones lay resting on each other. Through that subtle sympathy which binds together all things, and to stumps and rocks gives a speech which even we can understand, the night spoke to the little child the sweet words of comfort which she had looked for in vain in the brown Testament. She left off thinking and only sat and listened, and the sweet night wind blew in through the broken pane and touched her softly, till the weary eyelids closed and the little head found rest once more on the window seat.

Of course Undine was late next morning, late even for Sunday morning. Socrates, in despair of ever getting his breakfast, sat disconsolate on the top of his box, making believe to eat his tail, and every now and then raising his hands to his head and slowly rubbing them across his forehead, as if still suffering from the effect of too much moonlight thought.

It was going to be a sweltering day; even now it gave one an unpleasant sensation to look at the little hills of red round stones scattered here and there and acting the part of great reflectors; as though man and herb were not desiccated and burnt red enough without their help. Indoors the blue flies buzzed. In spite of the soothing effect of more than half-closed shutters all sat down to breakfast feeling mortally aggrieved, though hardly knowing in what respect, and, according to their several dispositions, desiring to have it out with some one or lapsing into silence.

When Undine came to the table she was met with the usual: "Late again, my dear; surely going to bed when *you* do, you *might* get up a little earlier. It is this sleeping so much that makes you so incurably stupid. Sannie and Annie were up hours ago," said the governess, casting an approving glance at the two little maidens opposite, who by their earnest patronage of mutton chops and fat were incontrovertibly proving their Africander origin.

"They went to bed much later than you and were up earlier, and have done their hair much better than you," continued her instructress, whose ideas were so truly correct, feminine, and orthodox, that they might all have been placed in an ordinary breakfast saucer and left there forever, without the least fear of their ever running over.

The meal being ended, the farmer went out to bully the herdsmen for not having let the sheep out earlier, and to saunter about till the heat should drive him in; while his wife hied to the nether regions, where bitter and clamorous war was being waged between Hendrik and Gobalee as to the possession of the sheep's-head-and-feet. The two little

Dutch girls stood in the kitchen doorway, and for once the dawning of a light, which if it had arisen might have been called animation, shone in their placid countenances as they drank in every word and even now and then inserted one.

Undine collected some bits of bread, took half a green mielie [1] and a cup of water, and, putting on her great brown kappie, went out to visit Socrates in the yard. He was glad of the contents of cup and plate, but quickly satisfied himself and began playing with his mielie, [2] now throwing it from him with disdain and gazing up into the sky with an air of deep abstraction, as though completely unconscious of its existence, then seizing it up, taking a bite and hugging it to him, with an expression of earnestness so comical it might have set a Methodist parson laughing on his way to class meeting. Undine did not laugh; she sat down on the ground beside him and looked at him, wondering if he really felt so happy, or only played so wildly because his heart was heavy. She wondered if he ever wished to be anything in the wide world but himself, and yet didn't see anything that he liked better; wondered if he ever longed to die, and yet wished never to die, and nothing in the world ever to die; wondered if it made him feel queer to look up at that little white fleecy cloud in the blue sky overhead; wondered what the little cloud meant and how it came there and why it came there, and why anything was where it was, and why the world was the world, and the sun the sun, and she, she; and why—

She could not wonder any more, for two strong hands were shaking her so that the little white cloud, Socrates, the blue sky and red earth, were all jumbled up together.

[1] The mielies ("corn") being on the cob.

[2] Used them in S. Africa both for a single "pip" and for the cob with the pips on. Here it is obviously used in the latter sense.

"Do you wish to ruin your complexion completely, you wicked child, that you sit here staring up into the sky as if you had never seen it before and were bereft of all your senses? Get your kappie from that ape and come into the house at once."

For Mr. Socrates had possessed himself of the large brown kappie and seemed in no hurry to restore it. Finds are keeps according to the code, and it was only after a world of persuasion had been lavished upon him that he very gingerly descended from his box and, with an air of melancholy resignation and a touch of condescension, delivered it to its owner. Then he sat gravely following with his eyes the little blue pinafore and brown kappie as they vanished into the house, and, there being nothing left worth his looking at, he then clambered up into his box to take a doze.

The sheep's-head-and-feet quarrel had been settled, and when Undine entered the front room she found the two little Dutch girls demurely seated on two chairs with their hymn books in their hands, learning their Sunday lessons. Undine, too, got her hymn book down from the shelf, but instead of following the virtuous example before her, she placed her book on the floor, laid herself across a chair, and in this very highly unorthodox position had just composed herself to learn, when she was asked if she had not yet rested enough and were going to sleep again. Of course there was nothing for it but to sit up and learn away steadily till the hour arrived at which, every Sunday morning, the three scholars were marched off into a side room to receive such religious instruction as was suited to their limited capacities and tender years. The first part of the program, which consisted in the recitation of lessons, was soon over. Then bibles were produced. The little brown Testament was not one of them—false friend it might sometimes be, but friend for all that, and not to be brought out for common eyes to gaze on.

The stiff and upright individual sat in a large armchair, and before her the two little Dutch girls on high-backed riem-bottomed chairs, while Undine took possession of a green waggon-chest that stood near the door.

The chapter chosen for their perusal and consideration was the twenty-fifth of Matthew, and when it was concluded each was in turn required to ask some question bearing on its contents. The eldest of the Dutch girls—on whom the heat, the darkness of the room, and the exertion of spelling out the long English words had had an almost stupefying effect—sat for some moments gazing at the face of her oracle with an expression of hopeless vacancy. At length a happy thought occurred to her: Were the virgins men or women? The mental effort required for the birth of this question seemed so completely to have exhausted all her powers of mind as to make it highly probable that the reply of the oracle was lost upon her and that she remained forever in total ignorance on the momentous subject of her inquiry.

It was now the turn of number two, who, with astonishing brightness, asked if the bridesmaids wore white muslin dresses and carried eau-de-Cologne bottles in their pockets. This searcher after truth having been satisfied, it was Undine's turn to in- inquire quire and learn. But that young lady sat upon the green box, noiselessly tapping it with her heels and fixing on the skin carpet that attention which should have been bestowed on her worthy instructress.

"Well, Undine, my dear, what have you to ask?"

"I understand that chapter," said Undine, without raising her eyes to the face of her interlocutor.

"You do, my dear! Well, then I suppose we had better reverse the order of things and I will question you. What was the oil which was generally burnt on all such occasions in the East?"

"I don't know," said Undine, very composedly.

"I thought that you understood everything that this chapter contained. I very soon find that you do not. You are wofully ignorant, my dear," said the teacher.

"I did not notice that there was anything said about the kinds of oil," responded Undine; "otherwise I should not have said that I understood it."

The questioner was fairly at her wits' end, but she shifted her ground. "What does the thirty-first verse speak of, my dear?"

"The judgment of the world," said Undine.

"And what does he say to the good people on his right and the bad on his left hand?"

"He says to the good people, 'Come, you blessed, inherit the kingdom prepared for you from the foundation of the world'; and to the others, 'Go, you cursed, into the everlasting fire'."

"And what lesson does this teach us, my dear?"

"That God has prepared a heaven for the people he means to save and a hell for the people he means to burn," said Undine, very gravely, never raising her eyes from the carpet on which they rested.

There was a pause; then came the remark: "Hardly the right way of putting it, my dear. It teaches you that you should be a very good little girl, so that when you die God may take you to heaven and not send you to hell to burn forever and ever."

"I would much sooner be wicked and go to hell than be good only because I was afraid of going there," said Undine, now raising her eyes from the carpet and fixing them on the horror-stricken countenance of her instructress.

"Undine!" gasped forth that unfortunate individual. "Undine, what *do* you mean? You were always an evil and wicked child, but you grow viler every day."

"Yes," said Undine, getting off the box, with a face alternately as red as the sprigs on her little print dress and as pale as her little white pinafore—"yes, I don't want to go to heaven, and, if God wants to, he can send me to hell and I will never again ask him not to, *never*. I know I'm very wicked, but I'm not half so wicked or so cruel as he is. Nothing is, not even the devil. The devil is glad when we go to hell, but he did not make us on purpose to send us there, and he did not make hell, and he did not make himself, and I'm sorry for him. I believe he tries to be good and God won't let him, that's what I believe," said Undine, who, with her wild dark eyes and clenched hands, looked more like some spirit who had just arrived from the regions of which she spoke than a carefully-brought-up little Christian receiving her Sunday lesson.

If she had been Medusa her gaze could not more completely have paralysed her opponent, who sat there as if turned into stone; while the two little pudding-faces looked from one to the other with wild astonishment in their big grey eyes.

Undine clasped her little hands behind her and walked slowly out of the room.

It was the first time that she had ever given utterance to the evil thoughts with which her small and, as she believed, devil-ridden soul was haunted; they were fiendishly evil thoughts, all of them, she knew; but, if they were hers, why should she not give them utterance?

Her little heart swelled so it well nigh suffocated her, but it was with a sense of freedom and strength that she was pacing up and down her little room, when she heard the key turn in the door.

It was pleasant enough to think of having a day all to herself with no fear of interruption and no company but her books; but to think of that clink of the key and know that, wishing it or not, she was a prisoner, made her stamp her feet upon the ground as she walked up and down and to rebel in her bitter little heart against all powers, human and divine.

The world was not the place for her, she was feeling persuaded; she was not fit for it. Why then had she been made so bad, and put into it? It was no use saying she ought to be good; she couldn't. The devil did not come to other people and make them think such thoughts as he made her. She felt herself very much aggrieved by these attacks from the infernal regions, and presently became very wrathful. Then reaction set in and she grew sleepy. Lying down upon the floor, she was soon sound asleep, dreaming of the glorious time when she would be a woman and would know everything and be loved by everyone, and when she would be free.

The ringing of the dinner bell wakened her; and, finding that nothing in the shape of food was sent her, she kneeled down before her little bookshelf in search of refreshment of another order. There were delicious fairy tales—*Arabian Nights* whose old torn pages seemed to emit an odour of myrrh and roses caught from the gardens of Bagdad—Hans Andersen's beautiful song in prose about the mermaid and the young prince—but these and others were of course not to be looked at. It would have hurt the child's conscience as much to have read a fairy tale on Sunday as to have told a lie; one of the crimes which always came to haunt her in the dark watchful hours of the night was her having read, on one never-to-be-forgotten Sunday afternoon, a part of that story of "The Mermaid and the Prince."

So Undine, rebel though she was, touched not, looked not, at the wicked thing, but from its hiding-place behind the other books brought forth a large, dull-coloured, leather-bound volume.

It was *A Careful and strict Enquiry into the Modern Prevailing Notions of the Freedom of Will, which is supposed to be essential to Moral Agency, Virtue and Vice, Reward and Punishment, Praise and Blame*, by Jonathan Edwards, A.B. They would have laughed at her for reading such an old man's book and one with so grandiloquent and lengthy a title, so it was always stowed safely away behind the others where there was no fear of its being discovered by prying eyes. The faded ribbon place-marker had already found its way into the middle of the book, and the child was soon deeply absorbed in sections eight, nine and ten of section two, in part three. She did not get through more than these, for each sentence was found so pregnant with profound and misty thoughts that she was obliged to read it carefully, and often re-read it, before it could be dismissed.

There was a strange contrast between the little reader and her great brown book as she sat there on the floor on that Sunday afternoon. The child so warm, with the wild blood dancing in every vein, looking out so eagerly into the world, so ready to give and take—the book so old, so dead, with the life thoughts of another generation petrified in its old yellow leaves, now probably being read for the last time.

The book had belonged to her own father, who, much to the grief of his father, had turned aside from the paths of truth and Arminianism, to the ways of Calvinism and error, and in those evil ways had died.

About three o'clock the key turned and one of the little Dutch girls put her face in at the door.

"You can come out when you like," she said. Undine did not even raise her eyes from the book, determining to show that she by no means objected to being made a prisoner in her own room; and she would in all probability have remained where she was until called to tea, had she not suddenly remembered Socrates. Of course pride must be swallowed and his wants attended to; so with an air of extreme indifference she made her way through the front room and, having got a mug of water and thrown a large damp towel over the brown kappie, went out into the yard.

She found Socrates lying on the floor of his box, quite exhausted with the heat and very glad to get under the shade of the damp towel. Loosening him from the stand, she carried him down to the little dam, where, under the scant shade of the willow- tree, her brother Frank lay reclining on his back. He had thrown open his jacket and waistcoat, more from force of habit than from reason, one would think; for the wind, like the breath from an oven, seemed, in place of cooling, to blight and desiccate all it touched. He was a fine specimen of an English Africander, tall and broad, with a fair handsome face, though rather sleepy-looking just now as he lay with his legs raised against the trunk of the old tree and his hat pulled half over his eyes. With one hand he kept it there while with the other he picked up small bits of baked earth wherewith to pelt the miserable ducks who, red, dirty, and hot, were endeavouring to swim in diluted mud by way of improving their condition.

Undine sat down close to the trunk of the tree, for that cast a small shadow if the branches did not; and for some minutes nothing was said.

"Had him that time," muttered Frank at last, as a more than usually lucky hit caught the old drake in the eye.

"I wonder why you do that," said Undine; "everything is miserable in the whole world."

The only response to this observation was another throw, but presently he said, "So you've been in the wars today, little woman, eh?"

Undine made no reply, but stroked Socrates softly the wrong way.

"Too bad to make you go without your dinner, little woman, wasn't it?"

"I don't mind that one bit," said Undine, "but I wish I had never been born. I'm miserable, and nobody loves me."

"Why, I do, and we all of us do, though you are such a queer little coon," answered Frank lazily.

"Yes, that's just it," said Undine, gravely tying Socrates' tail into a knot as she spoke, much to that gentleman's dissatisfaction. "Yes, that's just it; you only care about me because I'm your sister; you call me queer and strange; you don't like me one bit—only Socrates."

"Well, that is good. How do you know that Socrates likes *you*, and not the bread and butter you bring him?" asked Frank.

"I know he likes me," answered Undine, very indignantly. "Can't I see it? Don't I know it? When we sit together of an evening, I can feel he is thinking just what I am, and when I talk to him he understands me. That is what I hate," said Undine, twisting at the tail more vigorously than ever; "people don't know anything about it, and they say he hasn't got a soul. How do *they* know, I should like to know? If only people would not talk till they knew, I think the world would be a much nicer place."

Frank said nothing, but laughed, and directed a bit of mud straight at the tip of Socrates' black nose, who merely opened his eyes and closed them again very solemnly.

"I wish I were one of those ducks," remarked Undine, presently.

"I don't; they look hot," said Frank; "and I thought you said, just now, everything in the whole world was miserable."

"Yes, but not so very miserable because they don't think; at least, perhaps they do; but they've no bibles, you see, and I don't think the devil ever tempts them. It would not be worth his trouble, they are so small."

"If he paid visits only on account of size, I expect you would not see much of him," said her brother, with an amused expression on his face. "Are bibles your great trouble?"

"Yes," said Undine, unhesitatingly. "Sometimes I feel quite good, and I am sitting and reading, and I come to something that is quite different from what it was somewhere else. Then the devil makes me think, How can two things that say the opposite both be true? And then I feel wicked and I can't go on reading any more. Sometimes, too, when I'm praying and I feel as though I loved God very much, I remember all at once how it says in the Bible that he never forgives anyone for nothing, but always makes some one suffer pain first; and I remember all the other cruel things it tells about him; and then I hate him, and for a long time I can't pray again. Oh dear!" she said after a little pause. "I wish the world belonged to me. I would make it much better; I would let all the devils out of hell and love them and make them good, so there would be no one to tempt the people any more. Did you ever feel so wicked as I do when you were little like me?" asked Undine, looking earnestly at him, as though with the vague hope that his answer might be in the affirmative.

"No, I should rather think not," was the answer. "I used to make little clay oxen and train kids in an old box and enjoy myself; that is what I used to do when I was your age."

Undine heaved a little weary sigh and looked at the ducks. "I wonder if there are any people in the world who feel like I do and who have such wicked thoughts," she said at last.

"Of course there are, and much wickeder, too; there are people who don't believe the Bible is true, or anything else, and they write books also."

"Do they?" said Undine. "I wish I could read them. Have you ever?"

"No," said Frank; "it's too much bother; but I will, when I'm a man;" and pulling his hat lower over his eyes, he either made believe to do so or really went to sleep.

Undine did not go away, but sat at his feet, nursing Socrates and watching the ducks, till the koppies began to cast long shadows and the fast cooling air told that sunset was not far off.

By and by the back door of the house opened and the whole family appeared equipped for their Sunday evening walk—all, with the exception of the smallest Dutch girl, who, complaining of a headache, was left to keep Undine company.

"Take care of everything; get into no mischief; and above all remember that it is Sunday," were the parting injunctions which they received as the group, which now included Frank, moved off.

The two children stood still watching them till they passed out of sight. Then Undine, after crying and praying half the night, and reading Edwards and meditating half the day, began to discover that, she was neither anchorite nor saint, but only a very young animal with much wild blood in its young veins that needed circulating. It may have been the evening's cool that made her conscious of this, for it seemed to have an inebriating effect upon Socrates, who leaped, grinned, and turned somersets in a manner truly astonishing.

"I wonder," said Undine, "if Socrates and I were to run a race, which of us would beat"; and without waiting for a reply, she set about testing the matter at once. With one end of his chain held firmly in her hand they set off, but had not gone thirty paces when it had slipped out and Socrates, chain and all, was making his way to the nearest koppie, with jingling, screeching and leaping, much to the mingled horror and delight of his little pursuer. The delight soon vanished, however, for, the koppie reached, Mr. Socrates felt himself quite in his own element, and absolutely refused to be cozened by soft words or specious promises. Seating himself on the top of a large round stone, he would very leisurely stretch out his legs, scratch himself, and then look up into the blue sky with an air of melancholy abstraction; this till his breathless pursuer was within half a foot of him; then, with a whirl, a cry, and a somerset, off to another and more inaccessible stone, round which his little pursuer might dance and beseech in vain, leaping to catch the tip of the chain he left hanging almost within reach of her fingers. It is uncertain how long this game might have continued had not the idea entered Socrates' small head that more fun might be got from scampering over the roofs at home than by remaining where he was.

Accordingly, he was off like an arrow, while Undine followed him breathlessly, minus one shoe and with more rents in her garments than could well be counted. Arrived at the house, she found the exemplary Sennie standing exactly where and as she had left her; except that she had placed one finger in her mouth and partly turned her head to look at Socrates, who was now on the roof of the house, busily occupied in pulling out thatch and working away with the greatest dispatch and precision.

Undine quickly saw that, if this were allowed to go on for many minutes, he would have worked his way into the loft and perhaps to a bloody death as the reward of his evil deeds.

What was to be done? She looked at the little Dutch girl in despair; the little Dutch girl looked at her.

"He is naughty," said that little maiden at length, and then slowly replaced the finger she had taken out of her small mouth. Undine turned away in disgust; there was no help to be got from her, and nothing for it but to climb the roof herself and capture him.

With much difficulty a long ladder was brought which reached just to the top of the wall; and this was soon mounted. Once there, how to get on to the ridge was the question; for at every touch the old thatch crumbled away by handfuls, and she had not crawled many inches before it seemed inevitable that she should soon find herself deposited among the skins in the loft or with the thatch upon the ground.

"You will fall down and die," said the little Dutch girl, very deliberately, as she watched Undine's perilous ascent with almost as much interest as Socrates, who had now taken his seat on one of the gables, and with his chin resting on his hand was contemplating her movements most attentively.

Undine took no notice of either, but continued to climb, doing more harm at every move than Socrates in twenty. The ridge was gained at last, after infinite trouble, but not so Socrates. He waited till her fingers touched his tail; and then, with that appendage cocked high in air, walked off very quietly to the other gable, where he ensconced himself far more comfortably than his little pursuer found it possible to do at hers. There was no getting down again, for the first step down would have been on the ground; there was nothing to be done but sit still and wait. Consequently the appalling and shocking spectacle which met the eyes of the upper powers, on their return home, was Undine, shoeless, kappieless and torn, seated on the ridge and holding on with one arm to the gable, while at the other end Socrates, with clanking chain and tail in air, was dancing a true devil's quadrille. Never were worthy parents and instructors, on their return from a quiet Sabbath ramble, met by so horrific and wrath-rousing a sight.

A second ladder was quickly got and Undine safety deposited upon the ground, where she was instantly marched off into the house to answer for her evil conduct.

"How did you get into this plight, you wicked, wicked little girl?" said her mother.

Undine stood with her hands crossed and her eyes fixed on the one little white toe that had forced its way out of the stocking.

"I did not mean to," she said, feeling very contrite and not a little ashamed of herself.

"Did not mean to! Of course not! You never mean to do anything that you do. The wind loosened Socrates and blew you both up onto the roof of the house! Of course it did; we all know that it did."

Undine felt very much inclined to say that she was sorry and was not going to do so any more; then she remembered that saying so might make her punishment less, so she stood still and looked down at her toe.

The lean and lanky individual now struck in her note.

"Undine, my dear Undine," she said in a very low and subdued voice, "if you continue this course of action, what will become of your immortal soul? What will become of it?"

This was too much for Undine who had stood still to receive her bullying, filled with contrition and repentance; it raised all the evil in her nature. "I know I'm wicked and I don't care, and I don't care what becomes of my soul, and I'm not afraid of anything," said Undine, lifting up her face and throwing back her long tangled hair defiantly.

"Was there ever in this world so evil disposed and ungodly a child?" said her spiritual guide, shaking her head solemnly. "Go to bed, Undine; go to bed; I shall say no more to you."

"Good-night," said Undine and she walked off to her room with almost a smile upon her face. But once there and alone, she flung her tired little body across the foot of the bed and cried bitterly.

"Oh, I wish I was dead! I wish I was dead! There is nobody like me, and nobody loves me. Oh, I wish I was dead!" And at last, without undressing, fell asleep.

II.
UNDINE'S JOTTINGS

'TWAS a bright summer afternoon, just three weeks after my arrival in England. We were expecting visitors, and Aunt Margaret and I had taken our needlework out among the rose trees in the garden.

My brother Frank lolled beside us on the grass, pulling flowers to pieces and showering the leaves over Aunt Margaret's golden hair and white dress. He had changed in the three years that had passed since last I saw him, and had grown noble and handsome enough, I thought, even to possess the beautiful woman on whom his eyes were resting. In my estimation no one else was worthy to own her; certainly not my grandfather, whom I could not learn to like. He reminded me, when I first saw him, of the ox hides so often seen lying near the little dam at home, which had once been damp but by dint of lying in the sun had been reduced to a stone-like mass of wrinkles and lines; and he was so tall and thin. For a long time I never could see him rise from his seat without having recalled to my mind the image of an earthworm creeping out of the ground, which unfolds and unfolds itself to unimagined lengths. He had more resemblance to the skin than to the earthworm, however; for he was mentally as ossified and incapable of growth as any ox hide under the sun. Only in connection with Aunt Margaret did there seem a trace of softness in his nature, and it could not be otherwise. Nature gives to a few persons to have the influence of sunshine on all they touch—silently softening, warming, melting it—and she was one. I worshipped her; for in those days I had not eaten of the tree of knowledge, and worshipped and thought perfect all I loved.

I did not care for my grandmother nor yet dislike her. She was a weak, nervous little old woman, who had had all the soul pressed out of her long ago, and whose trembling little hands I never saw at rest for an instant, except she were asleep.

On that summer afternoon we three sat there, feeling very happy. They because they were together, and I because the roses were beautiful and the sky blue and they glad. The work had dropped from my hands and I had just got into a delicious dream, in which rosebuds, princes and spirits were largely concerned, when Frank tossed a great white rosebud into my face.

"At your old work again," he said, laughing. "You've no idea," turning to Aunt Margaret, "what evil thoughts are always fermenting in that little innocent-looking head. It's my decided opinion that in a pre-state of existence she was a Buddhist philosopher, or something else equally disagreeable and full of contemplations, and at her rebirth she did not become quite rejuvenised or lose all her old habits; otherwise

I can't account for her," said Frank, turning round onto his back, while Aunt Margaret and I laughed.

"It's all very well to laugh," he continued, "but she is awfully bad, much worse than I am. She is only a little girl and she has not any right to have thoughts at all. It's all very well for *me* to think that it's a hard state of affairs when a poor fellow has to be called into existence for the purpose of being sent to fire and brimstone; but it does not do for her; it's highly improper, *highly*," said Frank, rolling round onto his face again.

Aunt Margaret opened her big blue eyes and looked at me. I had been so shy and said so little since I came there, that I think they all thought me a particularly childish child; and I was glad of it. I was young, but I had learnt a little worldly wisdom—enough to tell me that, if a man is unfortunate enough to have ideas of his own, he had best keep them to himself. I was tired of being called queer and strange and odd, and all those other epithets which I had so learned to hate; and here was Frank dragging all my weaknesses out into the sunshine that the old names might be branded on me again. What I should have said I don't know, but at that moment, greatly to my joy, our expected guests arrived. They consisted of a parson, his wife, an old young lady, and a certain Jonathan Barnacles, whose wife had been a cousin to my father. All these had come to assist in the stirring up of the deadened consciences of my grandfather's congregation.

From behind our wall of roses we could, without being seen, observe and criticise them as they walked up the long garden path.

The advance was led by the Rev. Joseph Goodman and his portly spouse, both tall, both fat: she decidedly good looking, with large brown eyes and a Roman nose; he, decidedly greasy and with a dirty white choker. I was struck dumb with horror at the way in which the good lady turned her head from side to side, evidently bent, as I thought, on discovering our whereabouts, but, as I afterwards learnt, merely from a long-acquired habit and a wish to overlook no one.

Close at their heels was a little angular figure, dressed in a very fashionable and juvenile manner, whose head and face were completely enveloped in a blue gauze veil. Frank said she had taken to attending revivals and staying to prayer-meetings only since the arrival in their circuit of a young assistant preacher whose mother she was old enough to be.

The rear was brought up by Jonathan Barnacles, Esq., at whom I looked with more interest; for, after the Dutch fashion, might he not be called a relation of mine? He was a lean, bony man of about two-and-forty, with large calm blue eyes, lanky and scanty hair and beard, and an enormous mouth—a mouth that seemed forever hungering and seeking after something. I wished he were no connection of mine when I looked at it, little child though I was. Looked at from the lip upwards, he might have been an angel; looked at from the lip downwards, he might have been a devil. He was dressed then—and I never, in all the years I knew him, saw him in anything else, except on Sundays—in a rusty brown jacket and a pair of dark green-and-blue-plaid trousers. To me those trousers have become so a part of the man that I can never see any like them without being unpleasantly reminded of him.

As soon as the visitors had gone into the house Aunt Margaret rose to follow them, and Frank and I were left alone. He asked me if I were going to the revival meeting that evening. "You had better," he said; "it's great fun. I always do: I take my notebook and pencil; one hears things worth remembering sometimes. Besides, you'll get into hot water if you don't go, and pretend to be edified, too. There are just three grand crimes according to your grandfather's creed—to give expression to an idea that has not been propounded at least one hundred times before you were born; to believe in the pos- possible sible salvation of a Roman Catholic; and to absent yourself from a little heaven below: "I have been there, and still would go, 'Tis like a little heaven below—" hummed Frank as he rose to go into the house, where he would no doubt look up his "Golden Light," as he nicknamed Aunt Margaret.

I went to the revival meeting that evening, for I had never been to one before. Aunt Margaret and I started some time after the others, so we had a pleasant long walk all to ourselves. Frank, in spite of the sage advice of the morning, did not go. I suppose, having got what he wanted, he did not care whether he pleased my grandfather or not, and could not make up his mind to leave an easy chair and cigar for "those purgatorial Methodist planks," as he irreverently called the straight-backed pews in my grandfather's chapel.

We walked on in silence at first through the quiet twilight. At last I said: "Do you like going to revival meetings? Do they do you good, Aunt Margaret?"

"I don't know that they ever did," she said, hesitating a little, "but Christ does show himself wonderfully sometimes; and I feel, if only one soul is saved, it must be God's own work and I must help it. Think, if only one soul be saved from endless pain and sin, what a glorious work."

The twilight gave me boldness, so I said, "I wish you could feel as I do, that our Father will let nothing he has made be lost forever. As long as I believe as you do I could not love him, nor serve him; but since I have left off looking to the Bible, and listen to what he says in my own soul, I love him and I am happy."

"I wish you could make me think so too," she said, "but I know it is wrong even to say so. If once we listen to our own hearts and use our reason, we go away from God. Yet do you know, if some one whom I loved very much were to die not loving Christ, I think—I am sure, I should go mad, quite mad. It is so terrible that you cannot pray for them, that you cannot do anything for them when once they are gone. We must pray for them now, now," she said, with a passionate earnestness that astonished me; she was so bright and placid generally.

I looked up into her face, and I fancied there were tears in her eyes, but I could hardly tell, for it was so dark. I knew of whom she was thinking, and long after I remembered her words.

The chapel was dimly lighted. Only round the pulpit there were two or three candles, whose light served to make clearly visible the three principal actors in the scene about to be performed.

In front of the pulpit stood Cousin Jonathan, and when he spoke I could look at nothing but that mouth, that dreadful mouth, that seemed to have a horrible fascination for me. On his right he was supported by the Rev. Joseph Goodman, who stood with eyes turned heavenwards and fat hands folded meekly across his greasy and distended waistcoat. On his left stood my grandfather, his cold hard eye engaged in critically examining the scattered occupants of the different pews.

The proceedings were opened by the singing of a hymn, in which the torments awaiting all mankind, except that infinitesimal portion who are believers in Christ, were set forth vividly, and in no bad verse. That being ended, my grandfather engaged in prayer. The prayer was very much in the same key as the hymn had been, but a little bolder and weaker. When it was ended Brother Vickers prayed. He was one of those who most frequently called Frank's notebook into requisition; and if my grandfather's way of treating fire and brimstone was cool and calm, so certainly was not his. The good man fairly worked himself into a profuse perspiration and dragged away at the pew-back before us with both hands and with such fervent energy that I momentarily expected to see him fly, pew-back and all, against my head.

Brother Vickers' prayer ended, another hymn was sung, and then Brother Jones was called upon.

Some men must think the Almighty very ignorant, for they never kneel down to speak to him without feeling themselves called upon to explain to him the whole plan of salvation, creation, and damnation: subjects on which, one might almost suppose, he would be better informed than themselves. Brother Jones was one of these. It may have been that my mood was not very charitable that evening, but it certainly seemed to me that, in place of praying to any other being, he was laying out for his own personal edification and satisfaction the whole circle of his theological knowledge.

When we rose from our knees, before Cousin Jonathan gave out the next hymn, Mr. Goodman came forward and told us that, if the spirit of God had touched any of our hearts during the preceding prayers, we were requested to come up.

"Do come up, dear friends, *do* come up," he said.

The hymn finished, the spirit still remaining inactive and no one having accepted the invitation, it was repeated a second time, more urgently than at first.

"Do come up, dear friends, *do* come up. While Brother Stiles engages in prayer, do come up."

Brother Stiles began, Brother Stiles ended; no one moved.

Before Brother Stubbles engaged, the invitation was again renewed:

"The time is young, dear friends. Will no one begin? Will no one come up?"

No one would; so Brother Stubbles began. Between every verse of the hymn that followed Mr. Goodman continued to ask, at last almost with tears, if no one would come up, if no one would lead the way. "Do come, do come," he cried, as he moved both hands unctuously to and fro; and my heart was touched with pity for the unfortunate man. I looked round the chapel anxiously to see if there was no sign of an upward movement, but could discover none.

Brother Snappers, who prayed next, seemed to have been moved in the same way, for he scolded quite rabidly: If there were any there that evening (and he knew there were such) whose hearts God had touched, let them beware! If they refused to accept the invitation, if they refused to come up, that night, that very moment, the spirit of God might leave them; and that day year, or that day month, or that day week, nay, by that time tomorrow, they might be in that place from which there would be no coming up forever. He did not say so, but he left one the impression that he would not have many tears to weep if such *were* the case.

Brother Goodman himself prayed next, a rambling, meandering sort of prayer, which would have been just as suitable at a funeral, a coronation, or a wedding.

Then Cousin Jonathan, after a last vain appeal, closed the meeting with a prayer; and that prayer, sweet, tender and earnest, seemed strangely out of harmony with the rest of the evening's proceedings. 'Twas like entering a silent sunny cove after being tossed among black breakers. He prayed for those who had not yet felt the love of Christ, that to them it might speak with its glorious power, till at length, perfect in purity, they might become but the living reflection of that unfathomable love. Perfect purity, perfect truth; through every sentence the yearning for it breathed; and when we rose from our knees and I looked up into his face, I could not see that the mouth was always craving something; I looked only at the serene eyes and brow.

When the meeting was over we all walked home rather silently, for it had been a failure to all of us. As for myself, I had made up my mind, even in spite of Cousin Jonathan's beautiful prayer, never to attend another; never, come what would. On our way home the Goodmans turned in to have a chat at Brother Vickers's, Frank and Aunt Margaret went for a stroll on the beach, and when we got to the house my grandfather and Cousin Jonathan took themselves off to the study. There was nothing else to be done, so I curled myself up at one end of the great parlour sofa with Wolf's fairy tales. I still enjoyed them as much as I had done when I was eight years old, though I had such an old, old-womanish feeling sometimes.

Presently my grandmother and Miss Mell came in and sat down at the other end of the room. I think they soon forgot my presence; Miss Mell kept up a constant flow of talk, while my poor nervous little grandmother put in a timid little yes or no when she thought it required, and pulled away at the fringe of her crochet wrapper. She was old and not beautiful, but she looked so beside Miss Mell who sat opposite her in her juvenile dress, with her wrinkles and her sharp nose and chin, over which the skin was drawn so tightly that a little more would surely have caused it to crack. At first I was too much engrossed by my book to pay any attention to what they said; but when my tale was ended I sat and listened.

"A pity she praises up those great fat girls so," Miss Mell was just saying of Mrs. Goodman. "They are the ugliest girls in the village, but she can't see it. She has a very good opinion of herself, too," continued Miss Mell, seeing that my grandmother gave no response; "and she imagines there is no other minister's wife to be compared with her, and I know that she takes good *care* never to go where there is any infectious disease, and—"

Here the door opened and Mrs. Goodman's face, with its beaming smile, presented itself. "Did you think I was very long gone, dear?" she said to Miss Mell; and, kissing my grandmother affectionately, added, "It was a shame to leave you, but the dear good creatures would have it so, and I came back to you just as soon as I could, dear, just as soon." She seated herself close to my grandmother and, taking one of her hands, proceeded to pat, smooth, and caress it during the whole of the conversation which ensued.

"What were you talking about, dears, when I came in? I am sure it was something *very* entertaining; Miss Mell's conversation always is so entertaining. As Sarah Jane said to me yesterday afternoon: 'Oh, Ma! There comes Miss Mell. Shall we not have a nice afternoon!' And we had a *pleasant* time. Had we not, my dear?"

"Very. Did I tell you that Alice Brown had come back?" asked Miss Mell.

"No, dear, you did not; but when I was up at Mrs. Barnacles' this morning she told me of it, and that she has grown into such a beautiful girl! Is it true?"

"Beautiful!" said Miss Mell, with a sharpening in her voice that made it very fit company for her nose. "I should beg to be excused from such beauty! She's as large as an elephant and a great deal coarser, and as for her forest of hair—the best thing she could do with it would be to cut it off; it's as black and coarse as a horse's tail!"

"I don't know what she *looks* like," said Mrs. Goodman, shaking her head, "but she's been very badly brought up."

"Brought up!" interrupted Miss Mell. "Why, she has not been brought up at all. They were the lowest people in the place till they got this money left them, the lowest and the poorest; and she is the worst of them. Did you ever hear of that affair with young Mr. Blair?"

"No, my dear, I heard nothing," said Mrs. Goodman, in her great interest for a moment forgetting to caress my grandmother's hand.

"It's about two years ago now," said Miss Mell. "Mr. Albert Blair was swimming in the great pool near Brown's house and got cramp. He called for help, and the girl (she was then about fifteen) happened to hear him. You will hardly credit it, but in place of going for some one, she actually had the immodesty to tear off her own clothes and leap in; and, as if that were not enough, she actually carried him in her arms up to their house. You may believe me, for I had it all on the best authority; my servant was very intimate with the Browns in those days, and she told me all about it. She said, too, that he sent her ever so many presents afterwards, and thought nothing of stopping to speak with her in the streets—the brazen-faced creature."

"Is it possible, my dear!" said Mrs. Goodman. "How wanting in modesty and self-respect! How very shocking!"

"It's not the worst thing we shall hear of her, mark my words," said Miss Mell, with a gleam of intense satisfaction in her grey eyes as she gave utterance to this prediction; which, considering its nature, was by no means unlikely of fulfilment.

"Ah! this is a sad, sad, wicked world," said Mrs. Goodman, gazing fixedly at the wall opposite and shaking her head slowly. "As I said to Sarah Jane only this morning, if once we depend on our own weak selves how miserably we shall fail, fail, fail!"

Miss Mell, not perceiving the exact bearing of these remarks on the subject in hand, sat still; but my grandmother uttered a timid, "Yes."

"Ah! you may well say yes, dear. I have had a dreadful blow this evening. Oh, it is a wicked, wicked world in which we live. If my dear girls had not given their hearts to Christ, I should tremble for them, yes, even for them"; and the tears that had been gathering in the good woman's eyes rolled slowly down her cheeks.

"What have you heard?" said Miss Mell, who already scented something good.

"Oh, you know all about it, no doubt, dear—about Dr. Harper, who I always thought such a dear, good man, and Mrs. Harvey."

"Dr. Harper and Mrs. Harvey! I've heard nothing," said Miss Mell.

"You don't *say* so, my dear! I'm *so* grieved I said *one* word about it. I made sure you knew it *all*. You know I never talk about such things, never, never; but, oh! it is the saddest, *saddest* thing I've heard for a long, long time; though I always knew that that Mrs. Harvey was not a good woman. I said so long ago—at the time she left our chapel for the church. Mrs. Lovedy was nursing her when her first boy was born, and she told me things, dear, dreadful things; she said—" and there followed the relation, in minutest detail, of things such as I had not even dreamed of, whose hideous shadow had never yet been thrown across my young life. From my lonely African home I had brought an ignorance of evil (and of that which, holy and pure in itself, man's folly has made so) that might have been thought strange in a child of six years. Much that had been cause of vague speculation and wonder was made clear to me that night, and I was wretched; for, alas! is it not the old, old story—that the tree of knowledge is the tree of pain, and that, "In the day wherein thou eatest thou shalt surely die" stand written on every fruit of the wonderful tree?

The gentlemen came in after a time to say good-night, and I slipped off the sofa and went to my own little room, for I did not feel in the mood to be spoken to by anyone.

When I got there, it somehow seemed that all was changed; nothing looked as it used to look; the very light did not produce its old effect when it shone on the white bed curtains; and my beautiful bunch of roses told quite a different tale from that which it had whispered in the morning. I felt sour and bitter, and I took the poor bunch I had gathered with such care and flung it out of the window; then I partly undressed and sat down upon the floor and set my candle down opposite me. It did me good to look at its wicked red flame flicker and flare. Before that night I had often felt sympathy with my candle; but then it had seemed to me a poor soul always striving to grow higher, and never succeeding; now it looked red and bad, like the new world that had been opened to me. This was a wretched earth, and perhaps, after all, there was a place of endless sin and therefore of endless pain; it would only be the world a little more worldly, I thought.

Aunt Margaret came in to wish me good night just then; she had a crimson wrapper over her head, so I knew she had just returned from the beach. She looked more beautiful than ever and happier than I had ever seen her; but she seemed to have changed, just like the roses and the light.

"I thought I should find you in bed," she said, stooping down over me. "Which are you studying—your little bare toes or the candle?"

"Neither," I said; "but I wish I was not a woman. I hate women; they are horrible and disgusting, and I wish I had never been born rather than to be one."

"Why, darling, what is the matter now? I am very glad I am a woman; it is so sweet"; and a soft smile played round her mouth as she spoke.

"Did you like the revival meeting this evening?" she asked me after a pause.

"No. It was horrible. I am never going to another," I answered, briefly.

"Oh yes, you will. You will make papa so angry if you do not."

"I can't help it," I answered. "There are some places that make one wicked, and it's not right to go to them. I feel tonight as if everyone in the world were a hypocrite, and I shall be one too, if I go to these places just for the sake of pleasing some one else—as bad as Miss Mell and Mrs. Goodman.

"You are tired tonight, darling; tomorrow things will look brighter to your poor little eyes. You have sat up too late. Good night, sweet;" and she went out and I was left alone with my red light. I soon got chilly and sleepy and crept into bed.

I remember that day because, first, on it the joy and peace I had lived in for two years began to break; because on it I first entered the shadow of that cloud in whose darkness I was to walk for years, hoping nothing, believing nothing, trusting nothing.

III.
THE MAN WITH THE MOUTH

AS AUNT MARGARET had said, things looked brighter in the morning—the beautiful morning that throws its veil of misty light over the great ugly truths which, in all their hideous nakedness, have stood staring us in the eyes and riding us on the breast all night.

Undine, as soon as she was dressed, ran down to the beach; there the tiny waves danced laughing on the sides of the big ones, which in their turn chased and overtook one another, tossing their heads high into the sunny air and turning to white foam, or making a mad dash for the land and dying away in laughing ripples on the sand.

On such a morning, on this side of twenty, with no ghosts to haunt one and come in between the happy sunshine and the eyes, who would not forget that there are such things as revival meetings, and good people who always say one thing and mean another, and jealous old maids and unfaithful wives, and dry hippopotamus-hide-like old men? Who would not forget that underneath this green, laugh-laughing ing, merry old world lies fire and brimstone, into which a fall from any rock may send one in a moment? Undine forgot this and everything, and grew at last as wild as the dancing waves. She had brought poor George

Macdonald with her for company, but now she threw him down upon the sand, where the waves caught him and made fine sport of his Unspoken Sermons and almost ran away with them; while she leapt from rock to rock, and finally pulled off her shoes and stockings, the better to keep her footing and capture the queer little beings which every wave left behind it in the rocky hollows.

She was very busily securing an extraordinary little monster, with a multiplicity of tails and feelers, and, with her head some two feet lower than her feet, was in no small danger of having an unexpected bath in the shallow pool, when she heard a voice at her elbow.

Rising to her feet with some difficulty and throwing back the wild hair from her eyes, she saw, standing beside her none other than the man with the green-plaid trousers and the mouth—Cousin Jonathan.

He asked what she was looking for; and when he understood very soon captured the queer little fish.

The presence of a second person had in an instant taken all the exhilaration and life out of the morning and brought her back to the disagreeable human world, in which wild hair, wet clothes, and bare feet were terribly disgraceful things. She felt conscience-stricken and looked down into the little pool, wishing she were one of the little fishes swimming there.

Cousin Jonathan held out the fish he had just caught with one hand; in the other he had poor George Macdonald, looking almost as wet and disreputable as its mistress.

"I find your name in this book, so I suppose you must have dropped it," he said as he gave it to her. "The waves were very nearly stealing it, as I fear they may you one of these days, if you continue such a very zealous little naturalist."

"I'm not a naturalist; I don't know anything about fishes or about anything else," stammered Undine, hardly knowing what she said.

Cousin Jonathan smiled, not an unpleasant smile of ridicule, but one of quiet amusement.

"They say, when we know our own deficiencies they are half rectified. You would like to know all about a strange little fellow like this, would you not?"

"I would like to know something about him," she answered, the kind, quiet manner of her companion already beginning to set her at her ease. "When I was at home I used to try and learn a little about plants and insects, but I never had anyone to help me and I had not the right books."

"Perhaps I could help you a little," he said; "at least I am sure I could, with books; but if you do not wish to study them, what makes you take such trouble to catch them?"

"I don't know," said Undine, "but I never see anything beautiful without wanting to have it, especially if it's very hard to get. It's not beautiful now," she said, turning over the poor little fish in her hand.

"I never can see some beautiful things without wishing for them," he said, and when he spoke those words he spoke the truth.

He helped her over the rocks, with that respectful kindness with which even little children like to be treated; and, when they reached the beach, sat down beside her and let his talk wander on, from a description of the nature and habits of the little creature in her hand to that wonderland which the microscope makes visible; and Undine sat and listened till she forgot his mouth and forgot even her own bare toes.

"We must go home to breakfast," he said at last, and Undine went in search of her shoes and stockings. Cousin Jonathan never forgot when it was time for a meal.

On their walk home he changed the conversation and tried to draw her out; for the study of character pleased him, and he felt attracted by the queer, babyish, womanish creature. She was an orphan, too, and almost friendless, and he pitied her. More- Moreover over, had she not looked lovely as she stood there on the rocks with the hot blood in her cheeks and her exquisite little feet clinging to the rough stones. Cousin Jonathan liked beautiful things—of the feminine gender.

Undine as she trotted beside him had little idea that he or anyone else could see anything in her to admire; but with a woman's quick perception she felt intuitively that whatever she might say, it was all right, it would be well received; and accordingly her ideas and words flowed forth in such a stream as would have astonished anyone who knew her as the shy awkward child in whose throat even yes and no seemed usually to stick.

Undine passed the day almost entirely in Cousin Jonathan's society. Aunt Margaret was busy, and when she had time to spare was with Frank, who was returning to college the next day. In the evening Cousin Jonathan left, for his wife was an invalid and he could never be from home long. At parting he told Undine that he would send her books and that, in return, she was to write and tell him what she thought of them. When he walked down the garden path, she stood looking after him and feeling almost as though an old friend were going.

IV.
GOING TO CHAPEL

EVERY house has its smoky chimney, its draughty room, its creaky door; every life its own haunting shadows; and every state of life its own small troubles. It may be, when we arrive in a new place or enter upon altered circumstances, the sky is all serenely blue above us; but 'tis never long before the discovering eye perceives the tiny cloud—the cloud on the horizon, at first no bigger than a man's hand, which, growing greater and never quite dissolving, hangs over us, forever ready to rain sorrows on our heads. The direction from which her storms were to arise was soon made clear to Undine. After Cousin Jonathan left she took her work and sat down at one end of the pantry dresser where Aunt Margaret was busy making cakes for tea. Every now and then Aunt Margaret looked down at Undine and wondered what was knitting her brow and making her little hands work away with such desperate energy.

Undine herself could hardly have traced the gyration of the thoughts that were tossing in her own small head, but the result was an unalterable determination that she would go to chapel no more. It was her duty, yet she could not go, she thought; and wondered wearily if she were always to be afflicted with senses of duty driving her into paths where no one else would or could walk.

The Goodmans and Miss Mell had been asked out to tea, so there were none but the family round the table that evening.

"You must make haste," said Mr. Roch, "and get your tea done; the meeting begins in three-quarters of an hour."

"You must take care to wrap yourself up warmly," said the grandmother; "you are not accustomed to our climate yet."

"I am not going," said Undine.

"What do you say?" asked her grandmother, in whose throat the words stuck so fast that not even Frank, who sat next her, could hear them.

"I am not going to the meeting this evening," she answered, staring very hard at her plate as she spoke.

"Do you feel ill tonight, dear? You look very pale," said Aunt Margaret.

"I am quite well, thank you; but I would rather not go tonight."

"I wish all my household to be there," said the dried hide, straightening and elongating himself in his seat.

"Perhaps she wishes to stay with Frank, as it is the last evening," said the poor nervous little grandmother in an apologetic little whisper.

"Frank is going with Margaret," said the dried hide, with his leathery, intonationless voice. It sounded so terrible to Undine and filled her with such tremblings, that the brown Wesleys and Fletchers in the little bookcase behind her grandfather seemed to go up to the ceiling and come slowly down to the floor, and she wondered if everyone in the room could not hear her heart beat.

"I would rather not go, I don't mind staying alone at all," she said at last.

"Why do you not wish to go?" said her grandfather, fixing his cold eyes upon her.

"I don't think it is—I mean—I don't get any good from going, and, I—would—rather—stay—please." Her voice had almost died away as she spoke the last words.

"Why do you not wish to go?" repeated her grandfather in his usual calm voice.

The blood came back to Undine's cheek, and with it her spirit rose.

"Because it would be wicked of me," she said, and then, feeling that anything would be better than the silence that ensued, she went on, "I can't go and pretend to be serving God when all—"

"Be silent," said her grandfather. "Little children who act in this manner should be whipped and taught how to behave themselves. It is a pity you are not a few years younger, Undine."

The child looked up at him, with eyes almost blinded by rage and hatred, and trembling in every limb; then suddenly there came to her a thought—the thought of One who bore all things in meekness, wrongs in silence, who returned cruelty with acts of mercy, and the hatred of evil with the love of a god. Through long years of ceaseless dreaming he had become to her no vague shadowy existence of the long past, but a present living reality, ever aiding and ever sympathising, to whose influence were ascribed all her higher thought and better feeling, no matter from what source they arose. She thought of him, and no answer rose to her lips; and in place of the fury only a cold fainting at her heart was left. She sat here so quietly, breaking up into little bits the bread in her plate, that Frank, remembering the Undine of the old African days, gazed at her in astonishment, expecting an outburst. None came; and when her grandfather rose from the table and told her to get ready she quietly went to obey him.

"Conquered," thought the old man as he put his coat on in the hall; but perhaps he would hardly have thought so could he have seen what was passing in the heart of the conquered. "It is very hard and bitter to have to go after all this, but because it is bitter it must be right to go just this once, at least as a punishment to myself." So she reasoned as she walked beside him on the way to the little Methodist chapel.

The meeting passed for Undine very much as the last had done; only that this evening, on the seat in front of her, sat a tall, gaunt old woman in a black bonnet who from time to time pushed and pulled at the shoulder of the sallow girl who sat next her, in an endeavour to drive her up to the rails every time the invitation was uttered afresh.

"I don't want to go," the poor creature whispered, drawing back; and she would, Undine thought, have kept her ground had it not been for Mrs. Goodman, who, leaning over the back of the bench, whispered loudly in her ear, "Go up, my dear; go up."

The girl looked round with a startled expression. It seemed as though all things, above, around, below, were combining to send her "up." The poor preacher calling from the rails, the prayers hurling anathemas at those who did not accept the invitation, the hand of her companion persistently applying physical force in the direction of salvation, the mysterious voice from the gloomy depths behind urging her upwards: these were forces which she had not strength to resist, and rising slowly she went up.

Undine wondered what she found to tell him when Mr. Goodman's greasy head was bent down over her.

She was the only fruit that evening, but as they walked home Mrs. Goodman expressed her joy that the blessed work of Christ had begun and that she had been the humble instrumentality in his hands for beginning it.

"A word in season, my dear Mrs. Jones, a word in season; let us be thankful when the dear Lord allows us to speak a word in season, allows us poor weak voices to speak a word for him."

Mrs. Jones, whose road lay in the same direction, was accompanying them part of the way. She fully acquiesced, and at parting begged Mrs. Goodman to come and spend the next day with her. Mrs. Goodman was deeply grieved, but the next day they were returning to Greenwood; she would not see more of her dear Mrs. Jones. That lady was, in her turn, deeply grieved at hearing this, and bargained that Sarah Jane and Elizabeth Ann should be sent over to spend a week with her.

Mrs. Goodman said there was no one in the world with whom she would so gladly have her treasures as her dearest, oldest, friend, and they should surely come. Mrs. Goodman's dearest always was the person whom she happened to be addressing at the moment.

They parted with an affectionate embrace, and Mrs. Goodman was still wiping her cheek from the traces of Mrs. Jones's rather moist salutation when she remarked: "What a dear, good creature Mrs. Jones is! What a pity she should think so much of dress at her age; and oh, the adornments of the outer man, what are they, my dear Miss Mell, what are they?"

"Yes, indeed," said Miss Mell, "yes, indeed."

"And her poor husband, my dear," continued Mrs. Goodman, "he can't stand it, my dear, he can't stand it. Did you notice the really *su*perb silk she had on—really *su*perb."

"I don't think it was silk; it was alpaca," said Miss Mell.

"Alpaca, my dear! You are quite mistaken. She sat close to the rails, and I was looking at it from the time she came in till we went out, and what a lovely brown it was."

"I think you are mistaken about the silk," said Miss Mell, determined not to yield her point.

"I know it's silk, my dear," replied Mrs. Goodman. "We were in the middle of the first prayer when she came in, and I heard the rustle of the silk as soon as ever she opened the door. I thought, 'Whoever is that!' So I just looked up as she went by."

"Well, it might be," said Miss Mell. "I know she is as extravagant as she is stingy."

"Yes, it's a great pity; she is such a dear, good creature," said Mrs. Goodman, with much earnestness; "it is a sad, sad pity she should be so close: the fly, the fly in the pot of ointment, my dear. Ah! that fly!" And so the good souls continued their conversation all the way home.

Arrived there, Undine ran away to her own little room, tonight to study not her candle, but the little brown Testament. She sat reading a little and dreaming a great deal till she had worked herself into a state of beatific felicity; and in this state Aunt Margaret found her when half an hour after she entered the room.

"What is making you so happy?" she asked. "You look like one of the little angels I used to dream about long ago."

"Nothing," answered Undine, the golden light fading as quickly from her face as it was from her heart. Heaven on earth is only found in perfect solitude, whether by saint or by poet; and 'tis only a step from the heights of the celestial mountains to the depths of the valleys below.

When Aunt Margaret had left her she began slowly to pull off her boots; and it seemed as though the thought of last night, mingled with today's bitter feelings, all came back to her.

She could just catch the sound of her grandfather's voice as it rose in prayer from the room below; and as she sat there listening, the old hobgoblins of doubt who had been silent for so many months began their dance over her once more. They asked the old unanswerable questions, and new ones, more unanswerable still; and dared even to lay profane hands on the words that had just been transporting her into the seventh heaven.

When, however, the prayer below was ended and she had got into bed, she put these suggestions of the evil one from her. She had been reading too much, she had been thinking too much, she had been turning her eyes away from Christ. For a whole month she would touch no book but His word and think no more, and so resolving she fell asleep.

The cloud, the little cloud, at first no larger than a man's hand, waxed greater as the months went by—grew in the end to be so thick and heavy that at last even Aunt Margaret's sunshine was absorbed by it.

Undine went quietly to chapel Sunday after Sunday; and a meek, sweet, quiet child she was, they all said, even if rather dull and stupid. They little knew how those still eyes made food of their every action; how forever they were being hung in the balances and dismissed to have that unchanging "Tekel" written up against them in her mind.

She kept her resolution, and except when at her lessons allowed no book to tempt her but her little brown Testament; that she pored over daily for hours, just as she had done in her little whitewashed sanctum at home.

Was the Testament most to blame, or the inherent wickedness of her own small heart, or the good women with whom she came in contact in her grand- grandfather's father's house who, when not in chapel or talking of their neighbours, were thanking the Lord that they were not as their sisters in the mire?

Whichever it might be, at the end of three months this small heathen in a Christian land had made up her mind to go no more to chapel, had come to the conclusion that neither prayer-meetings nor their cousins, the class-meetings, were the gates of the Golden City, but rather the entrances to that other way that, beginning with a short circumbendibus, at last leads one straight to the gates of the city whose walls are of groans and whose pavements of sighs.

Having now a very decided hankering after that Golden City and a very decided impression that she was bound for it, it could not but be that she should eschew those entrances. She did not believe that at the gates of the Golden City stands a great winged angel:

"How old are you?" he asks of the applicant for entrance.

"Thirteen years."

"Have you always tried to do as your conscience told you? But, no, stay. Had you no one who gave you bread and butter and shoes?"

"Yes."

"Oh, then they kept your conscience. If you only tried to obey them— Well and faithfully done, enter into joy, and sit down on a throne."

This was what she did not believe; and so one Sunday morning she came downstairs with a laggard step and slow.

When she got to the door of the breakfast room she ran back again, to pray one prayer more, for it was a terrible mountain she had to cross that morning.

The window of the breakfast room was wide open and the morning light forced its way in, gilding for once the brown Wesleys and Fletchers in the bookshelf, and playing over the little bunch of flowers Aunt Margaret had put beside her plate. She ate little, and before breakfast was half over had strewed the carpet with the leaves of her broken flowers.

Aunt Margaret wondered what was wrong with her little niece, and made vain conjectures; while Undine kept repeating to herself the nice little speech she had prepared to make to her grandfather, which she had even taken the trouble to write down the night before by way of strengthening her memory. She would tell him that she could not go to chapel, because it did her harm; but she would tell it him so humbly and in such terms that even he must forgive her.

But alas for human plans! Every time she essayed to begin, the words stuck fast in her throat; the precious moments sped and breakfast was over without one syllable of her carefully prepared little oration's having got further than the region of her heart, where it lay, heavy as lead.

When, however, her grandfather had risen to go, and had passed out into the passage, she also rose quickly and, standing in the doorway, said, "Grandfather."

He turned round slowly and fixed his cold eyes on her.

"What is the matter?" he asked.

Seek of the dumb an answer, and you will as easily find it as Undine the words of her precious and laboriously concocted little speech. They had hopelessly vanished and gone, and in their place came only these—"I am not going to chapel."

"I thought I had given you clearly to understand, Undine, on a previous occasion, that I wished you always to go. I allow no disregard of my wishes in this house." So saying, he turned round to enter his study, but Undine passed him quickly and stood in the doorway before him.

"I am not going," she said. "It is a wicked cruel world in which one human being has power over another, but you cannot make me do what I think is wrong; and if I go to chapel just because I fear you I shall be a hypocrite like all the others who go there; and I will not. All people who love Christ should keep away from such places, which only bring disgrace and shame upon his name. If he came to earth today he would denounce them as he did the pharisees and priests in his day. It's all a mockery and an empty show, and I shall never go again, never, never."

Her words followed one another in a quick incoherent stream while she pounded away vigorously with one little hand in the palm of the other, till both were furiously red. Her grandfather stood silently looking down at her. In his heart horror and wonder largely mingled with hatred were moving, but his face told nothing. For one moment he felt a wish to strike her, but she scared him, as she had often done her old opponents, by her wild earnestness. He looked at her again, and then, without making an effort to enter his study, walked out the front door, conquered for the first time in his life; conquered by a little child.

And Undine, the conqueror? Alas! Has not the victor's fate been, from the beginning, to lie down and weep? She went out into the garden and dropped down onto the soft green turf among the rose trees.

The sweet Sunday bells were ringing loud; through the clear morning air their music came to her, sounding strangely soft and sweet now that she knew they would never summon her again. For all others they were calling, but they had no word for her; she was one alone, without kinship or fel- fellowship lowship among men—so she said in her bitterness. Had she been born with a curse over her head? Would it be so wherever she might go, that her hand should be against every man, and every man's hand against hers? Or was she really so much worse than others that, wherever she might go, love and sympathy would be denied her? Would she have to walk on alone, alone, unloved, misunderstood, right on to the end?

She was sobbing and digging away with her toes into the soft earth when Aunt Margaret came and kneeled down beside her.

"Go away," said Undine, fiercely. "I am alone. *Leave* me alone."

"Undine darling, what have I done to you? What has anyone done to you? Undine, you say you love Christ and are trying to be his child. Don't you think you were wrong to speak as you did just now?"

Undine threw from her the soft hand that was caressing her hair, and said, though more gently, "Please go away"; and Aunt Margaret rose and left her.

Long after, Undine thought, with tears bitterer than those she then shed, of the hand she had thrown from her that morning; but they were bitter enough to the little child—the little child, who had not yet found out, as we all must sooner or later, that the path through life in which each soul must tread is single; that no two walk abreast; that where one soul stands, never has stood, and never shall stand, another; but that each man's life and struggle is a mystery, incomprehensible and forever hid from every heart but his own.

V.
A SUNNY AFTERNOON AND A WILD NIGHT

IT WAS summer again; a dreamy, hazy, delicious summer afternoon. Three sat upon the brow of a small grassy hillock near the beach—Frank, Undine, and Aunt Margaret.

The grass was rich with great golden-eyed flowers, and he picked them as he lay there, to fasten in the golden hair of the woman he loved—long silky yellow hair that hung about her, soft and fleecy as the small white cloud that lay dreaming far away to seaward.

Undine, sitting a little apart with her book, looked up ever and again to watch them; they were pleasant to look at as the blue sky overhead or the green grass and shimmering light below. Every now and then she caught a word of their conversation; they were making little plans for the spending of the long good years that were coming to them, when they two should be always together. At last they called to her: "What shall the colour of the study curtains be—red, green, or yellow?"

"Blue," said Undine—"blue, just the colour of the sea where it lies at rest, far away."

"No, no; not that colour," Aunt Margaret answered, quickly. "I never did so before, but this afternoon I hate it. Every time I look up and see it, I hate it."

"Look at that cloud," said Undine; "when we came 'twas a tiny speck we could hardly see, and now 'tis like a great fairy snow-ship in the sky." Then a silence fell on all three; but by and by Frank fastened more golden flowers in the yellow hair, and Aunt Margaret's merry laugh was heard mingling with the rippling of the waves and the hum of the brown insects in the grass. Undine sat looking at the picture before her, all green and gold. Surely it must be that in such a world life and love are alone realities, and death and pain are but the fevered dreams of our own minds."

There were withered flowers lying among the grass stalks; there were heavy shadows growing in the valleys; the fairy ship was growing darker every moment and would come with the storm wind and the hellish grin of the lightning, to plough up the smooth face of the sunny sea before morning, but they saw none of those things and sat there smiling in the sunlight.

"Delilah, you are bewitching me," said Frank at last, as he sprang up from the grass on which he had been lying with his head in her lap. "I promised to be at Leeford tonight; must be there, in fact."

"It's too late now," said Aunt Margaret, shading her eyes with her hand to look at the sinking sun; "if you walk ever so fast you cannot get there before dark."

"I shall not walk; I shall hire a boat in the village and two boys, and shall be back again by ten o'clock."

"It is the last evening, Frank," she said, turning her bright childish face up to his, "the last for four whole weeks. Be sure you come back."

He stooped over her and whispered softly for a moment, and then with a good by to Undine sprang down the green slope and over the rocks along the beach.

Just as he was passing out of sight he paused for an instant to look back at them and call out, "Only till ten o'clock, you know, only till ten o'clock."

The two left rose to go home then.

"Shall I pull the flowers out of your hair?" asked Undine.

"No; I leave them there; I feel like only a little child tonight. Oh, Undine, I hope you will one day be as happy as I am."

She had reason to be happy, Undine thought; in a few months more he would have finished his studies and was to settle as doctor in Greenwood, and they were to be married; reason enough, but so had most women. How glorious it would be when she, too, was one!

Later on in the evening Undine kneeled in the seaward window of Aunt Margaret's room. Aunt Margaret stood behind her with her arms twined round her, and both were looking into the darkness. Except the flash of the distant lightning, nothing was to be seen, nothing to be heard but the faint roll of the thunder and the roar of night wind as it flung the mountains of water it had created against the cliffs or hurried them madly over the rocks.

"It is no use looking out any longer; he will not come tonight, Golden," said Undine, using, as she often did, his pet name.

"No, no, you do not know him as I do. He would do anything rather than disappoint me," she answered.

"But the boys, the boys," said Undine; "they would never venture out on a night like this."

"Then he would come alone." The words were said in a calm, measured voice utterly unlike her own; and Undine looked up at the white face above her and out at the darkness, and shuddered.

"What time is it?" Aunt Margaret said at last.

"I don't think it's very late," said Undine, with a piteous attempt at a smile that faded instantly when she had left the room and was making her way through the sleeping house.

As she stood before the great clock in the hall it struck the hours slowly; and then the solemn ticking was renewed. She thought of the things it might once have spoken to her, concerning the bright brown face that had looked back at them from the rocks—the rocks where now the wild water was foaming in the darkness—and was glad that it could speak them no more.

When she got back to the room, Aunt Margaret was kneeling at the side of the chair on which the candle stood, with her two beautiful hands clasped over her head.

"It is just twelve," whispered Undine as she sat down beside her. "He will not come tonight; it is too late."

"Too late, too late!" Aunt Margaret hissed the words from between her clinched teeth. "I never prayed for him as I ought, I never kept on praying till I felt God's answer, and now I can do nothing more for him, nothing more. It is what I deserve, it is God's punishment on me for loving a man who mocked His name, who had no faith in Christ; but, Undine, Undine, heaven will be no heaven to me if he is not there. I would give my soul so willingly to reclaim his; I could bear all for him. Pray, Undine, pray. I cannot."

And Undine prayed—prayed as we pray for that which we are losing, for that for which we fear the day of prayer has almost ended.

"Talk, Undine, talk," said Aunt Margaret. "If you are quiet I cannot bear it." And Undine talked on, the words of her own sweet dreamy faith—talked on till Aunt Margaret fell asleep with her head in the child's lap. Then at last Undine leaned her forehead against the chair, and slept also.

When she awoke next morning the world was laughing, the sky all blue with not one tell-tale cloud, the hills all green and glittering in the morning light, and the blue sea beyond them rippling in the sunshine, with a smile like the dimpled smile of a beautiful wicked woman after she has broken hearts and sucked the sweetness out of human lives.

Undine, before she was well awake, smiled back at the picture that laughed back at her through the open window; then wondered what this heavy weight about her heart might mean, and remembered all.

Had he come? Where was Aunt Margaret? Glancing round the room, she hurried out to look for her. As she passed her grandfather's door he opened it and called to her:

"Do you know who went out at the front door last night and left it open? I felt the cold wind blowing in, and had to go down and close it, about four o'clock."

He felt pretty sure the culprit stood before him; no one else in the house was given to wandering out at night, and in the dark. It would only be of a piece with all her other eccentricities, which had at last brought him to the conclusion that the child whom he thoroughly detested, yet could not get rid of, was not quite in her right mind.

She gave him no answer to his question, but asked hurriedly, "Has he come?" And seeing from his face that he did not know, she passed on.

Where was Aunt Margaret! Not in the garden, not in the house. Soon everyone was in full search of her except her father, who went into his study to prepare next Sunday's sermon.

She had angered him last night by asking him to send some one over to Leeford to hear if Frank had left. He hated his future son-in-law with a hatred only less perfect than that which he felt for his little granddaughter. A Freethinking child of the devil, he had more than once called him to Aunt Margaret, and he would never have had her had it not been that from his mother he had inherited something.

Gold is like charity; it covers a multitude of sins; it maketh a cloak wherein even Freethinking may array itself, and its nakedness shall not appear.

Two hours later he came out of his study with a troubled look. His wife had been to tell him that Margaret was nowhere to be found, and that one of the boys had returned from Leeford. Frank with the other had started in the boat at eight o'clock the night before, hoping to reach home before the storm broke.

If there was one thing in the world the dried-hide loved, it was his daughter; and in the search that followed no one looked so anxiously or so earnestly as he.

He had refused to send anyone last night, and she had gone herself, he thought; and so thinking he set out on the road she must have taken. Undine went to search where she knew Aunt Margaret's own heart would have taken her—to the little green hillock where the yellow flowers he had picked lay withered here and there, where she could see the rocks on which he had stood to wish his last goodbye and the placid sunny sea which murmurs on so softly, telling no tales of the beauty and the strength it has devoured.

Undine could not bear to stay near it and hurried back to the house and the dear old rose-filled garden.

Her grandmother met her at the door, crying and wringing her poor weak hands: "Oh, he is dead! Poor Frank is dead! They have found his body, and the boy's that was with him. And my darling, my poor darling, where is she? It will kill her! It will kill her!"

Undine did not stay to mingle tears with her, but passed from room to room like one in a dream, searching where yet she did not hope to find; with the restless moving water ever before her eyes as she wearily closed and opened door after door.

The door of her own room stood half open, but she only glanced in, and was just leaving it when her ear caught a sound from the corner near the window. There, with the sunlight streaming full over its yellow hair, crouched a naked human figure. The knees were drawn up till the chin rested on them, and one arm was clasped tight round them; the other was stretched out, and one finger pointed to a crack in the boards. The eyebrows were drawn down till the eyes were hardly visible, but they opened slightly every time the mouth twitched nervously to one side or the other.

Undine stood motionless in the doorway and watched it. Had sorrow touched her reason? Was she mad? Or was that really what she looked for—that thing with the faded yellow flowers in its hair?

"Ha-ha-ha!"

'Twas a hellish laugh that filled the room and rang out across the rose trees in the garden. The finger was still pointing to the crack along the boards.

"Ha-ha-ha! There they come—one, two, three; there they come—the devils that have got his soul, hundreds of them, thousands of them. That is the door they took him down, there. I asked God to take me instead, but He would not, and now they have got me too. He used to say there was no God, and no hell, but God will show him now. Ha-ha-ha! How they come! Little devils—one, two, three!"

Undine uttered a low cry and dropped down onto her knees beside her.

The yellow thing, with its faded flowers, crouched down lower, crouched till its chin rested on the floor, and its half-closed eyes glanced furtively now on this side now on that. Then springing to its feet, with a cry, it seized Undine with both hands and bore her to the ground. Kneeling on her and putting its lips close to her ear, it hissed forth: "I know you, who you are. You look like Undine; but you are the devil; the devil to whom God gave his soul. I know, I know. You left his body lying there upon the beach, and you tore it with your cruel hands that I might not know it when I found it lying there in the grey dawn: but I knew it, I knew it." She fixed her teeth in Undine's arm and clasped her to her breast until Undine's cries were smothered and she became unconscious. When those who had heard them entered the room, Undine lay upon the floor insensible, and in the far corner crouched a thing that licked its red lips and cried exultingly as it pointed at her: "I have killed the devil! I have killed the devil! Ha-ha-ha!"

A week after, and Cousin Barnacles had taken Undine to his house in Greenwood.

It is not time which makes old men and women of us. Undine's childhood lay buried in the grave upon the hillside where a form which the sea had given up was laid, and in a dark strong house far off where a mad woman grew wilder still if they showed her a bible or a yellow flower.

Ignorant of the world, shy, childish in her manners, yet for her childhood was forever of the past. She would never again dance with naked feet among the rocks and wonder how, in the world of green and gold, men ever sigh and pray for rest beneath its crust. For her, henceforth, the merry laughing children would be you, and grave-eyed men and women, we and us.

VI.
GREENWOOD

IT WAS a white lifeless face that Cousin Jonathan brought with him to Greenwood. So ghastly and pale that even Mrs. Goodman and Miss Mell, if they were not moved to pity, could not find it in their hearts to exercise their tongues upon it.

All day Undine used to wander in the old wood that lay between Cousin Jonathan's house and the village; used to wander there when the dried leaves were falling down in showers and piling themselves up in little grave-like heaps at the roots of the great trees; used to look at them and fancy, with a kind of apathetic pleasure, that, when the spring came with its young green, she, like the leaves, would have vanished away. She thought her heart was broken. Perhaps it was; but she did not know that hearts are only Time's china cups—china cups which the old father is forever throwing hither and thither, cracking and smashing in his wild reckless way, and then carefully picking up and cementing so cleverly that the old scar does not even show. They may ring a little dead if you strike them—but that is all.

Not knowing this, Undine wondered at herself when she found out that she intended to live, and to grow strong, and pretty too.

Then the women in the village began to say malicious things, and to find out that she was stupid and conceited and unchildlike; but she cared nothing for what they said, and read her books and curled herself up to dream for hours among the roots of her favorite old tree by the little bridge in the woods. At first they were sad, unearthly dreams, but when the year grew older and the golden colour came creeping over the hills, it crept into her dreams also; and she would sit there smiling and glad; then she would wonder at herself and go home slowly, thinking of the dark lonely house and the Goldenlight that was buried there forever.

Cousin Jonathan tried to cheer her, buying books for her, a horse, dresses and trinkets, and everything wherewith man seeks to comfort and delight the heart of womankind. But, as his wife remarked to Miss Mell, he might as well have saved his money and spared himself the trouble: she never showed the least pleasure at receiving his prettiest gift, except it happened to be a book that pleased her, and then it was only in a staid, old-womanish way.

Three years had passed by, and Undine the child had changed into Undine the woman—pretty, very pretty, even Miss Mell was obliged to allow that, "for those who like that style of beauty." But she was stupid, terribly stupid and old-fashioned. All her female acquaintances were agreed on this point. The most ravishing dress could not win even a glance, the most delicious piece of scandal the least attention. No little party or picnic, however heart-subduing in person or purse the gentlemen who were to be there, could ever awaken in her the faintest enthusiasm. People left off having anything to do with her at last.

"I'm terribly anxious about her," Mrs. Barnacles would say. "It's not that she is old; she is a mere child; but I don't see what's to make her change; and if no one ever sees her, who's to marry her?" Mrs. Barnacles was a yellow-faced big-nosed invalid, who passed her life on a sofa and was apt to take a dyspeptic view of things. "She has need of all her good looks, if she is to go off; men don't take readily to those queer, dull sorts of girls; and with those idiotic ideas of hers, on religious matters, too, half the men would not have her as a gift."

"Of course they would not," Miss Mell would here strike in; "and I believe it's all put on too—her not going to chapel and all the rest of it—just to be peculiar. It's all nonsense. What does she know about such things? For clever learned men it's all very well, but a stupid child like her ought to be well whipped and fed on bread and water for six months; that would take the nonsense out of her better than anything else."

"Yes," Mrs. Barnacles would assent, "for men it's all very well, as you say; but a woman, and one who lives on charity, ought to keep them to herself if she has ideas of that unwomanly kind."

She used to tell Undine all this, to her face, sometimes: "Go to chapel and give up reading those nonsensical books, and act like other people even if you don't think like them. It won't answer, it won't answer at all; and you had better give up all this sort of thing before it's too late. You'll repent it if you don't."

Then Undine, half bitter, half indifferent, would get away from her to the dear old world of inanimate nature, which never calls us queer and strange or advises us to wear a mask. It was well for her that she cared for that at least, for dark loveless times had fallen on her, and she cared for nothing else. Cousin Jonathan was good to her, did all in his power for her, but she liked him less as the years went on. She had never loved him, and the intellectual help which he had been able to give her ceased to be a bond between them when she had reached his ground and even passed beyond him. So now Cousin Jonathan shared the fate common to all lovers, and gave out his gold, such as it was, for dust.

One afternoon late in the summer Undine sat half buried among the long grass at the foot of her old tree. Mill's *Political Economy*, with its face turned to the ground, lay at her feet, while a little black beetle scudded hither and thither among its pages, all unnoticed. Her hands were busily employed in picking off small bits of dried bark from the trunk of the old tree; while her thoughts were in the same key, and as sweet and impossible of fulfilment, as ever were little Ellie's when she sat alone 'mid the beeches in the meadow.

It may be true that the man who has never dreamed with his eyes open never can know what disappointment means; but it is also true that he never knows what heaven is like. Undine's stay there was not of long duration, for by and by Cousin Jonathan came sauntering through the woods in search of her.

She was so enwrapped in her own thoughts that she did not notice his presence till his hand had been passed softly over her hair.

"Where are your thoughts wandering?" he asked as he seated himself softly beside her on one of the great knotted roots of the old tree which had forced its way out of the ground.

"Nowhere," Undine answered wearily.

"That is the answer you always make me now," he said, very gravely; "you don't make a friend of me now as you used to, Undine."

"Because I can't. There never was much sympathy between us on any subject; there is none now."

"It is you who do not understand me," he an- answered swered, passing his fingers softly through her hair and letting his hand rest on the back of her neck.

There was something in the action, simple as it was, that she did not like; and a feeling of disgust came, as it had often done lately when he kissed or caressed his little daughter, as he called her.

She threw his hand from her as she would a toad's claw, and sprang lightly to her feet.

"What is the matter?" he asked, looking up at her with his serene blue eyes; and Undine felt ashamed of her ingratitude and foolishness.

"Nothing is the matter," she answered, laughing, "only I am not quite so old as you and believe in perpetual motion."

Standing on tiptoe, she caught one of the overhanging boughs and swayed herself gently backwards and forwards. Cousin Jonathan thought, as he looked at her, that never, even on that first day when he saw her standing with her little naked feet upon the rocks, had she looked so deliciously lovely: as round, as downy and inviting as any golden peach that ever schoolboy eyes looked at and, looking, thirsted for, because it was unattainable.

"How dared you intrude upon me in my private residence!" she said, still laughing. "Is it not enough to make me disagreeable? Why don't you wait till I invite you?"

"I should have to wait a long time, I fear," he replied, still looking at her.

"Perhaps so, but death may make me more agreeable and sociable; and, as I am sure to die long before you, when you hear that I have departed this life you may come and hold converse with my spirit under this tree. I mean to haunt it, if the old monster does not quite dissolve me into nothingness." She rattled on thus, not knowing what to say and not wishing to be silent.

"You have a queer mind," said Cousin Jonathan. "As surely as you seem to be in one of your merry moods, you drag in some grim and ghostly thing to spoil it all. I don't believe you know what it is to be gladly happy."

"Perhaps not. I know that when I was a child and used to romp most wildly and do mad things that none of the others dared, it was just because I was not happy. Whenever my thoughts and miseries were too great for me, I used to let off steam by doing something terribly naughty; and when I had been lying awake all night under my bed, in the greatest agony about my sins and other people's, I used to get up and have the most desperate of romps all by myself. I remember one day, when I was only seven years old, having the story of Cain and Abel for my Sunday lesson. It made a great impression on me. If God accepted Abel's sacrifice not because of its value but because of his faith, why, if I only had faith, should not fire come down from heaven upon my sacrifice at Wilge Kloof. [1] I could think of nothing else for days, and so I waited till one day when I was very hungry and there was very nice meat for dinner. I thought the sacrifice must be one that had cost me something; so I would not touch a mouthful, but saved the nice little chop that was put on my plate till dinner was done and everyone had gone to take their siesta. It was a broiling day, but I went out to the shady side of the house and collected twelve little flat stones and piled them up neatly in a square heap; then I put my meat down on them and kneeled down to pray. I trembled with ecstatic joy when the prayer was finished, for I felt sure that, when I looked up, the flames would have descended and devoured my fatty chop. I was almost afraid to raise my eyes. When I looked up and saw the chop lying just as I had left it, I felt astonished, but my faith was not at all shaken, and I set to work again, praying with all my might. I looked up again after a long time, thinking I would see the chop and perhaps the stones themselves, like Elijah, licked up by the heavenly fire; but it was just as I had left it, only the sun had made the fat melt a little and run down the stones. I kept on praying till the people in the house began to stir, and then I threw down the altar and gave the chop to the dogs, and felt ever so wicked and miserable as I walked up and down in the shade of the house. I knew I had prayed with faith, and I thought the only reason why the fire had not come was because God hated me, as he had done Cain. By and by I went down to walk by the kraals, and saw one of the Kaffir girls fetching cattle dung to smear the floor of the house with. I thought smearing must be delightful work, and I could not bear to think about my poor altar and my chop any more; so I found a hard flat piece of ground at the back of the kraal, fetched some water in a broken oil can, and mixed up the water with the dung nicely, just as I had seen the black girls do. I worked so hard that in half an hour I had smeared a place the size of a room, and my clothes and face too. I was just beginning to feel quite better and as though I did not care so much that my offering had been rejected, when some one came and caught me in the middle of my dirt and happiness, and I was perched up on the top of a great box till bedtime."

[1] Wilge Kloof—pronounced Vilgerkloof. Wilge means willow.

Undine paused to take breath at the end of this long relation. She did not care much for Cousin Jonathan's company nowadays, and the fear that he would feel it and be pained made her very voluble generally.

"You have changed strangely since those old days," he said. "I don't think you are troubled with too much faith now; you believe in nothing under the sun."

"That only proves what I said just now," she answered. "You don't understand me. I believe more truly in some things than you do."

"In what, for instance?"

"Oh, in more than one. You said yesterday that there was no such thing as a love that must live while the soul lives; that wrong or neglect *can* change the love that can be felt but once in a lifetime for one human being and which is the best of earthly things. You pooh-poohed it and called it dreaming, not reasoning. I merely return the compliment."

Cousin Jonathan did not like this enthusiastic speech, and smiled a sneering sort of smile. Beautiful men and women can afford to sneer; Cousin Jonathans cannot, and he looked grotesquely ugly as he did so.

"With your magnificent intellect and your profound reasoning faculties whereby you profess to test everything, one might almost expect you to show a somewhat deeper knowledge of life and human nature. But after all you are only a child, and will grow wiser, when you have seen more of the world, than to believe that love can live without hope or return, any more than a body without food or air."

Undine hated to be told she was but a child and had no knowledge of the world, because there was so much of truth in the assertion. The little man knew this and therefore he told her so, for he felt angry with her that afternoon, though he hardly knew why and his blue eyes never showed it.

"You read all manner of trash and sentimentality till your mind is completely enervated; you came down here this afternoon to read some of Mrs. Browning's poetry and effete nonsense, I have no doubt."

"There lies what I have been reading," she said, pointing to where Mill still lay upon the ground. "There is nothing very sentimental in that, I fancy."

"You are likely to get just as much good from this style of reading as from the other," he replied as he picked up the book.

"You are difficult to please, my old father," she said as she caught the bough again and rocked herself gracefully to and fro.

Difficult to please! Of course he was. There was one thing in the world that would have pleased him, and that thing he could not have. The little man felt, as he sat there among the long grass, with his mild angel eyes and his seeking mouth, as though he could have killed her, for he knew that she would never love him. She hung as far from his reach as the rose that hangs on the topmost branch of a bush is from the worm that creeps up and down on the rotten leaves below. He hated her, and yet he loved her with a love that had grown with her opening beauty and her softening figure, as the worm grows while the rose but swells. It is a long way from the dirt to the rose; but may it not be climbed?

Was he asking himself this question as he sat looking at her? Undine thought he looked ugly and strangely out of place among the dreamy flowering grasses on which were dancing the sunbeams which had made their way through the thick foliage. The little brook that murmured all the more sweetly, because almost buried out of sight—he could not understand what it was saying, and why had he come to disturb her quiet? Her conscience was just beginning to give her the most unpleasant twinges for thinking so ungratefully of one who had done more for her than any other being, when steps and voices coming over the bridge made her look round. There were two gentlemen crossing it, and Cousin Jonathan rose to his feet and went to meet them. He introduced them to Undine as the Mr. Blairs, father and son. There must have been at least thirty years' difference in their ages, yet as far as form and feature went there was a strong resemblance between them. Both were short and very broadly built, with round noses, round faces, blue eyes, scant beard, and sandy-coloured hair; but here the resemblance ended. In place of a painfully flexible and sensitive mouth, and eyes more soft and melting than a woman's, the father had thick, firm, pressed lips that told of a strong animal nature and an iron will, while the eyes above were so cold and dead that the great stone in his breast-pin gave out more light and warmth than they did.

The path through the woods allowed only of two abreast; Undine had what half the girls of Greenwood would have given their little fingers to gain, a long walk and tête-à-tête with Mr. Henry Blair.

"Are you fond of reading?" he asked her, noticing the book in her hands. When a man opens conversation by this remark you may make pretty sure of one of three things—he wants education, he thinks you a fool, or he is one himself.

Undine decided at a glance that neither of the first two was the case, and that consequently the last must be.

"At times," she answered him, in a very indifferent voice. Books were her meat and drink, her friends and lovers, but she was not going to tell him so.

"You have Mill's *Political Economy* here, I see," he remarked. "I am just going through his works with very great pleasure. They are beautiful, are they not?"

"Very," said Undine, smiling inwardly.

Her companion then went on to state how he delighted in reading, how he spent his whole time in it. There was no work of note in English, French, German or Greek that she could mention, which he had not read. He liked philosophy, he revelled in poetry, he studied history, he worshipped science. He was a wonderful man, with a brain crammed as full of facts and ideas as a brain could be; and yet not one of them had ever been able to reach him. Just the backboneless, warm-hearted, weak character which nature had given him he had, and would have to the end of his days. 'Tis small use trying to graft an orange tree on to a Coonie. [1] If you have no thought of your own, those of other men will find nothing to which they can fasten themselves; and you will have to carry them about with you—if carry them you will—much as you do your rings and your gloves, rightfully or wrongfully yours, as the case may be; but always outside of you, and never part of you.

So Undine walked beside her companion, with his black-blue woman's eyes and his soft voice, feeling a kindly contempt for him, in spite of his infinite superiority to herself in knowledge and acquirements of every kind.

"What do you think of them?" said Cousin Jonathan, when after a somewhat lengthy call their visitors had taken their departure.

"Nothing," said Undine. "The son has not a bone in his whole composition, and the father is all bone, or something harder."

Cousin Jonathan smiled, not displeased to hear her express her disapprobation of other men.

"I wonder if you ever did meet *anyone* whom you approved of," he remarked, smoothing her soft hair.

[1] The "c" is a click. Coonie is a tree (shrub).

"You are quite right with regard to the father, however; he is not troubled with too much tenderness of heart. The first time he married it was to a lady of very good family, whom he married just on account of her blood. He led her a very fine life, and when she died at the end of two years he married a woman who was immensely rich and whom he liked still less and treated still worse. She left him all her money when she died; but I believe he hates her son, who was here this afternoon, just because he is hers. I never saw them together before."

"Has he any other children?" asked Undine.

"Yes, Albert, his eldest. In my pedagogue days, before I married Mrs. Barnacles, he was my pupil. He is here now, and is sure to call and see me in a day or two."

Albert Blair! Yes, that was the name of the man Miss Mell had talked about as having been saved by a girl from drowning. Albert Blair—yes, that was the name; then she took up her book and thought no more about it.

Next morning Undine rose early and took her morning walk onto the little hill that lay behind Cousin Jonathan's house. The grass was still heavy with the great glittering dewdrops, and the fresh clear air reminded her of the mornings in her old African home when she used to get up early and go to pray behind the little koppie. There it was so still and beautiful that it was easy to pray and to believe in God's love. She wondered if the dew lying on the English grass were really as lovely as the great drops that used to stand trembling on the bushes and silvery ice-plants among the stones of the koppie. Her thoughts went back to those old days—not longingly, for there hung over the memory of her childhood little of that free gladness which to most men causes it to lie behind them, a land of light and song, to be looked back at across the thirsty steppes of life with vain longing and sore regret. She had looked out onto the world with eyes too grave and earnest ever since the time when, a little child of six years, she had kissed the leaves and cried among the thorn bushes, because when chopped down and burnt they would die forever. She had found griefs and mysteries where other children see only playthings, and had passed a tearful solitary childhood in a home of love and plenty. There was no wish for their return in the eyes that looked back to those days; but they had about them that subtle charm which death alone gives to men or times. With all its intense solitude, its tears and doubts and bitter prayers, there had been hours of happiness in her childish life, hours when the heavens had seemed open and the angels of God had descended, and ascended from the earth.

Her thoughts wandered on from those old days to the first year of her life in England, to the glad love that had lived before her and which had been so suddenly put out.

The impression those days had made upon her, extinguishing all hope, all faith, all trust, had somewhat faded, but a strange deadness seemed to have settled down upon her; and, with an intellect vigorous and alive, it seemed as though all emotional vitality had died within her.

Cousin Jonathan had said, "You believe in nothing." He might with as much truth have added, "and love nothing." Not Cousin Jonathan's extinction or disappearance into fire and brimstone, or that of anyone else, would now have cost her one tear; and even for herself she had but a kind of apathetic indifference. In a way, it might be, she loved her books and nature; but her feeling for Spencer's *First Principles* was not like the love which had poured itself out in hot kisses on the leaves and cover of her little brown Testament.

It was the sense of this coldness and deadness that made the days of passion and feeling look so beautiful to her now, and that almost brought the long-stranger tears into her eyes as she looked down on the glittering dew and thought of those early mornings behind the koppie. Agony, anything, would be better than this dreadful coldness and indifference. Would it never end, never break? If only I could love something, she thought, as she passed slowly over the wet grass. To love some- something thing, to believe in something, to worship something, even if that something were only herself—to look at something with eyes other than those of calm indifference—it would be worth sleepless nights of tears and prayer.

She walked on with her eyes fixed on the ground, and was surprised when she looked up to find herself at the top of the hill. It was not a very stirring or striking scene that lay before her, but calm and bright. At the foot of the little hill on which she stood lay Cousin Jonathan's house, and beyond that the little wood in which grew her old tree. The white houses of the village were visible on the other side of it, and beyond that again the large mansion of the Blairs with its roof glittering in the sunshine. Not a soul was to be seen except at the edge of the wood, where a man and woman were standing. It looked as though the woman's head were resting on his arm, but they soon parted; he turned back among the trees, while the woman took the little path that led straight up the hill. Undine sat down, listlessly watching her as she came nearer; then she saw it was not a face she knew or had ever seen before in Greenwood. 'Twas a young face like those that sometimes haunted Undine's waking dreams and made her wish she were a painter, to fix them everlastingly on canvas. The woman was of more than middle height, with a magnificently developed yet graceful figure; her features were regular and almost of a Jewish cast, while her long curled eyelashes drooped over cheeks as dark and brilliantly coloured as the rare hothouse flowers she wore in her bosom. Undine looked at her as she passed, filled with genuine admiration, but the woman seemed quite unconscious of her presence. She loves some one, and she is happy, thought Undine; if I could love I would be happy too.

When she sat doing her needlework in Mrs. Barnacles' room that morning, she asked her who the beautiful stranger was; for that lady was kept well informed in the doings and sayings of all Greenwood by the indefatigable Miss Mell.

"You must mean Alice Brown, I think," said Mrs. Barnacles, after a moment's consideration; "they say she is growing more and more beautiful. It's very queer, but whenever the Blairs are here, she is. Generally she lives with her grandmother."

"I should like to know her," said Undine.

"Oh, they are only common people," said Mrs. Barnacles. "We don't associate with them."

That afternoon Harry Blair put in his appearance. As a rule he was careless enough about his dress to be mistaken for the greatest genius living; but on that afternoon he had arrayed himself with punctilious care, and had come to invite Cousin Jonathan and Undine to look at some fine pictures which had just arrived. Undine had said she was fond of pictures, and these were really beautiful.

Of course she could not refuse to go; and Cousin Jonathan went, for he followed her steps as smoke follows a train.

George Blair was a rich man, and no miser; a man who valued his money only for the status it gave him in the eyes of his fellow men and the ease and luxury it might bring him. The erection and adornment of this house at Greenwood had been the employment and delight of the last twelve years. He would pay away hundreds of pounds for a picture or a statue that was said to be good, though he was about as well able to understand the one or the other as would have been one of the thoroughbreds that stood in his stable.

It was the first time Undine had been in the house, for during the three years she had been in Greenwood the owner had been travelling abroad. It was aristocratic to travel on the Continent, therefore he went. He had married his first wife because she knew who her great-grandfather was. He would have sold his own soul to be thought refined and of blue blood, but he never succeeded in producing the desired impression.

Perhaps it was the sense that where he so deplorably failed his eldest son was by gift of nature preeminently successful, that gave rise to the feeling of dislike he entertained for him. This, if not so strong as the feeling with which he regarded his younger son, was to say the least unfatherly.

It half amused, half disgusted Undine to see the little bloated, leaden-eyed creature standing among the elegancies and beauties which his money had bought, talking of *my* pictures. My pictures! As if anything with a trace of beauty could ever belong to him. He might lay out his money for them; and if they were pictures they might hang on his walls, if they were women (a luxury in which he still largely indulged) he might dress them richly and buy their smiles and obedience; but possess them—never! The flesh-incrusted soul that looked out through the hard blue eyes in their setting of red fat, would know nothing of the possession of that which had beauty. Undine thought as she looked at him how unenviable was the fate of both women and pictures. But she soon forgot him before a large oil painting. It represented a battlefield. Horses and riders, dying and dead, lay around in wild confusion, while in the foreground, stretched out upon a heap of the slain, lay the figure of a man gorgeously clad in the knightly costume of the olden days. His plumed helmet lay at his side, filled with blood; and the beautiful face, so faultless in feature, so pitilessly hard in expression, was turned upward to the dark evening sky. At his feet, clasping them with both hands while it crouched upon the ground, was the figure of a woman, its delicate and voluptuous development being hardly concealed by the coarse, scanty clothing it wore. On the face there was a wild look almost of joy, though the lines about the mouth were those of speechless agony.

"You seem fascinated by this picture," said Harry Blair, gently, as he stood behind her. "It is my favourite also, but I confess I like it only because of the woman's face; I can make nothing out of it."

"It seems to me to tell its own story," answered Undine, speaking softly, as though more to herself than to him. "He was a noble, high-blooded lord, and she a poor serf, with only her soul and beautiful body to give him. He hardly cared to take them, though it was for nothing; and now, in the hour of death, she has followed him and found him lying dead; and she is crouching at his feet in agony because he is gone, and in wild joy because he is hers alone now, hers and no other's, if only that she may lie at his feet and die there."

"A very desirable fate, certainly," said a voice behind her that was far too melodious and well modulated to be that of either Harry Blair or Cousin Jonathan, whom they had left in the next room.

Undine looked round quickly from her slaughtered knight and passion-filled maiden to behold, standing behind her, that "Piece of divine perfection" as his lady admirers were wont to call him—Mr. Albert Blair.

He was a man of somewhat more than six feet in height, with a lithe graceful figure and a head of beautiful yellow-brown curls. His moustaches, of the same colour, were so delicately curled that one felt surprised to see the firm powerful lips under them. His features were delicately chiselled, and from the regular white teeth to the small round ear there was neither fault nor flaw to be found in him, unless it were his eyes. They were of a pale cold blue, and would not have been small had he not habitually kept the lids more than half closed. There was nothing lost by that proceeding certainly, for when now and then on rare occasions he lifted them, the gleam shot forth was as icy and chilling as a moonbeam falling on a glacier. It was one of these that fell on Undine as she looked round, and it instantly froze her. She knew without looking at him that the cold light was falling on the small rent in her glove and on her ruffled hair which she had not smoothed before coming out.

There are some men and women in whose society we instantly feel a sublime indifference as to the cut of a coat, the dust on our sleeve, or the sit of our necktie; while there are others who, the moment we see them, set us running over all the flaws and defects in costume and person, from the want of blacking on our boots to the broken nail on our forefinger. There are men and women in whose presence we seem to be released from ourselves and to be possessed of ideas and powers of expression which till then we never dreamed of; while others seem to shrivel us up and leave us standing without an idea or a correct word in all our vocabulary on which we can lay hands. One of these latter was Albert Blair.

Everyone on whom the cold beam fell felt awkward, ill-dressed, and ignorant. Elegant dandies felt in his presence that their whiskers were too long, the set of their coats execrable, and their way of handling a cane simply clownish and disgraceful. Ladies, however well contented they had been with their own appearance the moment before, discovered that their dress was all in shocking taste, their knuckles were too large and their sleeves too short, when the blue eyes were turned upon them. And Undine in the hour that followed thought of nothing but her split glove and ruffled hair and, while she stared at the pictures, saw as little of their meaning as did the Piece-of-perfection who walked at her side, with his deferential manner and his disagreeable eyes, passing commonplace conventional remarks upon all they looked at.

It was a great relief to her to get away from him into the fresh evening air, and walk down the green lane between Cousin Jonathan and Harry Blair.

An hour or two later that young gentleman was seated in the smoking-room, with Mrs. Browning's *Portuguese Sonnets* open before him. His feet were drawn up under his chair, his elbows rested on the table, his head was stretched forward, and his great eyes fixed on vacancy. His brother Albert was at the other end of the room, reclining in an easy-chair with his legs stretched over another. His glass, lamp, an elegant cigar-stand, and a pile of blue papers lay at his side on a small round table.

Presently he took the cigar from between his lips and, throwing down the last of the blue papers, said with one of his graceful inimitable little yawns: "You seem to find your book singularly entertaining this evening. You have not looked at it once in the last half hour."

His brother started, and answered quickly, "Quite as entertaining as those everlasting blue papers of yours"; and then added, after a pause, "Don't you think Miss Bock is very like the woman in that picture?"

"What woman, and what picture? You should *try* and be a *little* more explicit if you wish for an answer," said Albert

Blair, now really closing his eyes and puffing the blue smoke softly through his lips.

"Of course—I mean the picture we were looking at when you came up this afternoon," responded his brother, in a tone that very clearly showed how unwelcome that coming up had been.

"Yes, possibly there is a resemblance; but your divinity has not nearly such a delicate hand; and a good hand ranks next to a good figure," retorted his brother, calmly.

Harry looked fire and lightning at him, and the Piece-of-perfection, who had a strange aptitude for seeing things without opening or at least appearing to open his eyes, said, as he puffed away serenely: "There is no occasion to excite yourself about what I say, my dear fellow. She is a very pretty little girl, an uncommonly pretty little girl; beats Lady Edith and her sister hollow; only rather too careless about her dress, and a little peculiar in her manner, that's all."

To think of comparing her to Lady Edith, a die-away beauty with no more soul in her than a fly, and to speak of her with that cool air of superiority, was a crime on his brother's part which put into poor Harry's hand a strong inclination to send Mrs. Browning in her red morocco binding among his brother's curls.

Other books had been so sent for smaller offences in their boyish days, and the sender had been invariably knocked over and coolly kicked out of the room. He was not one of those to whom experience teaches much, still on this occasion he was wise enough to take himself out of the way of temptation; and making his way into the garden he paced up and down the paths in the moonlight. Surely that thing of grace and beauty which in two days had filled the whole circle of his existence—surely it was now in like manner wandering up and down under the dark trees around Cousin Jonathan's house. For had she not said in answer to his ques- question tion that she loved walking alone and in the moonlight?

Now as it happened, on this particular evening Undine sat beside a little table darning Cousin Jonathan's stockings, listening and laughing at extracts from the daily papers and *Punch*, which the little man read aloud to her as he lay on the sofa.

When she stood up to put her work away he asked her what she thought of Mr. Blair number three.

"Think of him?" she answered. "He is only an equally proportioned mixture of ice and iron. With all his deference and politeness, he would freeze one or crush one to atoms with as little compunction as a fly, if one happened to stand in his path. I don't like his brother, I dislike the father, and I detest him," said Undine, as she threw the last stocking into the basket and thought of her torn glove. She sat down to mend it when she got to her room.

"What a contemptible little wretch I am becoming!" she thought when she had finished it, "to allow such trivialities to break into my real life and drive out higher thought. Am I no better than other women after all? I've no heart; if I lose my head what is to become of me?" She felt weary of herself and disgusted, and she could not now lie down on the floor and pray, till in an agony or an ecstasy, she should forget herself. She had taken the first bite at the forbidden fruit, and could see that the terrors which had haunted her were but the inevitable creations of the human mind, as it looked out in its ignorance on this world of suffering and wrong—could see that the visions which had entranced her were but the dreams of the human soul in its craving after happiness and truth. So much she saw; but saw no farther. Inevitably as to the soul in its search after its highest truth there comes a time of agony and of blood, so too there comes a time of deadness and of cold. The old life has been cut down to the roots, the new life has not yet arisen. So, too, in our childish vision of hell, we stand alone in a world of darkness and silence till the world around us and even we ourselves seem to become mere mocking shadows. Yet, could we know it, it is but the silence that comes before the dawning; it is but the darkness that comes before the day breaks; it is but the land of glittering glaciers that lies between us and the celestial city. And what if we should perish alone in its mist and cold? Better to die frozen, striving for the glorious golden city of

God, up yonder—better than here, in the land of Egypt, with the flesh pots and the onions, the leeks and the garlic.

That evening, while Undine sat mending her glove, Albert Blair still leaned back in his chair, sipped his glass, and smoked with his half-closed eyes, making calculations and thinking hard all the while.

Unknown to his father and without capital, he was speculating, as he himself would have allowed, in a rather wild and reckless manner. These speculations had for him the same irresistible fascination that the gaming table had for many, and only through their help, if ever, could he hope to free himself from his father's control—unless he should marry a rich wife; and to Albert Blair's proud palate a wife's bread would have tasted yet more bitter than a father's.

"Still, I must keep Lady Edith well in hand. If these speculations should fail, it must come to marrying her. She dresses in good taste and is in perfect style—but I would rather it were her sister," he soliloquized.

VII.
LOVERS

THERE be loves many and gods many; and happy the man whose god and love are one—happy for the time being; most miserable of mortals when the time of revelation comes and at one stroke both god and lover crumble into dust.

Harry's love for Undine had sprung into life, full grown and omnipotent, on that first afternoon when he met her in the woods; and if from that time it could not be said to have grown stronger, it had certainly grown larger, until at last the whole world animate and inanimate, intellectual and moral, was for him but one being, imaged and reflected in a thousand ways. Women's dresses and faces had a new meaning for him; for, though standing afar off, were they not like to hers? And the little wild forest flowers that she loved, were they not emblems of her, as they nodded their innocent white heads at one another? In the books that he read, he paused only when he came to some sentence that might have been hers; and all that was beautiful and sweet sang back her name to him. Dark days came for his well-worn bible, and for Beecher's *Life Thoughts* and a score of brethren who had been his daily study. *She* never read them; and they were thrown contemptuously onto a lower shelf, to lie there till the wheel of time should have turned.

"Why do you always change the topic when our conversation turns to religious subjects?" Harry asked Undine one day, some four months after their first meeting, as he sat in the low bow-window in front of Cousin Jonathan's house, with his feet resting on the gravelled path outside.

Undine stood behind him, mending a great rent in her dress, made as they had been rambling in the wood together in search of the wild flowers which now, tied into a great bunch, he held in his hand.

"Religion is like love," answered Undine. "It flourishes best in silence, and is to be felt, not spoken of."

"I don't mean merely what one may call emotional religious subjects," he answered, looking up into her face with his great pleading woman's eyes. "You were arguing last night with Mrs. Barnacles about the right or wrong of committing suicide. You never talk with *me* about such things; your conversation with me is always about the smallest trivialities, such as you talk of to Miss Mell."

The dark eyes above him looked down on him with that half-pitying, half-scornful look that was so often in them when they rested on him.

"You must be contented with what you get," she said.

"But you give me so very little."

There was something very piteous in the words and in the face that looked up at her which would have cut sore against the hearts of many women; but she cared nothing, only said: "I give light where I get it. When you enlighten my spiritual darkness, I shall try and do as much for yours."

She had a contemptuous pity for the great boy, with his manly years and his crammed brain, and his passionate love that had made him follow her about for the last four months and serve her like a dog.

"If a bird is only fitted to live among the marshes and reeds in the valley, why tempt it after you to the cold high rocks where the eagle finds a glorious life in the clear cold air?" So Undine said to him, and so thinking, she made no attempt to lead her poor wild duck to the heights for which nature had never fitted him, and where he must die of frost and starvation.

His ideas as to what her views might be were not very clear, but he had a vague notion that she believed in nothing; accordingly he had convinced himself that he also believed in nothing and he had not a little disgusted and very much astonished her by informing her, as he scraped up and down with his boots on the gravel, that he was an infidel, an atheist beside whom Hume was orthodox and Voltaire a credulous believer.

"I am sorry to hear it," was Undine's brief reply.

"Why should you be sorry that I resemble you?" he asked.

"I was not aware that you did so," she answered. "Will you please tell me the name of that little purple flower? I wish I had all at my finger ends that you have."

He told her the name of the flower and sat twirling the bunch round in his hands.

Undine stooped down for it, when the rent in her dress was mended.

"I wish you would choose out one flower and give it to me," he said, never removing his gaze from her face. "May I have one?"

"Of course you may," said Undine, carelessly holding out the bunch. "They are very pretty; choose which you like."

"I care nothing about it unless *you* give it me," he answered, in a deep passionate voice that always angered her.

"There," she said, pulling out a great gaudy dandelion, which in spite of his disapproval she had persisted in putting in the bunch.

"How long the shades are growing. I really must go and get tea ready. I'm very discourteous to dismiss you in this way, am I not?" said his angel, and with a laugh fluttered out at the back door.

"What a poor fool I am!" he said to himself as he sat in the window, looking at the gaudy flower in his hand and feeling a strong inclination to throw it down on the ground and tread on it. In the end, however, he fastened it carefully in his buttonhole and walked home moodily through the wood; for, is it not written on the iron leaf: "Who drinks of Cupid's nectar cup Loves downwards, and not up: He who loves of Gods and men Shall not by the same be loved again."

It was not often the case (and it showed the discretion of all parties that it was not) that they were alone together, the three Blairs, father and sons. On this evening, however, all three sat in the smoking-room and all three were smoking; for had not Undine said that "A man who does not smoke is as bad as a woman that swears." It was purgatory before that time to Harry Blair, but he stuck to his pipe with the resolution of a martyr.

There was a blazing fire in the grate, and at one side of it sat Albert Blair; while before it lay a great curly brown-and-white dog with his nose resting on his master's foot.

"You are leaving for London tomorrow, are you not?" he asked his father, who sat on the opposite side of the fire.

"Yes," was the short rejoinder.

"Be back at the beginning of summer?"

"Perhaps so. Depends on circumstances."

"When are you taking yourself off?"

"Don't know."

The master of the dog had more than one attraction in Greenwood, and a lady who must be kept in hand close by;

so, though the place was wretchedly dull, he was in no hurry to leave it.

"There is no need to ask when you go," said the father, turning with one of his most sinister smiles to his youngest son. "We all know you are booked for Greenwood till a certain individual, despairing of a richer morsel, shall consent to swallow you."

Harry Blair threw down his pipe, emptying its contents on his trousers and the carpet; and drawing himself up and making a tremendous effort to look dignified and serene, after the manner of his elder brother, he said with trembling lips: "I must beg of you to say no more upon a subject upon which you are in total and absolute ignorance."

His father laughed, one of his coarse brutal laughs; Albert leaned down to stroke Prince's head and went on curling his moustaches.

"As to my being in total ignorance," said the father, "I know nearly as much of your little beauty as you do yourself, and infinitely more about woman in general, I fancy. She would think no more of throwing you overboard, along with her books and her flowers, if by doing so she could gain a few thousand a year, than I do of knocking the ashes off the end of my cigar."

Harry Blair rose to his feet, knocking over the tumbler that stood at his elbow. His hot blood, which in schoolboy days had gained for him the highly appropriate sobriquet of "Fire Brain," was now fairly roused:

"If any man but my father had dared to speak those words," he said with tremendous passion, "I would have knocked them down his throat; as it is, I will only prove to you that they are a lie, a cowardly dastardly lie."

His father spoke with a quiet sneer: "You surely forget in whose house you are standing, whose money it is that causes women to look at you! Go and tell your beautiful Undine that your father has turned you out of his house, that you have not a penny in the world, nor the wits to make one; go and tell her that your father would rather see his money rolling in the gutter than that a penny of it should ever come to you. Go and tell her that, and see what her answer will be! Go, go at once."

There was no passion in the words; they were calmly, sneeringly spoken, as words are that have been lying on the tongue for years, ready for use.

Albert Blair sat lazily looking into the fire. He had known it would come to this some day, and he was glad; it gave him a better chance.

When he looked up his brother had left the room, and his father, sitting opposite him, was puffing away vigorously.

"The young dog!" he said after a pause. "He has all his mother's damned impertinence, and he shall learn a lesson or two yet before he dies. Young dog!"

Albert made no remark and a long silence followed, suddenly broken, greatly to his surprise, by a long-continued, deep chuckling laugh proceeding from his father. The Piece-of-perfection for once fairly opened his eyes and stared at him. His respected senior was not generally given to mirth, even of the demoniac order.

"I'll do it," he chuckled, "I'll do it." And then, seeming to remember himself, he rose, kicked the dog, and took his departure, leaving his son in undivided possession of the fire and his own meditations.

The next morning was cold and stinging and Undine half repented that she had not stayed at home, as Cousin Jonathan wished, in place of going for her morning walk.

She was just turning homeward when, hearing a step beside her, she looked round, and saw, to her great astonishment, no less a personage than Mr. George Blair, looking redder than usual and almost out of breath.

"I heard this was your favourite early walk," he began, after wishing her good morning; "and I have walked myself almost out of breath, fearing I might miss you. I have long wished for an opportunity of seeing you in private, and at last I have it."

A pause followed, Undine ransacking her brain to discover some possible cause for *his* desiring a private interview with her.

"I trust," he began again, "that you will not be much surprised at what I am about to say. I trust—I feel in fact convinced—that you have understood what the attraction has been which has led me so often to your cousin's house. Though so much your senior in years, I trust, my dear Miss Bock, that you will believe me when I assure you that the affection which I offer you is as ardent and as sincere as that which any younger man might give you, and that, with the will, I have also the power to surround my wife—and such, if you will permit me, I would make you—with everything which can induce to happiness. I cannot ask, I would not desire, an immediate answer. It is of course only right that you should first seek the advice of your friends; but will you not give me some hope, however faint it may be?"

He paused to take breath at the end of his pedantic little oration, while Undine turned on him a face in which nothing but blank astonishment was written; it changed to one of disgust as her eyes rested on the little red-faced creature. He saw the look and had expected to see it. He had had, as he said, great experience in woman, and knew that the handsome penniless young lover must hope to carry the day by storm or not at all, that time and reflection are fatal to his success; while the man of fifty, with his bloated face and bags of money, has nothing but these to rely on; and they work for him more surely when he is absent than present.

He took no notice of the look she gave him, but it made him swear in the fatty depths of his inmost heart that, come what would, he should yet have her as his wife. He drew the little scarlet cloak that was slipping back lightly over her shoulder, and fastened it with a brooch formed of diamond-studded flowers which he drew from his pocket.

"Pray do not," she said, as she wrenched it loose and held it out to him as though it had been a creature which stung her hand. "You do me a great honour," she said; "but it is quite impossible, quite."

The old man peered out at her from his rolls of fat, and before turning to leave her said, "Then I had best wish you good morning; but before I do so may I beg of you, my dear Miss Bock, to remember that if ever you should change your mind (and we never know what the future may bring us), *I* shall not have changed. I leave for London tomorrow," he continued; "and unless you should write to me, having altered your mind, as I sincerely hope you may do, it may be long before we meet again. Good-bye, Miss Bock." And without waiting for her reply he turned away and trotted down the lane. Undine stood to watch him as he rolled out of sight.

"His wife!" She laughed a merry, mocking laugh. "His wife!"

The idea of being any man's wife, of bearing any man's children, was absurd enough to her, to whom a lover was only a reality of the imagination, to be adored, worshipped, and endowed with every perfection mental and physical, but not to be seen, clothed in flesh and blood; just as we dream of heaven, but would laugh to scorn the man who offered to show it us.

Her merry mocking laugh would have sounded almost as derisive had it been Albert Blair, the son and graceful Apollo, instead of George Blair, the father, old and coarse.

"Money," she said. "What is money?" And kicked with her little foot a rotten stick which lay in her path as contemptuously as she had just thrown from her the wealth that a word might have made hers.

Aye, gold and love, what are they? The great gods that rule us! Gold, god of the body with its lusts and its clay; Love, god of the soul with its fire and its passions. As long as a human being lives shall they, too, not live and struggle and strive for the mastery?—the one ruling over the young and fresh, the other stealing his kingdom from him when he grows old and wrinkled?

"Money! What is money?" said Undine, derisively, for she had seen no deeper into life than love songs and dreams could take her; and she wrapped the little scarlet cloak about her and went home light of heart and singing.

She found a letter waiting for her on her bedroom table, but took off her things and stood warming her hands at the fire before opening it.

"Only from poor Harry Blair, about some book or flower," she said. "Poor" falls naturally before some names; it did before his.

She opened the letter and threw the wrapper into the fire, where it flamed up and turned to ashes, like a young heart devoured by that cruel merciless old God of Love.

At first as she read she looked a little puzzled, then angry, then amused, and finally with a mingling of all three upon her face sat down before the fire with the three great blue sheets in her lap.

It was as passionate an appeal as ever was penned by arrow-smitten man.

For her sake he had given up all—fortune, friends, rank—without a thought and without a regret. She alone could give him that for which alone he longed, that which alone could make him happy. Would she refuse him? No, she could not, would not; he felt sure of that. Nothing else was dear to him on earth, nothing else did he desire. So it ran on. It might be years, he said, before he could make her his wife, but all he yearned to know was that her heart was his, her head, her soul.

When Undine got thus far the disgust she felt got into her fingers, which sent the two sheets she had finished into the fire after the wrapper.

"The father asked for my body and offered me gold in return; *he* asks my soul, spirit *and* body, and has nothing in the universe to give but a pair of great staring woman's eyes, and a soft brain, crammed to bursting and without a particle of sense in it." So she said to herself, as she sat tearing up the last page, still unread, and letting the fragments fall in a blue shower at her feet.

Well was it for the hapless penman that he could not see this and was not where he longed to be—lying at her feet; better wandering the woods where now and then, as the wind swayed the leafless branches, he would catch a glimpse of the house which held her.

She had just finished writing him a few very cool and careless lines in answer, when the breakfast bell rang.

"I will say nothing about it to Cousin Jonathan. It must make a man feel wretchedly small to find that another knows his love has been thrown back at him. And I suppose it is a kind of love they both have for me," she thought as she rose to go.

Passing out at the door, she caught sight of her own face in the little glass that hung on the opposite wall, and for the first time that morning a womanly, or in justice let us say a human, feeling of pleasure came to her.

It is so nice to be desired by others, so nice to be beautiful.

When she entered the breakfast-room Cousin Jonathan was standing with his back to the fire, dressed in his everlasting salt-and-pepper coat and plaid trousers.

"I'm a little wretch," she thought as she looked at him. "Here is a man who has been more than a father to me, and yet whenever I look at him I detest him. And two men have told me this morning that they loved me, and I feel no sorrow that I can't return it as a true-hearted woman would. I'm a heartless creature and horribly hard, there's no doubt of it."

"You are late this morning," said Cousin Jonathan. "I suppose you have been writing your answer."

"To whom?" asked Undine.

"The letter you received was given me to bring. I know all about it," replied Cousin Jonathan, smiling. He felt no trepidation as to what her answer might be; for, if there was one thing which the little man had studied in the last three years, it was the character of the pink-and-white thing before him. He understood her better than anyone else had ever done, in many ways. He knew of that power of passion that lay dead and unawakened beneath the cold, feelingless shell; and he knew as surely that the day would come when it would be called into wild life, not by his hand or that of any Harry Blair, with woman's eyes and soft trusting nature.

"You have still got your red cloak on; I always like you best in it," he said, as he drew her to him to receive the morning kiss he had given her ever since she came to him.

Undine turned quickly from him and sat down to pour out his tea.

"Where is Cousin Jane this morning?" she asked.

"She is feeling worse than usual and has just sent for the doctor," he answered as he drew his chair near to the table and to her. "What answer are you going to give a certain individual?" he asked her, after a pause.

"There is only one answer I could give him," she replied, shortly, as she passed Cousin Jonathan's tea.

"And he gave up everything for you! His father has vowed to have nothing more to do with him; and now all the world will say that you did not marry him because he had no prospects."

Undine laughed her little scornful laugh.

"All the tongues on earth may clamour; they cannot hurt me," she answered.

When breakfast was over she dispatched the note, as cold and killing a missive as ever carried destruc- destruction tion to aerial castle. She did not love him, never could; would never care to be any man's wife; hoped they would always be good friends; hoped he would find some one to make him happy and love him; so the note ended.

All the morning she sat with Mrs. Barnacles who was really very ill; but when the afternoon came, bringing Miss Mell and Mrs. Goodman, she felt free to take her book and cloak and wander out.

'Twas cheerless and wintry enough, but the air was pleasant and fresh after the close room, and her book engrossed her attention.

Presently she heard voices, but did not look up until she found herself close to Albert Blair. There was no one with him but his dog, so she concluded he must have been speaking to it.

Master and dog made a pretty picture as they stood on a raised bank, with the leaden sky and leafless trees for a background. Both looked so strong and placid, so perfect after their types.

The half-closed eyes caught sight of her in a moment, and their owner came forward to meet her. He made some graceful remarks concerning the weather, inquired after her cousin; and they paused as they walked beneath the very trees where poor Harry had wandered in the morning.

"Here, sir! here!" he called to the dog, who bounded out of the little path in search of some imaginary game. The dog came slowly back and rubbed his head against his master's knee, who stooped down to stroke his head.

"How absolutely that dog obeys you," said Undine, feeling as she always did in the presence of the Piece-of-perfection, at a loss for an idea.

"I make most things which belong to me do that," he answered, quietly; and as she glanced up at the firm lips beneath the delicate golden moustache she felt it must be so.

How nice it must be to have something you must obey, something you cannot help obeying, whether you wish or not! I never have, she thought.

"Have you had that dog long?" she asked.

"About two years, and he never leaves me; sleeps at the door of my room every night."

"You would miss him now if you were to lose him," said Undine, thinking of Socrates.

"Perhaps so," he replied, carelessly curling the tip of his moustache; "he is an exquisite animal. I have been offered fifty pounds for him, but would not let him go for four times that sum." Again he stooped and touched the dog's head, who walked close beside him, proud and pleased.

Undine, walking at the other side, envied him.

"Will you allow me the pleasure of carrying your book? It is rather too large a one for you," he said, noticing the ponderous volume under her arm.

Taking it from her, he glanced at the title, and Undine saw the satirical lines at the corner of his mouth and eyes grow deeper; but he only said in his blandest tone, "Rather stiff reading, I should imagine," and stooped to loosen a dry branch that had caught in her skirt.

Undine wished the book buried under the highest pile of leaves that ever wind collected and left there to rot; though only half an hour before she had been so absorbed by it that Greenwood and the vanities of the present life were banished from her mind.

In the presence of all other men and women she could walk erect. Why in this man's presence was she bowed down, wishing only to do and say what he might approve? Others might ridicule her dress, her manners, her tastes, and she would cling to them with the greater tenacity; but if a line deepened round *this* man's mouth, she would have given untold treasure to be able to alter or disclaim them.

She was glad when the walk was over—as she always was to get out of his society—and yet, when she was alone before the fire, she took the great book and quietly tore out the leaves one by one and watched them wither and shrivel in the flames.

"I must be going mad," she said. "What makes me do this, and take such pleasure in doing it?"

Going mad!—of course she was, as we most of us go once in our lives and, thank the gods, not more than once.

Cousin Jonathan was sitting with his wife up- upstairs stairs; and when it grew dark Undine built up the fire, blew out the light, and lay down on the sofa.

Presently down the passage came Cousin Jonathan on the way to his study; quietly, for Cousin Jonathan's footfalls were never heard. As he passed he looked in at the door. The red coals cast a ruddy glow over the little room, and the chairs and tables cast long flickering shadows on the brown wall. On the sofa in the corner opposite the fire *she* lay, just visible in her white dress, with arms clasped over her head and dark eyes fixed on the firelight: not seeing *it*, but only a tall figure with a rough dog at its side standing on a leaf-strewn bank, with the wintry sky and barren trees for setting.

Long the little figure in its brown coat and plaid trousers stood watching in the doorway; at last it entered and kneeled down softly beside her.

He had loved her so long, he had loved her so passionately, with the best love his nature could give; and tonight this love spoke itself in words as vehement and startling as the passion itself had been long restrained and covered over.

She started up and threw him from her, and, quivering with rage, stood before him.

Still on his knees at her feet, the little man caught her hand and glanced up at the face above him. Even in the dim firelight, the look of intense loathing it wore was visible. It brought him back to reason.

Dropping the hand, filled with insufferable shame, he crawled from the room almost on hands and knees, as though to hide him in the ground. As he shuffled through the doorway he dropped one green slipper on the mat.

Undine stood as one in a dream and watched the little figure in its plaid trousers and brown coat as it glided swiftly from the room, to pass out of her sight forever. For the little man, in his green plaid, with his angel eyes and beautiful prayers, she was to see no more, though from afar off his shadow might fall on and darken her.

As she passed out at the door she drew up her skirts, lest in passing they might touch the shoe that lay there.

"'Tis a pretty little thing," soliloquized Albert Blair as he walked home through the wood the same evening; "a pretty little thing, and if she were trained might be good for something. She would not care to be any man's wife, she tells my poor fool of a brother. Well, if these affairs of mine turn out well and I am able to indulge a fancy, who knows? How should you like a certain little eccentricity for a mistress, Prince?" he said, touching with the tips of his fingers the dog's head. "Whether I ever let things go as far as that or not, I may see what I can do with her. Ha, ha! How wrathful the poor boy would be, and the old one too, for I think *he* had his thoughts of her." And Albert Blair smiled his quiet smile. He had but one smile for friend or foe, for prince and beggar, which meant nothing, told nothing, showed nothing.

The next morning, when Undine had fallen into her first troubled sleep, Mrs. Barnacles' maid came to rouse her.

Cousin Jonathan had been obliged to leave on some unexpected and most important business and might be gone for weeks. He had started before daybreak, and his wife was terribly cut up at his having left her when she was so ill. She seemed worse and wanted to see Undine at once, the girl said.

When Undine entered the room she found the poor invalid in tears. "It was so cruel of him to go away like this," she said, sobbing; "he knows how that hateful Miss Mell and Mrs. Goodman will talk and say he cares nothing for me, to go away and leave me when I am so ill, and yet he does it."

Undine tried to console her and felt she could not tell her, as she had determined, that in a few hours she also would leave.

In her cold way she felt pity for the poor woman whose husband cared as little for her as she did for him, who loved nothing, had no friends, and lived in the constant fear and dread of Goodman, Mell, & Co.

"I was thinking," Undine said, "of going to stay with my grandmother. Since my grandfather's death she lives alone and has often asked me to come to her; but I will not leave you till you are better."

So all that day Undine sat at her bedside.

"Why *don't* you take a book and read? You could turn up a corner of the blind," said Mrs. Barnacles.

"I don't care to read today, thank you," said Undine.

"Why, what on earth has come to you?" said the invalid.

Later on the servant entered, to say that Mr. Albert Blair had called to know how her cousin was.

"Tell him she is no better," answered Undine.

"But he wanted to see Miss Bock herself," said the girl.

Undine rose and went downstairs.

He was leaning against the mantelpiece in the parlour when she entered, and his dog lay at his feet.

She looked ill and pale, but he had never liked her aspect so well as he did at that moment.

"Your cousin is seriously ill, I hear," he said as he came forward to meet her; "and you look as though you had not found much rest last night."

There was kindly feeling in the words but none in the tone or in the face that looked down at her, only bland politeness.

"I had not to sit up last night; Mr. Barnacles left only early this morning," answered Undine.

"So I heard just now. Wouldn't you allow me to send some one to sleep here? You have no man about the place, and it is a long way to the village to the doctor."

"No, thank you," said Undine, wondering to find in him such thoughtful kindness. "You are very good, but we require no one."

"I am sure you will feel very lonely. Won't you let me leave Prince to keep you company?" He noticed that she had stooped to caress the dog.

"He would not stay," said Undine, smiling.

"He will do just as I tell him," said his master, touching the dog with his foot. "Here Prince, lie down!"

The dog lay down again on the rug, but watched his master with anxious eyes as he turned to leave; and was only kept from following him by another stern, "Lie down!"

"Poor old fellow! It's very cruel of me to keep you," said Undine, kneeling down beside him after his master had gone, and burying her face in his rough curls.

"I'm very cruel, but I am so lonely, and I love nothing, nothing at all. I thought I loved my books and nature, but now I find I don't care anything, even for them. O Prince, I wish I were you! I don't want to be loved; I only want to love something."

The dog looked up at her with his loving, trust- trustful ful eyes and tried to lick her face, till she buried it again in his neck.

Albert Blair called again the next day and every day in the dreary two weeks that followed, but he never stayed more than a few minutes, and sometimes did not even come in, only wanting to hear how the invalid was.

Undine as she sat before the fire, not caring to read or work, counted the slow hours as they passed, for they brought his coming nearer.

Prince stayed with her always. She had thought never to love another animal again when Socrates died; but our hearts are often larger than our wills, and the great curly dog had grown to be almost what the brown-eyed monkey had been to her in other days.

VIII.
BEAUTIFUL SNOW

IT WAS a cold wintry afternoon and the white snow clouds were lying low and heavy. Undine, after many almost sleepless nights, crept down to the little parlour and had a fire made there, the first that had been made since Cousin Jonathan left.

Miss Mell, now her friend was getting better, had offered to come and sit up with her; and Undine, as she nestled down in the great armchair, looked forward to a long evening of drowsy rest. Prince lay sleeping before her with his head at her feet, and she, half dozing, watched the little sparks as they fluttered up the chimney. So short, so warm, so bright; how pleasant the life of a spark must be!

"You seem to find something very absorbing in the contemplation of the fire this evening," said a voice beside her; and Prince, wide awake in an instant, leaped up to greet his master.

"You quite startled me," she said. "I did not think you would come tonight; it is getting almost dark."

"Yes; we have the promise of a heavy fall of snow," he said, as he seated himself in an armchair on the other side of the fire.

"You can have no idea what a charming picture this room makes, coming in from the cold outside," he continued, trying at the same time to repulse Prince, who in a transport of joy had put a paw on each shoulder.

"You must take him home with you tonight," said Undine. "I am not going to be so cruel as to keep him here any longer; and you must miss him."

"No, I never miss him. You had better keep him if he is any pleasure to you," answered the Piece-of-perfection, stretching out one delicate white hand to the dancing flame.

After a short silence he said, "Do you never wish to return to Africa?"

"No," she replied. "I know no one there. My stepfather has remarried. But I should like to see the old farm and my little monkey's grave again."

He was leaning back now with his face in the shadow; she could not see the lines she dreaded at the corners of his mouth, so she answered, "Yes, he was the best friend I had."

Another pause followed; then he said, more abruptly than was his wont, "I have a favour to ask of you, Miss Bock.

"You rather puzzle me," he said. "I never feel sure I understand you, and I do most men. At times I form an opinion of you, at times another, but I never feel sure that I am right. I wish you could satisfy my curiosity and explain to me how it is you come to have such extraordinary views and manners."

"Why do you not put some other word in the place of 'extraordinary'—say, 'pernicious,' 'reprehensible'? That is what you really think," she replied, using a freer speech with him than ever before, for in the firelight the bands of speech are loosed and the tongues of men and women do wonders.

He never paid her compliments or spoke to her as he would to another woman, so he answered quietly, "Those words would be almost too strong; say, unwomanly."

Another making this remark would have been answered by a contemptuous silence; or at best she would have launched out into a denunciation of that singular injustice which cramps and dwarfs a woman's mind, making it an unpardonable offence against her womanhood to entertain a thought or give utterance to an idea that has not been repeated and reëchoed till it is as stale and unpalatable as a last year's loaf. Tonight she only said: "Why are they unwomanly? What is your idea of what a woman ought to be?"

"You are asking me a question hard to answer," he replied, looking with his half-closed eyes into the fire. "A woman to be womanly should have nothing striking or peculiar about her; she should shun all extremes in manners and modes of expression; she should have no strong views on any question, especially when they differ from those of her surroundings; she should not be too reserved in her manners, and still less too affable and undignified. There is between all extremes a happy mediate, and there a woman should always be found. Men may turn to one side or the other; woman never must."

Undine said nothing when he ended. She could not help it; she had been born with strong and determined ideas on every subject, sub- and superlunar, and not one step of her sixteen years' journey had she walked in the happy mediate road. It was too late to change now. They had told her that the day would come when she would repent having done nothing to try to conform herself, at least outwardly, to the views of others; and she did repent it as she sat there that evening. She would have parted with all that was highest and best in herself to become a little less Undine, a little more like anyone else. Who was this man, what was he, that he should make her grovel so? she asked herself.

"You have not yet answered me," said the Piece-of-perfection, again stretching out his delicate hands to the blaze. "Are you going to satisfy my curiosity?"

It seemed so strangely delightful to do something at his request, and yet she seemed to have nothing to tell, nothing that she could tell *him*; and she said so.

"Nothing! And you have lived for sixteen years and in two continents, and certainly are not troubled with lack of ideas. You must excuse me, however. I have no right to press you in this way."

Undine sat leaning forward with her arms folded on her knees, looking into the bright flame that threw its light full upon her, and began, awkwardly and stupidly enough at first, to tell of the old African days—awkwardly and stupidly enough till she forgot the presence of the man who was leaning back in the shade on the other side of the fire and watching her with his cold blue eyes. Then she saw only Socrates and her governess, and the little Dutch girls, and the old red farmhouse in the Karoo—saw the little round-stone koppies, with their milk bushes and red sand, and was again the little child among them all, with the child's thoughts and longings.

Albert Blair sat and listened without the shade of a sneer upon his lips.

Most men have their moments of insanity, which belie and are at variance with all the days and years of the past and will find no successor in the future, moments when their thoughts and feelings are opposed to all they have ever deemed rational, right or possible.

Such moments came for the first time and the last to the Piece-of-perfection as he sat listening to Undine in the firelight.

A pity, nay, a passionate sympathy, filled his heart for her; for one moment he forgot that the soul which troubled itself further than to find and eat the bread and honey of this life was the soul of a fool—forgot that the only right of a woman is the right of the rose—to smile and be, not to think and live.

Forgetting all this, bewitched, befooled, infatuated, he stretched out his hand to the little figure opposite him.

"Your life has been lonely; no one has understood you; you may have had no one to guide you," he said, speaking for the first time and in a voice strangely sweet and unlike his own. "Will you let me be your friend and take care of you?"

She sat and looked at him as one in a dream.

"Come to me, darling," he said, holding out his hand to her.

Still she sat and looked at him; then he drew her softly to his arms, and she nestled close to him.

She did not kiss him or speak: only clung to him and rested with her arms round his neck and her head on his shoulder.

If she lay there hours or moments, she did not know; it was enough to be there.

"Why do you lie so quietly, darling? Why do you not tell me that you love me?" he said, turning her face round to his.

It seemed to break her rest, and she only answered him by putting her hand softly on his cheek.

"Are you not going to kiss me, my little girl?" he asked again, lightly bringing his lips down to hers and kissing them.

She kissed him and then buried her face in his shoulder.

"Did you ever care about anyone before you loved me? Did you, darling?" he asked her, running his fingers through her hair.

What was the past? What was the future? The present was enough. She answered, "No."

"You could talk so well a little time ago, and now you can hardly get out one little 'no'. Tell me that you love me, my little girl."

"I love you more than anything, more than everything," she said, holding his face between her two hands and putting her cheek softly against his; then she nestled close to him again.

"Are you happy now?"

"Yes."

"How astonished everyone will be when they hear who is to be my little wife," said the Piece-of-perfection as he thought with infinite satisfaction of the discomfiture of his father and brother, also of Lady Edith and others of his worshippers. How would she look among them all? Beautiful? His wife must shine and eclipse all women. Men must envy him his wife, as they did his dogs and his horses. Would it be so with this little girl?

"Undine, I want you to do something for me," he said, after a long pause. "I know you will do whatever I tell you. Will you not?"

"Yes," she said, creeping very close to him.

"You must not spend so much time over your books as you have done. I would rather you left them alone altogether. You must give two or three hours a day to your music, and learn dancing. I want my wife to be deficient in nothing. Do you hear?"

It was the cold Piece-of-perfection with the half-closed eyes that spoke these words, not the lover of half an hour ago, and they struck Undine a little chill; but she only whispered in his ear that she would do all he told her.

"Why do you tremble so, my little darling?" he said, as he stood her down on the hearth rug. "I must go now, but I will come again early tomorrow. How cold your little hands are. Warm them by the fire and then go to bed. Now you belong to me, I don't want you to have dark rings round your eyes, as though you had sat up all night. My wife must be always bright and beautiful, you know. Good-night, darling." So he left her.

Undine kneeled down before the low window and drew back the blind to watch him as he passed down the garden path.

The snow had fallen, the clouds had gone, and the full moon poured down her light on a white glittering world—so white, so pure, so calm. Even the iron paling had its coat of crystal, and the dark evergreens that grew beside the window were bent beneath their load. As far as the eye could reach stretched the silent white snow; only down the little garden path there were his footmarks in it.

IX.
TRODDEN SNOW

"UNDINE," said the Piece-of-perfection the next day, as he stood in the doorway putting on his greatcoat, preparatory to taking his departure; "did that little old cousin of yours never try to make love to you?"

"No," said Undine.

She hated him so, it would have given her such infinite satisfaction to have injured him; yet at the same time it seemed the height of meanness to speak against him—the man who had befriended her. The untruth seemed, in the darkness and confusion of the moment, higher than the truth, and it passed from her lips to bring forth the poisoned fruit which the lie bears, be it spoken for God's glory or the salvation of a soul.

She would have retracted it almost in the same breath, but he answered quickly, "I am glad to hear it; I have a greater respect for my old pedagogue than for almost any man I know, but I had an idea from the way he sometimes spoke of you that he cared rather more for you than a second cousin's husband generally does. I am glad it was fancy. I will come again this evening and take you for a walk." And he was gone.

He was gone, and the untrue word was gone also. She stood in the hall and buried her face in both hands, utterly humiliated. She had told a lie, and told it to *him*. In other days her sorrow would have been that anything could have tempted her so to demean herself. Now it was all swallowed up in this—it was to him.

She ran out through the little garden with nothing on her head and the sleet and snow falling thick upon her. He was just entering the wood. She paused when she had almost reached him at the thought of the cold light that would fall on her when she presented herself before him in such plight—paused, then turned slowly back to the house.

Evil times had fallen on her, and she asked no more, "Is it right?" but only, "Will he think it right?"

"This afternoon I will tell him," she said, as she walked, damp and chilly, up the garden path. "I wish he had never asked me."

It seemed so evil to speak against the man she hated, worse to leave things as they were; yet neither on that afternoon nor on any of the days that followed could she look up into the cold half-closed eyes and say, "I told you a lie."

The words were always on her tongue, always in her heart; but the white face with its wonderful crushing influence over her kept them unspoken.

"I will tell him tomorrow, some day when he loves me better, when he understands me, when I am his little wife," she would say to herself, whenever he had just left her. But a silent though not less abiding conviction was with her that the day never would come when he would know her better. Her one hour of light had passed that night in the little fire-lit parlour; henceforth, strive as she might to annihilate herself and be only what the man might choose, he would never come near her, they would never meet.

"I am afraid I made a great fool of myself," soliloquised the Piece-of-perfection, as he walked alone one sharp frosty evening. "No other woman ever made me lose my head, but I do believe the little creature bewitched me that night with her sentimental talk. She loves me, I can do anything with her, I shall make something of her in time; but I was a great fool."

"What are you doing here?" he asked, coming suddenly upon the subject of his thoughts as she stood below her old tree, wrapped in her little red cloak, with Prince at her side.

The dog rubbed his head against his master's foot; the human dog crept nearer him.

"You know I do not like your wandering about alone," he said, in the cold, unlover-like tone in which he had always spoken to her except on that first evening.

"I would not have come if I had thought you would not like me to," she said, glancing up into his face.

"I want you to go to church tomorrow," was his next and rather abrupt remark. "Your cousin is better; you will be able to go, will you not? You will have to go some day; I would rather you began now.

"Yes, I can go," she answered after a moment's pause.

"'Tis a matter of supreme indifference to me," continued the Piece-of-perfection, "what you choose to believe; but you must do nothing to make yourself peculiar. There is nothing so hateful in a woman as eccentricity of any description."

Undine had now heard this remark so often that she had no new reply to make to it, and walked on in silence.

"Were you very busy this morning, Undine?"

"No, not at all," she said. "Why do you ask me?"

"Because your glove is torn, and I was thinking you might have had some very important matters to attend to which prevented your mending it; but you have a weakness for torn gloves, I fancy."

"You will never see me with one again," she said, pulling it off quickly.

"I hope not," he answered, quietly. "There are few things which I admire less than a slovenly woman. If a woman cares to retain the affection of those about her, she will always be particular as to her dress."

"So that others might love her dress, not herself," said Undine.

"I will care for my wife just as long as she gives me reason to be proud of her," he replied, coolly.

"Just as you do for your horses and your dog?"

"Yes; I believe I care for that dog as well as for most things; but if he became disobedient or vicious, I should care nothing more about him."

He spoke gravely; Undine knew he meant what he said; and the life that lay before her seemed to look almost as cheerless and icy as the white frosty world that lay stretched out before her eyes. But, she resolved, I will be all he wishes me; he shall be proud of me, prouder than of all his dogs and horses, she thought, as she clenched and loosened the fingers of her little gloveless hand.

"What causes you always to move your hand in that extraordinary manner whenever you are angry? It is not very pretty, I can assure you."

"I am not angry; I was only thinking."

"What?"

"That I will try and be everything you wish. Do you believe me?"

"If I did not believe that you would try and that you would also succeed, I would not care to make you my wife," he replied. "You are a clever little woman and can do anything you wish."

And Undine felt more exultant at these equivocal words of praise than Lady Edith at his most honeyed compliments.

For some time after that they walked on in silence, only the sound of their footsteps on the hard frozen ground breaking the stillness.

At last she said, very suddenly and very hurriedly: "You know that if ever, at any moment, at any time, you change and would rather not marry me, if it were the very day before our wedding—you must feel quite free—you must tell me so—it will be all right."

"Are you changing your mind already?" he asked, glancing down at her.

"No, I shall never change," she answered.

"Nor am I in the habit of retracing my steps, either; but it is certainly better, if one does repent, to do so before it is too late."

They said no more till they got to the gate of the garden.

"Are you not going to come in and see my cousin today? She is up," said Undine, and while he sat in Mrs. Barnacles' little sitting-room she ran upstairs.

There was an ominous pulling about the corners of her mouth but she knew if she gave way to it her eyes would be red and swollen in two minutes; so she tore off her hat and cloak and, changing her dress, spent at least five minutes in arranging a black-and-red bow in her hair and a few more on her dress. It took her a long time before she was satisfied with her appearance; then she went downstairs.

He was satisfied with it, too, though she could not tell it from his face. Poor little fool! How she did love him! And he felt a kind of pity for her.

It was growing dark and the red lamp in the hall was already lighted when he rose to go. He had wished her good-night, and she was turning to go upstairs when he called her back softly. He uttered her name twice and drew her tenderly to him when she came to his side.

"Be sure you practise this evening; you are my own little darling," he said, and pressed a long kiss on her lips. "Don't sit up too late, and look as pretty and as sweet when I come tomorrow as you do now. Good-night, my little girl." And again the firm stern lips with their soft golden moustaches were pressed against hers as he folded her close to him.

It was late the next morning when Undine rose; for it is very pleasant, when one has delicious visions, to be dreaming and dozing in bed on a winter's morning. And her visions were sweet, sweet—though, God knows, they were childish and small enough. She would do her hair so; she would dress herself so; she would go to church; she would do this; she would do that. He would kiss her, he would kiss her, as he kissed her last night.

She was sitting on her bed side, as she had been sitting for the last five minutes, with one stocking half on and the other in her hand, when the maid knocked at the door and passed her in a letter.

The hand was his, and it was the first she had ever got from him: she tore it open quickly. It ran:

> MY DEAR LITTLE GIRL! I have just heard that my immediate presence in London is indispensable. 'Tis a matter of business and I can't delay. I have a note from Mr. Barnacles in which he tells me that he has been ill, but returns to Greenwood on Monday. As you intend leaving for your grandmother's as soon as he does so, I suppose I shall not find you here when I return. I shall try to run down and see my little girl as soon as I am able.
>
> Yours most affectionately, A. BLAIR.

She threw herself down among the pillows, and after half an hour rose slowly to begin her packing. When it was done she went to Mrs. Barnacles' room, to tell her that she was leaving that evening.

"It's just another of her freaks," said that lady to Miss Mell, who came to spend the afternoon with her. "No one could have been more kindly treated than she had been here;

quite spoiled in fact. There is no telling what she will take into her head next. I wish her grandmother joy of her, I'm sure."

"Don't you think Harry Blair's going away so suddenly, without making her an offer, may have something to do with it?" said Miss Mell, looking enormously sharp and green about the eyes.

"I am sure from what I have seen that she could have had him at any time she chose, but—you will not mention it to anyone, I know—his father has quarrelled with him and will have nothing more to do with him."

"Ah, I understand now," said Miss Mell; "that will have put my lady out just a little in her pretty little game. A poor penniless boy is not much of a catch. It serves her right. I always thought it shameful, the way she used to walk about everywhere with him quite alone. I wonder she had not more regard for her character than to act as she did. *I* would die sooner than be on such intimate terms with a man to whom I was not engaged; and even then I think a modest reticence *so* becoming in a woman." And Miss Mell drew herself up stiffly in her chair and drew down the corners of her mouth.

"Well, anyhow," said Mrs. Barnacles, sipping her tea, "I do wish her grandmother joy of her. There is something one can't help liking about the girl, but she is so peculiar and eccentric I shall be glad to have her off my hands."

"Don't you think she is trying it on in another direction?" inquired Miss Mell, with that wrinkling about the mouth which was all she had to show for a smile.

"I don't think she tries it on in any direction; that is just what I complain of," replied Mrs. Barnacles. "From what I know, I am sure she could have had old Blair if she had chosen. He is much older than she is, but a penniless girl can't be too fastidious, and he is terribly rich."

"As to her not trying it on, I don't know about that," said Miss Mell; "I don't think she would have said no, if he had given her a chance of saying yes, but perhaps she has higher game in her eye. What do you think some one comes here once and sometimes twice a day for?"

"Oh, he is polite to all women; his attentions mean nothing. He will look higher when he chooses a wife," said Mrs. Barnacles. Miss Mell smiled a far-seeing smile and broke her cake.

While they sat talking of her in the little parlour, Undine was standing for the last time under her old tree in the wood. It was leafless and bare now, and great white icicles hung from its branches. The little stream was silent and noiseless.

Next summer the green leaves would break forth on it and the little brook would run laughing past, whispering to the long grasses and white forest flowers, and among its knotted swollen roots the bright-backed beetles and busy ants would run; but she would rest no more among them. "Good-bye old tree," she said, breaking off a bit of its dry frosty bark. "Good-bye, my friend, my dear old friend. I have had such beautiful dreams beneath you; I have had such happy thoughts. They will never come to me any more; my higher life is dead, quite dead; I love only him and I must serve him now. Good-bye."

X.
MELTED SNOW

HOW white, how white and dazzling, that road upon the hillside lay!

All day she sat at the window, watching it. In the dusk, when no other eye could mark it, she saw it winding in the dimness. All night in her dreams it lay before her, in its white aching emptiness.

How slowly the chill weeks crawled over her—two, four, six, eight. Still she watched it till the colour faded from her cheeks and the bright restless light grew strong in her eyes. Her old grandmother would lay her work aside and, standing behind her, would stroke her hair softly with her old withered hands and say, "You are not well my child; you are lonely; the place is too quiet for you; a young life like yours should not be buried away here."

And Undine would answer nothing, and sit watching, only she knew for what.

The snow had vanished and the road lay, a white chalky line between the brown fields; only now and then a farmer's cart or a labourer from the next village would pass along it.

"Why do you never sit by the fire? It is so cold and cheerless at the window, and there is nothing to be seen," the old woman would say. But still she sat there, looking out and stitching away always at delicate white muslins with pink bows and dreamy blue and white stuffs, which the old woman thought made her look like an angel when she tried them on.

"The child has changed," she would say to herself, as she sat knitting and dozing in the firelight. "She never reads now and thinks only of dress and music; but I suppose it is natural; the young will be young."

The winter went early that year, and the first signs of spring were showing themselves. Undine did not count the days any more; she did not reason or ask herself any questions; she only waited, waited.

One day she saw a boy coming down the road. It was quite midday and the sun was shining with an almost summer-like warmth. She sat there with her hands folded in her lap, looking at him yet not seeing him till he came up to the open window and put a letter in her hand.

She started up and passed out through the next room, where her grandmother sat knitting in the sunshine of the opened door.

"What is it? What has happened?" asked the old woman; but Undine only hurried past her with the letter pressed tight in both hands against her breast.

Through the long leafless garden she passed, where the soft buds were just beginning to swell under the brown bark, through the rough uneven meadow beyond, and sat down at the side of the little cozy river that crept slowly between its muddy reedy banks. She sat long looking at the paper in her hands, with its great red seal; then she tore it open.

What that letter said she never could remember; but she knew, when she had read it, that the dream of her life had vanished, to return no more.

She put the letter whole into her mouth and chewed it fine between her grinding teeth; then she sat still and watched a tiny white feather that lay upon the muddy water bobbing up and down, up and down. Her mind seemed a perfect vacancy but for the thought of that little white feather. She wondered if it would be caught by nodding leaves of the reeds that dipped into the water, or whether it would be stranded on the oozy bank—looked at the little white feather and wondered, and ground the letter fine, fine, between her teeth.

Then, a sudden wild impulse seized her. She must rise—she must run—she must flee—she must go—somewhere, anywhere.

With nothing on her head, sinking ankle deep in the soft mud, she broke through the reeds and bushes and climbed up the steep bank with hands and feet. She did not pause an instant, but ran on to the rugged hill with its winding sheep tracks and sharp stones, climbed it, and ran on among the trees and rocks that lay scattered on its summit. She did not seem able to get further; again and yet again she thought she found herself in the same place; and every time she looked up at the great red sun it seemed a great, laughing, cruel human eye, looking down at her from the clear blue sky.

It was on her, on her, wherever she went, that great blood-red eye, and the great brown hill opposite with its white chalk road was like a leering human face that laughed at her, jeered at her, mocked at her; and the stones, and the trees—they had all a hidden sneer about them. "Fool! fool! fool!" they cried. And the blue cloudless sky overhead was so hard and pitiless, like a righteous human soul which has no mercy for the erring. "O sky, blue cloudless sky, have pity, have pity on me!" she cried in her madness; and she threw herself down and lay on a great flat stone in the footpath. Gazing up into the sky's blue depths, she looked straight at the dazzling sun with an unnatural strength of sight.

They drove her madder, madder, the sky, the sun, the earth; till she writhed in her pain, like a trodden worm, on the ground and stones. Then the old feeling came over her again, and she rose up and ran. Her sight seemed to grow dim and blurred at last, and she stumbled and fell again and yet again over the stones and stumps. Bruised, bleeding, she felt nothing, only knew she must run on, on.

Her grandmother looked out anxiously for her all day, and when it was growing dark that evening, saw her walking slowly up the little garden path, with her head drooping on her breast and her arms hanging heavily at either side.

"Where have you been, my child?" she said, coming out to meet her. "Are you not bitterly cold?"

"No," said Undine, wearily; and when they entered the little parlour with its cheerful lamp and firelight her grandmother noticed that the bright anxious light she was accustomed to see in her eyes had vanished.

"You look ill, my child," she said, resting her nervous old hand softly on her arm.

"I am not ill," Undine said, "only tired. No, I am not hungry; I only want to rest. I am tired, very tired. I want no light, thank you. Good-night."

XI.
A CLEVER LITTLE MAN AND A POOR LITTLE FOOL

IF THE ploughboy knew how the worm suffers that writhes beneath his foot, surely he would not crush it. If we saw the work of the cruel word, surely we should not utter it. If we could see the light of a life vanish and die out, surely we should be loath to extinguish it. But we never can see, never know, never watch these things; therefore blighting, cursing, and inflicting suffering, we go on our way rejoicing.

Albert Blair was not a cruel man. A man of high principle, the world said. A man to whom no one in trouble ever appealed in vain for help. A man who never gave his horse or dog a blow more than was necessary—a good master, a good man, as the world goes. Yet he felt no sorrow for the young life he had crushed. It had to be done, and he did it—as he beat his dog or discharged his servant when necessary.

He had meant to write to her from London, but important affairs occupied his attention; his specula- speculations tions were coming to a bad end—he had no time to think of her.

"I will run down and see her when I go back to Greenwood," he said. "'Tis a pity, as things seem to be turning out, that I ever let the poor little thing make such a fool of me, but it can't be helped now."

Lady Edith with her thousands would have mended matters at once, but what was the use of thinking about her?

The first night after his arrival at Greenwood, Cousin Jonathan came to see him. The little man had heard, on his return, of the frequent visits which had been paid during his absence. Passion has eyes, as far-seeing in the dark as love's, and he knew both visitor and visited so well that he soon came to certain very definite conclusions on the matter of these visits. He knew well that a hundred Harry Blairs were not so to be dreaded as one Piece-of-perfection, with his cold eyes and iron will.

It would be hard to say whether the little man started from home that evening with any particularly fiendish purpose in his head, but his heart was fed on by the green-eyed monster and his weak legs trembled and quaked beneath him as he thought of what *might* be—of what she might have told. Perhaps the reception from his sometime pupil would be a summary dismissal from a boot point. At any day all Greenwood might know that, in place of Jonathan Barnacles the saint, the holy man, and the blessed man of God, they had been bowing down at the shrine of a poor sinner, a man of like passions with themselves. For with the exception of one or two benighted individuals, Cousin

Jonathan stood highest of the high in the estimation of the Greenwood world. "He is so pure, so calm, so transparent. If there were more Christians like him, all the world would soon become Christian," one of his admirers was wont to say, when expatiating on his transcendent virtues.

It is a cruel thing they do, who fasten on a man too high a character. 'Tis a small hobgoblin on his shoulder, forever pushing and poking him into the wrong paths, leading more straight along the devil's road than gold, wine, or women. Having committed one action out of keeping with it, he must sin on eternally to make a grave wherein to hide that action.

Cousin Jonathan felt sick at heart as any girl when he knocked at the door and was ushered into the presence of the Piece-of-perfection, who met him just as usual, made him take an armchair, and offered him a cigar.

"You have been ill?" was one of his first remarks, noticing the pale face and troubled look in the usually serene eyes of the little man.

Cousin Jonathan declared he was in perfect health, in the best of spirits; and, after a few more remarks had passed, began to express his gratitude for the kind attention shown to his wife and Miss Bock during his absence.

"It was exceedingly kind of you," he continued, rubbing his hands together as nervously as it was possible for such a very unnervous little animal to do.

"It is quite unnecessary, I assure you," said the Piece-of-perfection, knocking the ashes from the top of his cigar into the delicate china stand. "You will understand that it is so when I tell you, as perhaps I should have done sooner, that in all probability, e'er very long, Miss Bock will become my wife."

The little man had a wonderful command over his features, and showed at this announcement no more feeling than that amount of surprise which it was to be expected he would experience.

"You really must excuse me," said Cousin Jonathan; "but I am amazed, astonished; it is so very, so altogether, unexpected. I—you really must excuse me, but I was under the impression that, if ever I had the honour of looking upon any member of your family as the future husband of my charge, it would be another."

"I do not imagine Miss Bock ever had any very great regard for my poor brother," he replied contemptuously, curling the corner of his delicate moustache between his finger and thumb.

"Has she not told you? But of course she will have told you more than even I know," said Cousin Jonathan.

"On what subject?" asked Albert Blair, closing his eyes closer than usual and playing with Prince's ears.

"About this affair with your brother; but of course it is all passed now, and I wish you both every blessing, every happiness," said Cousin Jonathan, apparently very much affected.

"I always understood from Miss Bock that she was perfectly indifferent to my brother, in fact rather repelled than favoured his addresses. I imagine you must have misunderstood her."

"Oh, yes, and there can be nothing gained by speaking now over things that are past and gone," said Cousin Jonathan; "and I cannot tell you how grateful, how relieved, I feel to think that the dear child will be in your care. When she seemed so devotedly attached to your brother, of course I did not like to interfere, but it was, I can assure you—it was a cause of great anxiety to me. If she were my own daughter, I could not feel a greater regard for her welfare; and she is so peculiar, so eccentric, that with all her noble qualities and rich and vigorous intellect she has never been able to get on anywhere."

The Piece-of-perfection sat passive, so Cousin Jonathan went on.

"It may seem, and I fear was, very selfish on my part, but I could not help feeling less concerned at your brother's trouble and departure than I should otherwise have been. It seemed wholly to change her mind, and as things have turned out I am thankful, how thankful I cannot tell you. He was very sincerely attached to her, but he would never have submitted to her tastes and ideas, as it would be absolutely necessary he should if they were to live together. But that is all past now and I cannot tell you how relieved, how thankful, I feel. I have loved her as if she were my own," said Cousin Jonathan, screwing up the corners of his eyes till they began to look watery.

A long pause followed, then the Piece-of-perfection said, "Perhaps I ought to explain to you that what exists between myself and Miss Bock is not a definite engagement. It is an understanding which either party may bring to an end at any time he or she should wish to do so, and it might be just as well to say nothing on the subject till matters are more definitely arranged."

"Certainly, certainly, if you wish it," said Cousin Jonathan; "but I do hope that matters will soon, very soon, be in that condition. I have often feared that she might be tempted for the sake of wealth and position to give herself away to a man who was utterly unworthy of her. She is so young, and therefore it is only natural that she should desire such things, and having also been brought up in circum-circumstances stances of almost more than poverty, they necessarily appear all the more alluring to her."

"I understand that Miss Bock's family, though not wealthy, was a very respectable one. Take another cigar; yours has gone out," said Albert Blair, passing his case.

"Oh, I know nothing, nothing whatever, against the character of any of her relations. Her father was a connection of my own, and as far as I am aware his family are all well to do. Of her mother I know nothing. He made a great mistake in marrying her, I believe. She was some woman he picked up in London and who married as her second husband some low farmer at the Cape. Her grandfather got her home when her mother died, but she could not get on with them; they did not seem to understand the dear child's little peculiarities and could not appreciate her."

It would not take more faith and prayer to obtain pardon for one lie than for twenty; and Cousin Jonathan, having told one, found that lies flow as easily as truths if only one is used to them. Cousin Jonathan held great faith in ghosts, but nowadays dead people do not rise out of their graves and come to avenge themselves, be they ever so slandered; and 'tis safe talking in an English smoking-room of an African farmer between whom and yourself there are some thousand miles of sea and a hundred of still more separating Karoo. Her mother had been the only daughter of a wealthy London merchant and had been disinherited for marrying beneath her; but does not every man who finds a wife pick her up, and had not her mother taken as her second husband a Cape farmer? He had only spoken the truth judiciously, of course, *very* judiciously, but only the truth.

"I feel so sure," he continued, "that you of all men will be able to overlook any small deficiencies in the dear child, when you consider all the adverse circumstances with which she has had to contend. There is something so original and strong, so noble, in her character, that if she were only a little more open she would be almost perfect in my estimate. Not that I mean," said the little man, apparently recollecting himself and speaking with great earnestness—"not that I mean to say she is not quite truthful, but she is sometimes not quite—so open, as one might expect to find her. Her nature is, I believe, a *thoroughly* truthful one in *every* respect, and it is only the effect of early mismanagement. And are we not," said Cousin Jonathan, falling into his preaching voice, "are we not all of us formed during the first few years of our lives? What is done then, can it ever be undone, ever?"

He seemed lost in thought for some moments, then he said suddenly: "But it is all right now; I feel so rejoiced to think that for the future she will be shielded and cared for better than I could care for her. I have felt very anxious about her lately, very anxious; I could not see clearly where the path of duty lay with regard to her."

"You're a very devil of wickedness or a poor fool of a saint," thought the Piece-of-perfection as he leaned back in his chair with the lamplight falling full on the inscrutable white face, the lines of which Cousin Jonathan was vainly trying to decipher.

"I may tell Mrs. Barnacles, of—of the understanding, may I not?" he said. "She has been much grieved at Undine's sudden freak of leaving us; and I cannot myself understand how the idea came into her head, unless she thought we were imposing on her by leaving her alone with an invalid on her hands. She never told you if that was her reason for leaving us, I suppose?" inquired the little man, casting a quick furtive glance at the face of his companion.

"No; she told me she was leaving because she was weary of the place and wished for change. You are surely not leaving yet?" for Cousin Jonathan had risen to take his departure.

If you wish to ruin a man's character, if you wish to have your revenge on an enemy, if you wish to blight a man's life because you have done him an injury, be sparing with your words. It is the small drop that falls in between the wine and sugar that poisons the cup.

So Cousin Jonathan, having eyes as far-seeing as they were blue and saintly, discovered that it was quite impossible for him to remain any longer, much as he wished to do so. There was a special prayer-meeting in his house that night, and his presence there was indispensable.

People remarked, as they walked home after the meeting, that never before had he prayed with the eloquence and earnestness of that evening for perfect purity, for perfect truth; truth that might challenge, not the dull eye of the world, but the deep-seeing, perceiving eye of conscience; truth in thought, truth in word, truth in deed, Godlike truth, he prayed for with passionate fervour. And let he who will sneer and raise the ever-ready cry of hypocrite. Through a long life free of temptation he had in the main been pure and truthful, as those about him deemed him; but the hour of his trial had come and he had fallen, as the son of the morning fell, to rise no more.

The greatest devil among us has his white spots, and the purest saint has ink-black stains which will be clearly visible if he do not keep his white clothing too tight about him.

When his visitor had left him, Albert Blair paced slowly up and down the room. Was the little man a fool, or a devil? He turned the matter over and over in his mind as he passed slowly from one end to the other, with Prince following close at his heels.

The poison took its full effect, and early the next morning he started for London. "I will write when there," he said. "The little schemer quite deserves to be kept waiting, and it gives her more time to forget me. They may say what they like, but I do believe the little devil likes me or at least my prospects.

"I don't know what's come over Miss Undine," said Nancy, her grandmother's maid, as she stood chatting with her lover over the gate one evening. "When she come first, why, there she'd sit from morning till night, stitch, stitch, stitch, at them lovely white dresses, and staring out of that there window. If we'd not 'a' made her come and eat, I believe she'd just 'a' starved. Well, all of a sudden, just four weeks gone, I went upstairs to make her bed, thinking as how of course she had been up and out hours; and there she was a-sitting on the floor in the middle of the room, never been in bed the whole blessed night, though one could see as she'd been a-laying on it, her dresses and ribbons and all her nice things that she'd been a-working at lying in a pile that high before her.

"'Nancy,' says she, sort of strange and quiet like, 'you can take all these things.'

"'Lor'! Miss Undine,' says I, 'what do you mean?'

"'You can have them,' says she; 'and if you don't want them you can burn them,' says she so quiet like, and walks out of the room with her arms a-hanging down at each side of her—like *this*—and her head a-lying sort of loose like on her chest, as though she'd gone and got her neck broken; and, Lor'! her back was bent as double as an old woman's. I never see anything like it, 'cept when my poor brother Jim got shot in the side by them horrid poachers and came back the night afore he died, looking just like that."

"And did you get the dresses?" asked her lover.

"Course I did," said Nancy, "and other things too. And Miss Undine she just goes on walking about in that 'ere sort of a way. Lor'! and she is queer sometimes; she takes a cloth and begins rubbing down the chairs and things in the parlour. 'I can do that Miss Undine,' says I.

"'No, I like to do it,' says she, and there she sits a-rubbing at one leg of a chair for five minutes or more, like as if she was in a dream like.

"'Don't you think that chair is pretty well about polished down now, Miss Undine?' says I.

"'Yes,' she says, and goes on to another. And, Lor' bless me, if she don't go and lie down under them trees in the garden for a whole blessed day sometimes, as still as a corpse. She is just that deep with blossoms when I come to call her in of an evening; and if I did not, why I do believe she would lie there till the morning," said the puzzled Nancy, emphatically.

It was not only Nancy who was puzzled. Her grandmother would watch her wonderingly as for hours she would sit under the great tree that grew before the cottage, gazing vacantly at the soft early grass and the budding hedges. It was no use asking if she were ill; she would only answer, "No, I am well—only tired—rather tired."

"The flowers of last year, when their stalks grew hollow and empty, fell to the ground, to give place and food to the fresh green shoots of this year; then why must we live on, when we are tired, so tired?" she would ask herself. Sometimes she got out the little wooden box where she kept her papers—little songs and allegories, fairy tales and half-written essays. They had lifted her up to heaven when she wrote them; now they were bits of blue paper, scribbled over and blotted, and she would put them away listlessly without ever looking at them.

One night, in the middle of the night, she woke up. Generally she went to sleep early, and slept heavily till morning, but tonight she woke and lay still, listening to the wind as it moaned around the house. Then before her eyes lay the little river, with its muddy banks, and the great trees knocking their bare branches together over it, and the brown still pool where the little feather had nodded up and down, up and down, on that afternoon.

It had moved very restlessly, but deep down, at the bottom of the pool, it was very still and restful. The mocking sun with his jeering blood-red eye could never look through to see what lay there.

She was tired, so tired; so she got up slowly and drew on her clothes in the dark. She was turning mechanically to feel for her little crimson cloak that hung behind the door, when, "Why should I spoil it?" she thought. So without wrapping anything around her, she went out into the night wind and the darkness, through the long garden, over the uneven field. She stood at last beside the muddy pool. Overhead the leafless branches rattled their dry joints together, and through the rifts in the cloudy sky a few stray stars cast their uncertain reflection on the water.

It seemed so still and quiet, it seemed to lure her to itself.

"I cannot help it—it is not cowardly—I am too tired—so tired. He does not want me any more. There is nothing in the world, and I am so weary," she whispered under her breath, as though excusing herself to some unseen judge.

"I shall never trouble him any more, down there."

She pressed closer to the muddy edge and stood looking down into the water. Then, sudden and unbidden, a thought came to her, as may have come the angel's touch to the lone prophet when in the wilder- wilderness ness beneath the juniper tree he laid him down to die.

Might I not serve him!

How or in what way, who could say? But life is very long, and the wheel turns strangely. How could she tell that he would never need her!

The prophet of old ate of the angel's bread and went forty days and forty nights in the strength of that meal; she also ate of angel's meat, the only food which the heavens now yield us, and went forty times forty in the strength thereof.

Back to the house she turned slowly; and no one ever knew how nearly she had found rest and quiet on that windy night.

What a small thing it is sometimes that makes life's kiss sweeter than death's to us—the light in a pair of blue eyes—a little applause for a picture we have put on canvas—a few comprehenders for a song we have written—the knowledge that our name means something when scrawled on the bit of paper which we call a cheque. These mean life for some of us. Take these out of life, and what an unbearable weight it becomes. We walk about in this rich teeming world as through an empty, howling wilderness; and if we do not fear to meet with something more wearying on the other side, how we seek to get out of it by way of a muddy pool, a bullet, or a few drops of arsenic.

'Tis very strange, very ridiculous, quite incomprehensible, no doubt; but some really do require something more to reward them for the trouble of living than black cloth, roast beef, and the power to use them.

XII.
SOLD HER LOVE

THE summer had come and the little cottage looked like a monster nosegay in its sheath of climbing roses. In the great tree that stood before the door the birds had built their nests and sang there all day long, and the blossoms in the garden had turned to fruit and the tender green leaves had grown dark and strong.

Undine had sat below them, working a little, dozing a little, all day. She was glad the blossoms were gone, for their smell made her heart heavy.

"Lor'! Miss Undine, you'll catch your death of cold; the dew's a-falling already, and there's a gentleman in the parlour a-wanting to see you," said the good Nancy, bursting with desire to give an account of the visitor's appearance, with her ideas thereon appended.

Undine, however, asked no questions, but, rising, walked towards the house.

The little parlour was almost dark when she entered it, and the man was sitting with his back to the window. Instantly she recognized the bald crown and tuft of hair belonging to George Blair.

"This is indeed a great and unexpected pleasure," he said, rising and taking her hand into his own fat and flabby palm, "a great and most unexpected pleasure. I have been in the neighbourhood for some days, engaged in inspecting a large estate I have just purchased, and it was by the merest chance that I heard of your being here."

Then he launched forth into strong and vehement denunciations against the roads and inns of the neighbourhood, directing his remarks principally to her grandmother. At last the old lady rose to order candles, and Undine and her visitor were left alone.

"Have you been to Greenwood lately?" she inquired.

"Not since the autumn." Then, after a moment's pause, "I have been hoping continually to hear from you since that time, but have been always disappointed hitherto."

This remark eliciting no response, he went on, drawing his chair a little nearer to hers.

"I trust I need hardly tell you, my dear Miss Bock, that in the months that have passed *I* have not changed in my feelings or wishes. What I then asked, I still most earnestly and truly desire."

The timely entrance at this moment of Nancy, bearing candles, saved Undine from the necessity of making him any reply. She asked him where his sons were.

"I know nothing of Master Harry's whereabouts," he replied; "and as for his brother, I *will* know nothing. He has gone in for all manner of mad speculations without my knowledge or advise, and of course has got into trouble and expects my help now. He shall not have it, though. I shall have as little to do with him as with his brother for the future. If he wants help he may go to his aristocratic relations, who, if they were sold up, blue blood and all, could not raise the sum he wants. *I* could let him have the money and never miss it," said the old man, very complacently, "but he has seen the shine of my cash for the last time, I can assure him."

A fat, disagreeable-looking old man, her grandmother, though not generally very discerning or critical, thought him, when she reëntered the room at the end of his speech.

Undine soon made an excuse for leaving them and went out at the front door and stood before the house. The evening air was cool and balmy and the smell of the cluster roses that covered the cottage was sweet, but she only dragged a bunch from its stem and crushed it in her hand till the thorns pierced it. The time had come, and come so soon, when she could serve him. Once or twice she paced up and down the length of the house; then she reëntered the little parlour.

She asked her grandmother to leave them alone for a few moments; and the old man looked at her in some astonishment as she stood before him pale and eager. Surely she was beautiful, this woman, with a beauty deeper than that of form and colour; and if she were so fair in her rough, careless dress, what should she not look like in the velvet and damask he might give her!

She crushed the flower in her hand till the blood fell in a crimson drop on her crumpled white dress; and, standing straight before him, said: "You asked me once long ago to become your wife. I told you then that it could never be; but I am willing now if you will give me what I want." There was something so strange in her manner and look that the old man, not knowing how to answer, sat still, and she went on:

"If you will settle on me, before our marriage, fifty thousand pounds in cash, to be mine absolutely, to do exactly as I please with, then I will marry you as soon as you wish. I do not love you, but I will be a good wife to you."

She looked at him and the old man looked at her. Many women had sold themselves to him before that night, but not the most abandoned in a more open and barefaced manner than this: "I do not love you, but you will have no reason to repent marrying me if you are willing to do so on my terms."

He hesitated for a moment, but his mind was soon made up. That she should consent to marry him for anything except his money he had never dreamed, and, whether the bargain were expressed in words or tacitly understood, where was the difference? So he answered her:

"Not only what you ask, but everything I have, shall be yours; though of course if you wish it, an arrangement such as that which you mention shall be made."

He stayed a little longer, and when he had kissed his wife that was to be, upon the lips, he left her.

They were pretty lips and he did not repent his bargain when he thought it over at leisure. They had answered him scornfully once; he might do what he would with them now. His son had coveted them once, but gold had won when youth and learning had failed.

So it must always be, he thought, as he rolled his fat joints into bed. Youth and learning and love, they are all convertible into terms of cash, and have their equivalents.

XIII.
A VERY WICKED WOMAN

A FEW weeks after the night of the bargain two notices appeared in the same paper. The first informed the world that on a certain day George Blair, Esq., and Undine Bock had become, till death should part them, bone of one bone and flesh of one flesh, by a holy and inscrutable mystery, two in one and one in two.

The second notice asserted that the like wonderful and miraculous though oft-repeated process had taken place between Mr. Albert Blair and Lady Edith Mountjoy.

"Did I not say so?" said Miss Mell, excitingly, as, seated beside Mrs. Barnacles' sofa with the paper in her hands, she read the two notices. "She was not half the poor little fool you all thought her; she understood her game when she let the son slip to catch the father; she knew where the meat lay.

"She has a nice nest of it," continued Miss Mell. "The old man is too stout and apoplectic to last long, and the sons are both in his bad books, where you may be sure she will take good care to keep them. She is an innocent little creature, only likes her books and her flowers, but she knows a thing or two. We shall have her here after a few years," continued the poor little woman, "a widow with her thousands, cutting a dash and riding roughshod over our heads."

She felt it was an unjust world this, in which one woman wins all the cakes and bon-bons and another nothing more than dry bread and weak tea.

An hour or two later Cousin Jonathan, sitting in his study, read them also, and as he read his heart grew lighter. It had been heavy, strangely heavy, of late.

"She could never have cared for him or she could not have done this," he muttered. "To marry for money and so soon: she could never have cared for him." And with these words the little man was wont to quiet unpleasant stirrings for months and years to come.

Albert Blair, taking up the paper to see his own notice, read what stood above it.

"What a merciful escape I have had!" he exclaimed, and for once the imperturbable calm that reigned within him was almost disturbed. It is never pleasant to find yourself a dupe where you thought yourself adored, and a fool where you thought your self wise; and what small pity he had felt for the little girl who loved him was changed into loathing for the woman who had fooled him. From that mo- moment ment his flickering faith in woman died and he held his father's creed—the creed that all women have their value in coins, though some mount high.

In a poor half-furnished room the owner of the woman's eyes and the crammed head sat beside a bare deal table. Before him lay an open newspaper.

"There is nothing worth loving, nothing true, nothing noble in the world," he cried, bitterly, and buried his face in the paper before him. When he raised it, it was wet with tears. She was not only as all women are, but lower than many: to sell herself, with her youth and talents, to an old and evil man for his money and lands.

"O God, my God!" he cried in bitterness of soul, covering his face with both hands, "and this is the woman whom I have allowed to come in between my soul and Thee."

In a richly furnished apartment, enveloped in a soft cloud of white lace and delicate azure ribbons, sat Undine Blair. Diamonds glittered in her hair and her little jewelled fingers strayed listlessly over the leaves of the paper before her. Around her on every side lay a profusion of those things in which a woman's soul delights—the bon-bons and cakes that the Miss Mells of this world sigh for.

She was sitting waiting for dinner and the arrival of her husband, and ran her eye carelessly over the sheet before her. There, below the notice of her own sale, stood that other notice. She read it and a burning mist gathered in her eyes. From her ears and neck she tore jewels that hung there and threw them on the ground at her feet. Signs of her servitude, worn for his sake, there had been a sweetness in their very bitterness. Now they were accursed—burning into her very sleep; she trod upon them with her foot. For nothing, all for nothing; he had no need of her. Poor childish fool, to think that ever he could stand in need of her or of her sacrifice.

"Dinner is ready and my master is waiting," said a servant who a few moments later came to call her.

"Say I am ill today and cannot come," she answered, and when the door closed behind him sank back in the chair and covered her dry throbbing eyeballs with her hot hands. She ground her teeth in futile rage and helplessness. Parched and very bitter was her soul that night.

Truly, a very fiend's had been the voice that had called her back to life from the muddy, reed-edged pool, called her back to life to pass from evil on to evil.

A soft pulpy hand rested on her bare shoulder and her husband spoke to her.

"Is my little pet ill this evening? What is the matter with her?"

She threw his hand from her with passion through which involuntary disgust was clearly visible, and, eluding the hand with which he strove to detain her, passed quickly from him.

"What do you mean by this?" cried the little man, and stood staring at the closed door by which she had vanished. His astonishment was great. In the three weeks of his married life she had taken all his caresses, submitted to all his wishes, as absolutely as though subdued by the most slavish passion. As an automaton is guided by the hand of its master, his will had moved hers, and of desire or inclination of her own she had seemed devoid.

Was his honeymoon to end so soon? Were his self-congratulations to end in this? Had he really purchased a scourge and a termagant in his fair young wife? As soon as he could leave the delights of the table, had he not hurried upstairs really concerned at the indisposition of his precious new treasure—puffing and red with wine, soup, and exertion? Had he not entered the room to caress and fondle her? And was he to be met so? Had he played the fool in his old days? he asked himself. For the first time in his long life he thought he had fallen into a bad speculation, but he changed his mind as time passed on. In the months that followed the scene of that evening was never repeated. She grew quieter, colder, but more passive and submissive every week. Whether it were to sit by his side, to have her lips kissed, to wear a particular dress, to attend a certain ball, the obedience she gave him was equally absolute, unquestioning, and lifeless.

He had paid his price for her faithfully, she realised, and it was not his fault if the thousands he had given her were of as little service as a handful of gravel from his paths. She had bartered her life for his gold and she must give it.

In the autumn they went to the seaside. The restless murmuring of the water stirred up old memories which she would fain have left buried; but he wished to be there and she said nothing. The winter and spring they spent in London; when the summer came they went to his new estate.

"I shall never be able to live in Greenwood," she said. And he paid deference to the one wish she had expressed.

"You never ask me to do anything for you," he said one day. "Ask me for something." And she, obedient in this as in all else, asked him to buy the little rose-covered cottage in which her grandmother lived. The gift came too late to profit the one for whom it was intended; for in the winter her grandmother died.

If she felt the loss, no one could tell, for she showed no feeling on that or any subject. During the summer their house was filled with guests of many kinds, not because either host or hostess had many friends or was well liked, but because there was good shooting, good living and good company to be had there. All admired the young wife and pronounced her lovely—even women. They had as little reason to feel jealous of her as of the silent statues that adorned her rooms.

"She is a cold, dull, heartless little creature in whom nothing can awaken the faintest spark of womanly emotion," said one who considered himself preëminently endowed with those charms of appearance and manner which cause disturbance in the hearts of women, and who, through a long morning ramble, had been vainly endeavouring to exercise his charms upon her. For him, for all, there was one constant smile that went no higher than the lips, and that had no meaning save when a little scorn showed itself. Cold, heartless, and surely money-loving must be one who could marry an old, bloated and apoplectic little man who had only gold with which to varnish himself and cake over his deficiencies.

"She dresses well and knows how to make herself look beautiful, but that is the only thing she has sense enough to understand," said the women. But none of them accused her of vanity. She was too supremely indifferent as to the impression she made on others.

No one offended her, no one cared for her: not her inferiors in spite of her lavish generosity to them. Her kindest actions were done in an indifferent, feelingless manner that made it as impossible to feel thankful for them as to the rain for falling or the wind for blowing.

Nancy, being now without employment, came one day to see if Undine would take her into her service. "And, Lor'!" said she, when giving an account of all that had passed to her lover that evening, "I did not know Miss Undine: she's grown so beautiful and dresses so grand; it kind of took my breath away to look at her. Then I just remembered how she used to lie under them old trees in the garden and rub down them chairs, and so I says, 'Miss Undine—Mrs. Blair I mean—I hope you'll be so good as to forgive me for making so bold, but I'm out of work now and I thought perhaps as how you'd be so good as to let me get some work, if as how you have any to give.'

"'Aren't you married yet?' says she, a-looking straight at the book in her hand.

"'Lor'! Mrs. Blair, no,' says I. 'I've not got anything to get married with,' says I.

"'If you had that little cottage my grandmother used to live in, I suppose you could do well,' says she; 'it's got a large garden.'

"'Lor'! mum,' says I, 'we could never have a house like that; it's worlds too grand for the likes of us.'

"'Well,' says she, 'if you think it would help you, you can go and live in it for nothing,' says she, 'and I'll see that you get work whenever you want it.'

"'Lor'! Mrs. Blair, you don't mean it, mum!' says I.

"'Yes, you can go in as soon as you like,' says she; 'but the housekeeper asked me to let a woman stay in the little shed outside the garden; you must not trouble her,' says she, and goes on reading as though there weren't no one in the room. My head was all of a-whirl like, so I just says thank you, mum, and walks out of the room."

A few days after Nancy's visit Undine made her morning ramble a longer one than usual. She was alone, and a solitary walk was a pleasure she had rarely enjoyed since her marriage. Mile after mile she wandered on till she found herself near to the little rose-covered cottage, very silent and desolate now with its flower-clothed walls and its closed shutters. She did not enter the garden, but passed round to the front of the house, thinking to rest on the bench beneath the great tree that grew before the door. The spot was occupied, however, and she stood at a little distance, watching its occupant who, not aware of her presence, was stitching quickly at the blue work she held in her hands. She was an erect, tall, well-proportioned woman with lustrous black eyes and glistening black hair.

She had been very beautiful once, thought Undine, more beautiful than I. But the young face was worn now and there were lines of suffering round the dark eyes and curved lips. Something hard, almost repellent, was in the expression of the face she bent over her work, but the look vanished when she paused for an instant in her work to throw down a bunch of green leaves at the baby that lay before her on the soft short grass, a pink-and-white thing with blue eyes and yellow hair. She smiled a soft, glad smile, and Undine felt sure it was not the first time she had looked at that face and smile, though where and when she had looked at them she could not tell. The woman was raggedly clothed, not even cleanly; the child was spotless, and neither in colour nor in features bore any resemblance to her.

She was just resuming her work when she noticed Undine and rose from her seat as the little silk-clad lady approached.

"Do not rise," said Undine; "the bench is large enough for us both."

She felt attracted by her, not because of her neglected beauty, not by the vague impression that they had met before, but by a look in the dark eyes which drew her, as a look sometimes will in the face of some passenger in a crowd or a woman behind a counter. We may never speak, have no communication, but we feel that we have come near to one who is of our own flesh and blood.

"Do you live here all alone?" asked the silken-clad little beauty as she took her seat beside her rag-clad sister, who, if she remembered meeting her be- before fore, did not show it and stitched on quickly with downcast eyes.

"No. I have him," answered the woman, looking down at the nine-months-old baby at her feet. "Having him, how can I be lonely? How can I want anything?" the look said; then she hurried on with her work again.

"Do you not feel very lonely, living here so far from all other houses?" asked Undine after a moment's pause.

"No," said the woman, shortly. "I like it."

Then Undine sat quietly watching the large, soft, brown hands that had evidently not been accustomed to hard work, the proud erect figure, the defiant sullen face, and the pink-

and-white thing that laughed at their feet. She was a woman who had come no one knew from where, with only a baby, and her story was not difficult to read. Her neighbours read it after their fashion and called her a wicked woman, a very wicked woman.

When Undine had rested a few minutes longer she rose to go, but first she kneeled down on the grass where the baby lay.

"One kiss, for the sake of your bonny blue eyes," she said.

As she walked slowly past the garden hedge she came to the shed where mother and child lived. 'Twas a miserable tumble-down place, yet Undine, as she passed it, envied them.

"I am not alone, for I have him, the child of love," the eyes had said; and Undine with her empty heart, and the knowledge that she, too, soon would be mother of a child, not the child of love, but of loathing—Undine with her riches and her good name envied the dark woman her disgrace, her baby, and her rags.

"Where have you been all day? Not climbing the hills and over-exerting yourself, I hope?" said her fat little proprietor as he met her in the door on her return; and for the rest of that day she was never free of him; neither on many days that followed did she find an opportunity for repeating that morning's walk.

The anniversary of their wedding day came. They had given a grand dinner, but the guests had departed early, and her husband, having indulged a little more freely than usual in that which makes heavy the heart of man, had fallen asleep on the sofa in his dressing-room. She stood at the low open window of her room, looking out into the oppressive night. There was that heavy stillness in the air that precedes the bursting of a great storm.

"You may go. I shall not need you tonight," she said to her maid; and when she had withdrawn, Undine threw a great shawl over her head and stepped out of the window, still dressed in black velvet and wearing on her neck the pearls that had made her the envied of many women that night. She walked on quickly, not caring which path she took and pressing her foot hard on the ground at every step. It had caused a greater strain than usual that evening to wear, without once dropping it for a moment, that mask of smiles that she wore till the lines in her cheeks grew stiff and hurt.

As she walked on, the lines of an old song she had liked ran through her head: "Behind no prison gate," she said, "That slurs the sunshine half a mile, Are captives so uncomforted As souls behind a smile."

"God's pity let us pray," she said.

Thinking of nothing, with these lines running, running through her head, she walked while the sky grew dark and yet darker. Presently gusts of wind came hurrying past her, and then the great storm whose forerunners they had been overtook her. Fiercely the wind shook the branches of the trees over her head, and the large drops fell heavily through them. She was too far from home to think of returning, but she knew her grandmother's cottage could not be far off. She would go and sit in the little porch till the worst was over, she thought, and walked on slowly while the fast-falling rain made its way through her shawl and drenched her to the skin.

As she passed near the broken shed she noticed light coming through its small crooked window and through the crevices and cracks in its old stone walls. When she passed the window she paused for a moment and looked in. Most of the panes of glass were gone, their place being supplied by strips of pasted paper, but through the two squares that still remained she could clearly see all that the hovel contained. In one corner stood a small stretcher which was now unoccupied, for on a small stool before the fire, with her back turned to the window, sat the woman, her head stooping low over the baby she held close to her. Before the window stood a small table in which a tallow candle fixed in a broken brass candlestick was flickering and flaring. In the hearth the smouldering fire was almost extinguished by the rain which came down through the chimney, and the drops which made their way through the roof gathered themselves together in pools on the uneven floor.

It was a strange reversal in the order of things—the honoured wife of the rich man in her velvets and jewels standing out in the night storm and gazing in with envious eyes at the home where poverty and shame had taken their abode.

There came a hush in the storm and Undine could hear the woman was murmuring to the child as she bent over it. The first words she did not hear, but some came to her through the crevices and holes in the crazy window frame: "My child, my little child, you will not leave me, you will not forsake me. You are all, all I have." Then there came words Undine did not catch, and then again: "If you will only stay with me, I will live for you, work for you, starve for you; you shall be rich and clever one day. I am not cruel to want to keep you. You must not die, you cannot die, my little baby. I loved you so before you lived. You are all I have of him. You must not die and leave me, my baby, my little baby."

Then the mad storm came back howling after its rest, and the words were lost. Uncertain whether to enter or to go on to the cottage, Undine paused for an instant, then knocked at the door. There was no response and she laid her hand on the broken latch. The crazy door, opening, let her in, with a flood of rain and a gust of wind that almost extinguished the quickly melting candle.

"I hope I have not frightened you," she said, when she had fastened it once more. "I have been overtaken in the storm."

The woman made no answer, but looked up at her with dull, lustreless eyes; then, recognising her visitor, she said, "You liked my baby; you were the only one who ever kissed him. He is dying now." She said the last words slowly and distinctly in a harsh whisper, and then looked down at the little figure wrapped in a great shawl that lay upon her knee.

Undine kneeled down beside her. She would have spoken words of comfort, but when her eyes fell on the little face, even by the uncertain light of the flickering candle and fire, she saw that death's hand was on the baby and the little life of love and shame would soon be ended.

In silence she kneeled by them, holding in her white jewelled fingers the tiny cold hand that rested on the shawl, while her long velvet train was curled up in one of the pools on the floor.

There was no word spoken in the hut for a long time. The storm shook the loose walls in its fury, the great raindrops killed the smouldering fire, and the two women sat watching in silence for the coming of the awful stranger.

At last there came a sudden hush in the storm. No sound was heard but the slow falling of the raindrops as they dripped from the roof into the puddles on the floor, and the candle flickered no more but burnt up straight and steady. Then the little child heaved a long weary sigh, and the clasp of the little hand relaxed, the closed eyes partly opened, and they knew that death had been with them.

The mother sat as one who dreams, looking down at that which lay upon her knees, and their breathing sounded loud in the stillness.

At last she rose suddenly and, dropping the child heavily into Undine's arms, turned towards the door.

At that instant the storm came back, loud and fierce after its rest. She went out into it and to the darkness, and in the hut Undine sat with the dead child on her knee.

The light fell full on the little face with its half-closed eyes that looked so strangely old and stern now with the shadow of death upon them.

As she looked down at it she seemed to see, not the face of the little snow-white baby, but that other face that haunted her day and night—the face that she would never forget, that came in between her and the blue sky when she tried to look upwards, and between her eyes and the sunny grass and flowers when they smiled upon her.

Was she not to look into the face of a dead child without seeing it even there, also?

It was like madness, she thought, and drew from beneath the small chin a white handkerchief that lay folded there, to cover from her sight the strange white face.

As she opened and spread it out, her eyes fell on a name beautifully worked on one corner. She read it and then sat thinking. After a long time she raised the little baby very gently and held it close to her. *His* dead baby. For she knew now that it was no madness that showed her the old haunting face in the features of the little child.

She knew now where she had seen that woman's face before, with its lustrous eyes and brilliant tints; remembered now the old hints and stories which she had regarded as lies but which tonight came back to her as truths. And she saw it all—the deep love of years, giving all things, denying nothing, pouring itself out at the feet of that stern strong man to whom it was only a thing to be used, drawn upon, and, when no longer needed, trodden on and forgotten.

His little baby! Cared nothing for—loathed, perhaps—but what a difference. *His* little baby still. If she had only known it while the warm blood ran in the lips that struck her cold and chill when she pressed them now. If she had only known it sooner.

She gathered it up in her arms and moved the pearls aside that it might lie close, close against her soft warm breast—close, as though she would have given of her life to bring it back.

Then she laid it down once more and sat looking at it, and when the candle fell into its socket she still sat holding it, and the grey dawn when it looked in still found her sitting here.

The storm had gone, and when the sun arose the earth was green and laughing. The fresh morning wind helped the green branches to shake off the glittering drops that still hung on them, the flowers opened their eyes by thousands, the warming earth sent up a delicious smell, and the heavy grasses raised their wet heads and the tender plants shot out of the moist ground through every crack.

The storm had gone; only here and there a strong bough hung broken, or a great tree lay upon its side, whispering of last night's work. For nature keeps her secrets well and hides away from the sunshine the things which she does in darkness.

Yes, well she keeps her secrets!

When the curious morning sunbeams forced their way through the tall reeds and matted boughs that grew over the muddy pool, they saw nothing, they knew nothing; *they* could not tell what it was that lay across the old rotten trunk deep under the thick still water, with its brown hair buried in the mud. They did not know it, and the small birds did not know it, or how were it possible they should sing in the branches overhead such joyous lies? "Life is sweet," they said. "Life is sweet, and love is long; it lasts all summer time."

"Tell me all about it, Nancy," said her lover as he conducted her home through the quiet fields that evening.

"So I will," said Nancy, "but Lor' bless me if I know where to begin, there's been so much a-happening today."

"Begin at the beginning," was her lover's very sage advice, which Nancy followed.

"Well, this morning, afore ever the sun got up, I went to the cottage to have a look at them shutters which we forgot to shut after we had been a-cleaning up last night and which I thought as how the wind would have blown off. Well, just as I goes past the little shed outside the garden, what should I see but Mrs. Blair a-standing in the door as large as life, and a great shawl over her head and all.

"'Good-morning,' says I, wondering how she comed there at this time of day.

"'Nancy,' says she, 'there's a little child dead in here. I wish you'd call your mother and come and see to it, and see to the mother, too.'

"'Where is the mother?' says I, looking in.

"'I don't know,' says she, and walks off."

"What do you think she came there for?" asked her lover, curiously.

"Lor'! I don't know," responded Nancy. "Nobody can't give no reason for her goings-on. I wouldn't be in no ways surprised to hear she'd been and gone and drunk poison, or gone up in a balloon, or been a-doing anything unlike other folks."

"Well, I went and called mother and we seed to the baby: and the prettiest fattest little thing I ever seed, it was.

"Mother says, 'Nancy,' says she, 'look in that there little box under the bed and see if you can't find no clothes for it. The woman don't seem to be a-coming yet.'

"'Yes,' says I, and pulls out the box. The thing was locked, but, Lor'! it was so rotten, afore you'd touched it it was broken open, and there weren't much in it, neether—just a pair of babies' clothes and the beautifullest little box that ever I see; and, Lor'! I do believe it's real gold and writing all over the top, and mother and I, we spelt out, Alice Brown and something about a drowning, but the other words were a sight too long."

"And what was in the box?" asked her lover. "Money?"

"Money?" said Nancy. "No. I just opened it afore I thought, and what do you think I seed in it? Why, the likeness of the beautifullest young man I ever set eyes on in all my born days. The man on the hairpin box ain't nothing to him, nothing. Curly hair and moustaches just the same, but a sight more handsome."

"Was that all?" said her companion, not feeling in any way entertained by the raptures of his lady love over the pictured perfection.

"Yes, that was all," said Nancy, "'cept a couple of bits of cigars, half burnt out, and an old glove a sight too big for her I should say, though she is pretty considerable big."

“What did she say when she came back and found you’d been a rummaging all her things?”

“Comed back! She *never* comed back,” said Nancy, “and it’s my belief she never will neither. She’s come from nowheres and she’s gone to nowheres. She thinks as how other folks can see to its burying, but it’s always the way with the likes of her. Women that do the sort of thing she’s been a-doing of, they never have no natural feeling,” said the virtuous Nancy. And her lover agreed with her.

“Did you tell Mrs. Blair about her never coming back?” inquired the swain.

“Well, that’s what I’m just a-coming to,” said Nancy. “At four o’clock I says; ‘Mother,’ says I, ‘hadn’t I better be going down to Mrs. Blair’s just for to tell her that the woman hasn’t come?”

“‘I was just a-thinking so,’ says mother. So off I went. When I gets there, ‘Can’t I see the mistress?’ says I.

“‘Don’t you know?’ says he.

“‘Know what?’ says I.

“‘That she’s a-dying, and the baby,too,’ says he.

“‘Baby,’ says I. ‘Lor! you don’t mean it.’

“‘Yes,’ says the housemaid, a-coming up, ‘she was took ill this morning, and the baby ain’t much bigger nor your hand and more like a rat nor a baby.’

“Well, afore I could say anything in comes the nurse.

“‘How’s Mrs. Blair?’ says I.

"'She's pretty near gone,' says the nurse, 'but she's asking after somebody. I can't hear the name very clear, but I think it's Nancy Grey.'

"'If it is,' says I, 'here I am,' and so she takes me upstairs.

"The room was so dark I could see nothing at first, but, Lor'! when I did it was awful sad to see her a-lying there so white and dead like. She didn't take no notice of me, so after I waited a bit she said as how I had best come out. And I was just a-going out at the door when the nurse brings her baby for to put it by her side.

'Take it away, take it away!' she cries out, quite strong like, and then I comed out."

"And what are you going to do with the other baby?" inquired Nancy's lover.

"Have it buried, to be sure," said Nancy. "Mr. Blair he'll pay for it if she's dead."

But Undine did not die. And the baby lived, a puny shrivelled thing, but still it lived. One Sunday afternoon, four weeks later, they carried her from her bed to a sofa, wrapped in a richly embroidered dressing-gown and a great shawl. Near her, in its white-and-blue-satin-covered cradle, they laid her baby.

Why would they always bring that thing into her sight and keep it near her? Was it not enough that its little weak cry had rung loud in her ears when she was insensible to every other sound and had made her lose all love of life, all wish to keep it, even more then than the kisses of its father had done.

For every few hours the little man would steal softly into the room on tiptoe, with his hands open and his fingers stretched out, and, breathing very hard, would come up to her bedside to see how matters stood. When the death scale seemed to be going down he was seriously concerned, and refused to find consolation in devilled turkey, allowing the gravy on his plate to congeal there several times before he touched it, an event wholly unprecedented in the past. Now, however, he could sip his wine at ease and smoke his cigar in tranquillity, for the doctors had pronounced her out of danger and the baby still lived. True, it looked as though the first ball coming its way must inevitably bowl it out of the game, but a baby is not very much. Babies are plentiful, and he had his wife and would have another baby some day.

On this Sunday afternoon he sat dozing peacefully in his chair, and the nurse sat by his wife.

"I think I shall sleep. I don't want to be disturbed," said Undine; and the nurse, not unwilling to take the hint, rose and left her. The room was very cool and still. A soft light came in through the dark-green curtains. She lay on the soft pillows with her face resting on her thin hand, and looked at the baby, a mere speck of red amid the blue and white. Her baby and his, therefore she hated it. Her baby—she looked at it, and then lay thinking.

It was strange to know its life had sprung from hers. Strange to have hung another tiny wheel in the great world machine that grinds on so mysteriously with its ever-jarring, never-resting wheels flying round forever. And what did it all mean? What were they all, really—that little life—the purple violets—the dark-green curtains—herself lying there and thinking? Were they all nothing, dreams, shadows? Or something? And, if something, O God! what?

It was the old question she had asked so often when she stood, a little child, looking at the dry Karoo bushes on the old farm; and it met, as then, the old oppressive silence for an answer—silence like the hush which comes when we sit by the seashore on a dark night and hold our breaths to hear the great restless waters running up and down.

Presently she moved her hand quickly across her eyes, and then rose slowly and moved with trembling steps to the cradle-side.

"Poor little soul," she said and stooped down over it, "life is too wonderful to hate in. Poor little soul, we are all too nearly bound for hating"; and she took the baby to her. When her husband came in half an hour later he was surprised to find his child in her arms and a bunch of soft violets clasped in its tiny hand.

"Why do you do that?" he asked as he sat down beside her.

"Because I am going to call her Violet," his wife answered, and looked up at him with a smile so bright and unlike her own that it made him feel uncomfortable for a moment. Surely she was not going to die.

But after that day he often saw it, and others saw it also. The very servants whispered that their mistress had changed strangely; and surely it was the coming of the baby that had changed her, they said, speaking like the little children who fancy that the swallows bring the summer.

In the long bright days that followed she would have an armchair put out under the great trees on the other side of the lawn, and would sit there all day with the child in her arms, drinking in the sunny beauty of grass and sky, as though birds sang to her what others could not hear.

Sometimes she read in those still sweet days; and books, which to her had so long been meaningless and dumb, had again voice and life. Whether they were the hot words of a passion-filled heart singing to appease its own intolerable hunger, or the calm record of things long past, or the exact statement of some savant concerning a flower he had dissected, there was life in them all and music. To her they were as food to one who wakes hungry after a long dark dream.

Oh, the beauty of those days, the glory of the brown that rested on the hilltops, the brightness that hung over the cut stones of the house walls!

So sweet was that first draught of a new life that she had no eye to mark shadows, and did not notice, as all others did, that the life of the little child was growing weaker and fainter as the autumn days drew near. She knew so little of children that its slow growth did not trouble her; it knew her, and would open its dark eyes and lie smiling up at her for long times together, as they sat out in the sunshine.

"My little friend," she used to call it softly, and whisper *all* to it of things which could not have been spoken in any other ear.

"My little friend, who loves me."

"Some one ought to tell her; she does not dream of it," they all said. "She will wake up some morning and find the child lying dead in her arms." The doctor said so, her husband said so, they all said so; yet no one cared to tell her.

At last one evening, when the sun was almost setting, the old doctor went out to look for her. He found her sitting on the grass with the baby on her lap, bathed in the rich regretful sunset light that warmed the soft tints of the flowers in the little wreath she had wound around the child's head. He looked down at the little face below the wreath, and wondered that love could look at it without reading it. He asked her very gently how it was.

Undine only smiled softly for an answer, and said, as she stuck tiny leaves of grass among the flowers: "She is so fond of flowers, and does not tear them to pieces as other children do. She holds them so carefully in her hand and turns them round and looks at them. We don't give babies credit for half wisdom enough," she said.

"It is growing very thin," said the doctor, taking its small clenched fist into his hand, "very thin."

"Not thinner than it was," said Undine; "and when next summer comes we will go to the sea; it will soon be strong and well then."

"That is a long time to wait," said the doctor, gravely. "Many things may have happened before next summer."

Undine looked up into his grave face, and down at the little one with its crown of flowers. After a long pause she said, "What do you mean?" And he knew she had read what was written there.

It was not needful to say much more. He soon left her sitting in the sunlight. "Oh, my little friend," she said; "is it to be always so? Are we only to lift our heads above the water to be pushed down again? Do we only rise up because, if we did not, we could not be flung down to earth? Is light only sent to make the darkness visible?"

She sat there till the last glow had faded from the hilltops and the grass on which they sat began to grow damp and cold.

"My little friend, I am very cruel to wish to keep you. Would life have more of happiness for you than it has had for me?—a little gladness out of colours and lights; a little sweetness out of dreams; one hour of bliss looking at footmarks in the white snow? Is that enough to make it worth keeping? Oh, my little friend, it will be better to go. You have made a little brightness. There is nothing better waiting for you if you stay."

"Not in bed yet?" said her husband when, returning late the next evening from a dinner he had been attending in the neighbouring town, he found his wife still up and sitting on a low chair with the child on her knees. "You might as well have gone with me if you meant to sit up so late. You will never get your roses back if you go on in this way.

"I cannot go to bed tonight," she said, quietly, smoothing softly the crumples in the child's little nightdress. "It is very ill."

"Ill? What's the matter?" he said, peering down into its face for a moment. "It looks just as usual to me. I suppose that fool of a doctor has been frightening you."

"No; he says there is no cause to be anxious just tonight, but I can see more than he can."

"Oh, we all know you can see through a wall, but it would be more sensible of you to go to bed and rest," responded her master, sullenly, as he turned away and left the room.

"Would not touch the baby at first, or have it brought near her; goes and makes a fool of herself over it now," he grumbled. "Couldn't see that it was ill, and thinks it's dying now. She's a queer composition."

It was a warm night for that time of year, and Undine had opened the great doors and windows on both sides of the room to let in the air. Yet the lamp that hung overhead burnt steadily and threw down its unwavering steady light over mother and child. On the mantelpiece the bronze clock ticked regularly, but the breathing of the child was so low it could not be heard.

Perhaps she was very foolish, after all; the doctor must know best; and she looked down inquiringly. There was just the faintest smile about the little mouth and the hands were crossed loosely on the little breast. As she looked the smile passed slowly and the child opened wide its eyes and fixed them on the lamp overhead—those large, unearthly deep brown eyes.

Undine would not move for fear of disturbing it, but the baby turned its head round slowly, and looked up into her face with those great calm eyes. Did they speak to her or did she only fancy it? Those dark awful eyes of her own little child. There was no dread, there was no questioning in them, but a calm, solemn light.

Undine looked deep, deep into them. She did not hear the clock strike or know how the moments passed, till the white lids dropped slowly. There was no sigh, there was no change, but when she laid her hand upon its breast she knew that the baby was dead.

She rose up and carried its body to the large white bed, and laid it down just as it was with its peacefully crossed hands. Then she dropped down on her knees beside it with her forehead on the ground, and the dead was not more motionless than the living.

The next morning when her husband, having been roused early and told of his child's death, went out in search of Undine, he found her sitting in the sunshine on the dewy grass.

"It is dead," she said, looking up at him with a calm, cloudless face, as though she had said, "It is asleep." He wondered, for how should he understand the love she bore her child, the passionless love, loving it in spite of its being hers? The baby I love, because it is mine; the woman I cling to against my reason—I must hear them, see them, touch them, or be devoured by a senseless gnawing; but the friend whose soul has reached mine, the thing I have loved for what it taught me, I let them pass without a tear, for my part of them remains with me, and for the rest, let it go.

"You have heard the news, of course," said Miss Mell one morning before she had entered Mrs. Barnacles' room. She was very much out of breath, for she was growing asthmatic of late. "Harry Blair has come. I saw him myself half an hour ago, and he says his father is dead. Did you ever hear of such a thing? Some people *are* lucky," said Miss Mell with energy.

"Why, I don't think he will get much. Did his father leave him anything?"

"Leave him anything! Of course he didn't. You may be sure she would take good care of that. I can see it now just as well as if it were past—how she'll come here lording it over everybody and marrying a big swell before the year's out. With all her money and her bold, free manners, men are sure to be taken by her. I am sure she has no good looks to talk of, but they are such fools they never see it. They are so easily taken in."

"Even if they are, I don't wonder that you never managed to do it," thought Mrs. Barnacles; but she only replied: "I don't know anything about her. I've never heard her mentioned since her baby died two years ago. I've never had but two notes from her since she left. Gratitude was and never will be one of Undine Blair's virtues."

Mrs. Barnacles refrained from making any further animadversions on the character of her connection; for it struck her that should Miss Mell's prognostications be verified, it would be just as well to have a smile for the young heiress and get the benefit of some of the fruit and game that would be plentiful at Blair House. Indeed, it would be rather pleasant than otherwise to have all Greenwood ridden over the head by a connection of hers, provided only that she were not included in the everybody.

Miss Mell, whose aversion for Undine was of the same nature as that of a cat for water, or a Kaffir for work, quite irrepressible, inherent and inextinguishable, continued to express her opinion of the character of her natural enemy with asperity that might not be rivalled. She was just remarking on the perfidy of her behaviour towards Harry Blair, when Cousin Jonathan's mild blue eyes looked in at the door.

"Do come in, Mr. Barnacles. You've heard the news, no doubt; perhaps you've seen Mr. Blair?"

"Yes, he called on me as soon as he arrived. He was on the Continent when he got the news of his father's illness, and came to find him dead."

"Poor fellow! Did he really expect to get anything?" said Miss Mell, in a voice expressive of infinite scorn at his credulity.

"No; he was astonished when he got home to find that the property was to be divided equally between the two brothers. He had no idea of any such thing."

"So the old man left her nothing?" said Miss Mell.

"No," assured Cousin Jonathan; "he left her everything, but she's gone off, nobody knows where, and has left an order that everything is to be divided between them. Harry Blair has come here to enquire whether I know anything about her."

"I should say the best thing would be to let her alone," said Miss Mell; "she has evidently got some nice little game of her own to play." But Miss Mell was discomfited. Hitherto her abhorrence of that red-cheeked, scheming affectation had been of a groundless kind, accountable only on the hypothesis of natural antipathies. Other girls as pretty did not arouse the latent feline propensity of her nature in anything like the same degree; it would not have given her half the infinite satisfaction to efface *their* beauty with thumb and finger nails that she would have had in operating on the cheeks of the scheming affectation. But now, to be proved a daughter of Belial, a false prophetess, by Undine obstinately refusing to commit the evil prophesied of her: was it not just cause for bitterness?

Saints made perfect forgive such injuries, but not a wrinkled woman on the rotten side of forty, with no money or intellect to keep the wine of life from turning sour in her bottle.

She sat there wishing Undine might be gone to the devil, as Alice Brown had gone in verification of her prophecy of six years before. She did not stay long, however, and found it hard work to change the expression of her countenance to one of serene affability as she passed young Mr. Dunstables in the street.

After she had gone, Cousin Jonathan sat down to smoke and read a sermon. It was a good cigar, but it hadn't any flavour; it was a nice sermon, original, by Henry Ward Beecher, but he didn't like it. He had not felt so many nasty twinges since he had read a certain marriage notice in the papers years before. "I am growing too studious," he said; "my nerves are debilitated, seriously debilitated. I must take a tonic. I must take a walk."

Exercise is good for debility of many kinds, and he came home feeling better.

While he was walking in a desperate hurry with flying arms up the hill, Harry Blair was wandering in a desultory manner among the trees below. Cousin Jonathan was more light of heart than he had been for many a brown day:

"She was not so evil as they thought her, not so mercenary," he said, and rejoiced.

XIV.
ON BOARD SHIP TO SOUTH AFRICA

ON THAT Wednesday morning the cause of the violent exercise of the former and the joy of the latter was standing on board a steamer bound for South Africa.

Undine was leaning over the side of the ship and turning back no wistful look to the fast receding English shores. Like a great impassioned living creature whose burning, striving heart impels it to wander on forever, the steamer passed over the blue, breezy, swelling sea, leaving its track of foaming bubbles to dance and die in sunshine. The wild free sea-birds, as they dipped their wings into the water and spread them out in the morning light, were glad and full of life.

It was such rest to stand and watch them, it was long before she turned her eyes to the little world on deck. There was motion enough there also, and happiness too for all that might be seen; but Undine looked back longingly at her sea-birds as they floated over the water, as though it might be pleasanter to be among them than among the wiser fowls that trotted on the deck.

Near her were sitting two Africander girls who had been sent home for their educations, and who were returning sublimely ignorant of everything in general and their own deficiencies in particular, to make a grand sensation in their little up-country town, to be worshipped and sought after by the sterner sex and woefully traduced and servilely copied by the gentler, who would for a short time look up to them as Young Lady's Journals in the flesh and worthy of all imitation from their collars to their walk.

Further off there was a portly dame wearing the stiffest of black silks with the stiffest of necks, who could by no conceivable effort bring her eyes lower than the great gold rings that adorned her short fingers, and who devoutly believed this ball had been launched into space and continued suspended there to serve as a floor whereon might be placed her well-shod feet. Long ago she had done her own ironing, and her own washing too at a pinch when no Kaffir maid was to be got, but her husband had been a lucky emigrant and those days were forgotten now. Her husband, who sat not far from her, looked as though the rolling of the ship were considerably more than he could stand and fervently wished himself in old Africa again: old Africa, to which he would return smaller and wiser after his travels, the truth having been revealed to him dur- during ing his wanderings that the world has greater things than a British settler. To his wife no revelation had been made, for the darkness that surrounds the female soul is dense.

A little to the right of this couple was standing a pimply young missionary, biting his nails and staring very hard at a very pretty blonde who was going to the Cape to be married and who filled his bosom with those gentle stirrings to which the sacerdotal breast is strangely prone. She looked not at him, but from under her black silk hat her dove's eyes glanced softly at a group of young Englishmen, birds of a feather, who stood together smoking and chatting. A fish in the hand is worth six at the hook, and more than one bride has come out to her beloved to find herself unwanted; so, if there were any golden fish on board, it might be as well to angle for them. The young gentlemen on whom her eyes were resting now were small game, however—puny, white-faced young Londoners, "raw Englishmen" they would be called out in the colony, where they would no doubt go into stores as clerks or become petty diamond-buyers at the Fields. There were one or two German Jews on deck, smoking cigars and sunning themselves, some going out for the first time and some returning to the Cape: not the little snivelling, weasel-like creatures who come out third class and, as soon as they land, supply themselves with a waggon and a couple of mules and become "smouses," [1] hawking false jewellery and damaged clothing among the Dutch farmers, and growing rich on it; but gentlemen Jews, with their polite foreign manners and their fascinating broken English, who will make you swear round is square and sell you to the devil before your face, and you shall never know it; who will squeeze you to pulp to get your last shilling today, and tomorrow, when your wife is starving and no Christian will help her, will give her ten.

There were men and women of all shapes and qualities to be seen, but nothing so pleasing as two little children with pretty faces who stood near to her. Innocent blue eyes and pink-and-white dimpled faces were surrounded by a maze of fine yellow hair. Presently a very diminutive and equally ugly terrier with a white body and little yellow ears came up, and received from the foot of the smaller of the two an astonishingly lusty kick.

"Oh, Lily, how can you!" said her sister. "It belongs to that lady in the black-silk dress."

"No, it doesn't, or I would not have kicked it," responded the little one; "it belongs to that woman with the plaited hair and the old grey frock."

"Oh, then it's all right," answered the elder, complacently.

[1] "Smouse"—hawker, peddler. Used in English, the word rhymes with "house"; in Afrikaans it rhymes with the English word "dose."

Undine stooped down to caress the shabby little creature whom the world ill used because its mistress had not a chin or a silk dress. Even in a morsel of humanity not three feet high, with a baby face and golden curls, must one find the world, the flesh, and the devil full grown?

She looked away from them to the woman with the plaited hair and the grey dress. She was shabby, dreadfully shabby. Her grey skirt had been turned not only inside out but upside down; her loose cloth jacket had once been black but was now brown, and, to judge from its cut, was the last relic of a long-deceased fashion. On her head she wore a great round hat ornamented round the crown by a piece of brown lace which must have been young when the jacket was black. Her black gloves were three sizes too large for her and yet did not conceal the knobby condition of her long thin hands. She had a weak, nervous mouth and sat on the edge of the bench, as though hardly sure she had a right to be there at all. Her hands were crossed in her lap and her eyes looked out across the water. Immense wonderful steel-grey eyes that were strangely out of keeping with the wrinkled wizened face in which they were set.

"I wonder who that woman in the grey dress is," said a gentleman standing in earshot of Undine to his companion, a military man who boasted an immense pair of moustaches and a most elegant drawl.

"Woman in grey dress? I saw one just now. Deuced pretty little thing. Tried to get up a conversation; couldn't. Best-looking thing on board."

"Then she's not the woman I mean," responded his companion. "She's not your style, would not exactly attract you, but she has marvellous eyes."

"Who has?" inquired the captain's pretty sister, coming up at that moment. Possessing a pair of eyes as remarkable for their brilliancy as the shabby woman's were for their shadowy deepness, she thought the remark referred to none other than herself.

"I can't say that I admire your taste," she said when the owner of the grey eyes had been pointed out to her. "A living song they are, you say? You who have so much of the poet's blood should really try and translate them into something intelligible to us poor mortals who see nothing in her but a piece of very shabby gentility. You poets should not absorb all the light that falls on you without reflecting a ray on us."

"I'm afraid it takes more to make a poet than nature has poured into my mould," he answered, laughing lightly, as he offered her his arm and walked off with the graceful black-eyed beauty. Undine thought his dancing blue eyes as pleasant to look at as the rippling waves, and stood watching as he passed to and fro, now stopping to throw bonbons to the children or stooping to stroke the yellow- and-white terrier they had kicked, then standing to chat with a lady or raising his hat and turning his face against the breeze to let it toss and play with his brown curls. A boy he seemed in his perfect enjoyment of life in spite of his rich brown beard, the only glad childish thing on board. Undine's eyes followed him and she forgot the shabby woman till she went down to her cabin and found that she was to be her companion there.

It was better than having the captain's pretty sister or any of the gay butterflies on board; and truly better she found it when, lying down in her berth, she did not rise from it for weeks. The strain under which she had lived for years, the excitement of the last few weeks, had told on her, and now when it was all past she broke down utterly. After a few days she was well enough to lie still and enjoy the quiet rest, but was weak enough to feel grateful for the silent constant attention of her companion, who sat beside her night and day.

"You are very good to me, very good," said Undine one day, when the woman sat bathing her head with vinegar and water. "You do everything for me so much better than the stewardess can."

"I ought to be able to," said the woman in a low, nervous voice. "I have been nursing for twelve years. I do nothing else."

All day Undine's occupation was to lie and watch her, for she never went on deck but sat there sew- sewing ing at innumerable little white shirts and petticoats, with those great marvellous grey eyes which always seemed looking beyond the object on which they were fixed to something far away.

She might have been any age between twenty and forty, for in spite of the wrinkles in her sallow face there was something more of the girl than the woman about her.

She never spoke unless spoken to, till one day Undine had scribbled half a dozen lines of rhyme in which she told what she felt when there had been rain in the night and she went out to see the roses knocking their faces together and sending down a second shower into the face of the moist sweet earth. She was looking radiantly happy, for it is as thrilling as a lover's hot kiss to have fixed on paper something that has looked beautiful to us.

"Are you going to some one?" asked the woman suddenly.

"Going to some one?" repeated Undine inquiringly.

"Yes. I beg your pardon," said the woman, seeming terribly abashed and speaking more nervously than usual. "I hope you will forgive me. But I meant—you looked so happy—and I—I thought you must be going to some one."

"No, I have no one to go to," said Undine. "Are you going to friends?"

"Yes," said the woman.

Undine leaned back wearily on her pillows. So it was only she who was utterly alone; even this queer grey woman had friends.

"Where are the friends you are going to?" she asked presently.

The woman waited for a long time, then she said, suddenly, "I have one; I am going to him." And then, after a short pause, "He is dead." And a smile as sad as the last red light that burns on the highest crag of a mountain passed over the worn face and the great grey eyes.

Undine asked no more questions. Some great sorrow has shaken her reason, she thought.

The next day the woman sat at her interminable sewing and, Undine, who lay reading felt as a generous child does who is eating something sweet and cannot understand that it could be less sweet to another. "Would you like me to read aloud to you a little? You must grow so tired of sitting here always and sewing," she said.

"Thank you," said the woman in a tone that was as far away as the look in her eyes. "Long ago I used to like books; they said it was that made me so stupid."

"How could that be?" asked Undine, resting her cheek on her hand and looking at her.

"I don't know, but I never could learn, and I used to sit in the window in the moonlight reading the books I liked; and they said it was that made me so stupid; but I don't think it was; I would have been stupid anyhow."

Then she remembered the work which had dropped from her hands while she spoke and she stitched on faster than ever.

"Reading makes no one stupid. They must be strange to say so," said Undine.

"I don't know. You see, I could only remember poems and tales, I couldn't do sums or remember the tables; I was very stupid, but I understood some of *them*; Shelley was the name of one man I used to like, but I did not understand him; I only felt sorry for him. It was wicked, I know, but I used to wish I could have seen him. I used to like him." She spoke this in the low tone peculiar to her, and more as though she were speaking to herself than to anyone else.

"I don't think he was wicked," said Undine. "It is so long ago, perhaps I have forgotten."

"I don't know, but I thought he and his wife went away from each other, and I thought he loved another woman; but I forget."

"He did love another woman, but I don't think that that's any reason for not liking him. It's always right to love, love as much as we can, and as long as we can, and as strong as we can," said Undine, emphatically, raising herself on her elbow and watching the busy fingers as they moved to and fro.

The exertion tired her, so presently she lay down again, forgot all about the book, and was following her roving fancies, when the woman laid her hand softly on her arm.

"Do you really believe it?" she said. "Say it again."

"Say what?" asked Undine, looking into the grey eyes which for the first time were really looking at her.

"That it is not wrong," she whispered.

"Not wrong to do what? Not wrong to love? How can it be? It is not wrong to feel warm or to feel strong, and we can as little help loving as feeling either."

"But if it hurts other people," said the woman slowly.

"Then it must be silent as the dead are, who they say live, yet we never hear them."

The woman sat with her hands folded in her lap. Undine lay and watched her wonderingly.

Suddenly, with the abruptness which was at all times common to her, she drew from her bosom an old gold locket that was tied to a black-velvet string, and put in into Undine's hand.

"Look at it," she said. "I never felt so before—but I would like to tell you. I never felt so before—but I would like to tell."

Like to tell! Yes, we all like it. It is not only the purple dove in the deep shade of the bush, it is not only the poet in his rhapsodies, talking to stones and trees, but the coldest hardest sinner among us who passes through life without giving a sign. We all like to tell, but, alas! too often find no comprehender, and walk through life dumb and mute with our burden.

Undine opened the old gold locket. In it there was the face of a young girl, a pretty, weak, sensitive face, with a setting of abundant brown curls and great, timid, fawn-like eyes.

Opposite was the face of a man—a dark, handsome, sensual face with bold black eyes.

Undine lay looking at the pictures, while the woman talked on in a low dreamy voice, so softly that a times she could hardly hear her.

"I was always stupid," she said. "I think that must have been the reason why no one ever loved me. They sent me to school when I was quite a little child to see if it would do me any good, but I used to get so frightened I could never remember when we had to come up and say our lessons, and so I always stayed in the classes with the little girls. I think they used to like me, the very little ones; I could dress their dolls and even help them with their lessons a little. You see, I was not stupid to them, but to the big girls, and they could not bear me, but they used to let me darn their stockings for them and, when any of them got into a scrape, then they used to come to me and say, "Don't say it's not you if the teachers ask, because you are sure not to get a prize anyhow." And I used to say yes, because I thought it would make them love me; but it never did, it only made the teachers hate me. One of them I thought liked me, she always talked so softly to me; but one day when I was shut up all alone in the dark room that opened out of the schoolroom, I heard some of the teachers talking. I think they had forgotten me and I heard them say I was the stupidest girl in the school and that they could not think how she could like me. "I do not like her," she said, "I feel sorry for her, she is such a poor thing; but there is not a girl in the school I care less about." Then I lay down and cried. I had been so happy when I thought she loved me, and when I came out the girls all laughed at me because I had been crying, and said I was afraid of the dark; and I was not afraid at all, I liked it, but I did so want some one to help me, some one bigger and cleverer than I was.

"Afterwards, when I grew a great girl, I left off trying to make people love me, because it was no use.

"I used to get away from the others whenever I had time and sit and read all by myself. I had not many books, only some books of poetry and a tale called *The Wide Wide World*, and some other little books that I forget, but I read them over and over till I could repeat them by heart. I don't know how it was I could remember such things and not my lessons. I know I tried to learn them, but somehow I never could.

"When I was grown and wore long dresses my mother died, and my father a little time after, so I had to go away from school, and I had nothing and no one to go to except one aunt. She had a beautiful little house close to the sea, with a balcony and a flower garden in front, with little white gravelled paths, and she and her three little children lived there alone. I thought I would be so happy there and make her love me, and I thought I would not read my books any more, because they said it was that made me so stupid that no one could like me.

"When I came there she gave me a pretty little green-and-white room all to myself, and she told me I should only have to teach the eldest two children and help her a little with her needlework; but I would make her love me if I worked very hard and tried to do everything I could for her. So I used to get up very early and help the nurse to dress the children and the cook to get the breakfast, and I used to work all day and late in the evening. When the children were in bed I used to get out the needlework; and when she used to ask me if I was not tired yet, I used to say no, though sometimes I was so tired when I went up to my room I used just to lie across the foot of my bed and cry for tiredness till I went to sleep. I knew it was very wicked of me, but somehow it seemed as though she would like me better if I said I was never tired. After a little time she sent the nurse away and I had to go and sleep with the children and look after them all day and take them for walks, and she never asked me if I was tired any more, however late I sat working. You see it was all my own fault. She believed what I told her, but it seemed so hard that she should not care about me a little bit. If she had sometimes looked at me as she looked at the children, I don't think I should ever have felt tired.

"At last one day she told me she was expecting visitors; a friend of hers and her husband and child were coming to board with us for six months, because she was very delicate and wanted to be near the sea.

"I was half sorry and half glad when I heard it. It would give me more work, but then I always fancied, before I saw people, that perhaps they would like me and not find me so dull as all the others had. By and by they came. She was a pretty woman and used to sit in the parlour all day, making wax flowers and baskets. My aunt used to sit and talk with her, but she never took any notice of me, even when I put fresh flowers on her table or brought her pretty seaweeds for her baskets; and her husband I was very frightened of. I could not bear him. He used to sit in an armchair on the balcony just before the schoolroom window all day, and I used to feel as if I could not teach the children anything, especially when he looked in. I was so afraid of him, I wondered how anyone could love him, till one day when I saw him sitting there with his little girl on his knee. Her head was on his shoulder and both his arms were about her, and he looked down at her with such a look in his face, and he was so strong, that I ran away to my room that the children might not see me. For I could not help crying; I wished so I was that little girl.

"After that, early in the mornings, when I used to walk on the beach with the children and his little girl, he would often meet us when he was coming back from his bath and stand and talk to his little girl and sometimes to me. I wondered he did not mind being seen talking to me by the other gentlemen who went past us, because I always had my aunt's baby and looked like a nurse girl. I thought it was very kind of him, but I did not like him and I was afraid of him. I went round another way when I saw him coming. He always talked so kindly to me. He said my arms were not strong enough to carry such a big baby, and he asked me if I was not tired. No one else ever did.

"One day he had brought a beautiful painting of a woman and hung it up in the parlour. I was passing the door with a cup of arrowroot for the baby, when he called me to come in and look at it. It was a very pretty picture.

"'Do you know why I bought it?' he said. 'Because it was like you.'

"I could not think how anyone could think such a beautiful face was like mine, so I looked at the picture again. Then I felt him take my hand softly in both his, and when I looked up into his face it seemed to have just the look that had been there when he looked at his little girl.

"I pulled my hands out of his and ran away to the children's room and knelt down by my bed and cried, I was so happy. I never thought anyone would look at me like that, and all the day I was so glad; I never felt tired or miserable. In the evening two or three gentlemen came to play whist with him, and my aunt told me to make some eggflip for them. He had showed me how to make them before and I could make them very nicely, but this evening he came into the dining-room just as I had finished, because he said he was afraid I would not do it right. We were all alone, and as he went out of the room he put his arm so softly round me and kissed my mouth. It seemed as if there were a great river running past my ears, and I sat down and put my head on the table. I did not think there was any wrong in it; I did not think at all. It was all so strange, and I was so happy. I did not think that day or for many days after. I had no time to think. You see, I was working, working all the time with the children or at housework, from early in the morning when all the other people were in bed till late in the evening, and at night I was so tired I could not undress. I went to sleep in my clothes. I only know that I was happy. They say when people are idle and have nothing to do they sin, but I think people do more sins when they have no time to think, because you can love without time, you see. One Sunday evening I had time to think. They had all gone to church and the little ones I was taking care of were asleep, and I could sit at the foot of the bed and think. I saw that his love for me was not like his love for his little girl, else why did he never kiss me when even the children were by? There must be something wrong in it. So I thought I would ask him to go away very soon. I did not love him; I hardly knew if I liked him, except just when I was talking to him; but I knew it would be very hard to lose him. You see, nothing else had ever loved me like that.

"Just as I was thinking so, I saw him standing in the door. He had gone with the others to church; I don't know how it was he came back. He came into the room and stooped down over me and asked me what I was thinking of. Then I told him, and he said I was a foolish little girl and told me there was nothing wrong in his loving me; he said some kinds of love between men and women were wrong, of course, but he only loved me as if I were his little girl. I was his little sunshine, he said, and he did not show his love to me before others because his wife was so queer; she did not like him to have a friend, even a man, though she did not care for him at all, he said. He had never had anyone to love him, and he longed so to have some one who cared for him utterly; he asked me if I would not. Then I felt as if I had been quite wrong to think it was not right to love him, and when he asked me to kiss him I did, though I never had before. Then I loved him better, and I felt quite glad and happy till the next day. I was dusting the parlour, and I heard his wife talking to him in the other room.

"'I'm not a fool, or quite blind either,' she said. 'I understand your small games by this time. I know very well why you bought that picture, and the meaning of your pleasant looks. Oh, yes, I am not such a fool as you take me for, nor she, either, with her flowers and her seaweeds and her pretty innocent little face.'

"I went out of the room then, because I did not want to hear more; but suddenly, I don't know why, the thought came to me that they were talking about me. I asked him that evening, and he said: 'You must not mind her; she would be jealous of your aunt if you were not here. It is only her nature.' I felt very unhappy after that whenever I had time to think and was alone, but when I was near him I was quite happy, and I got to love his little child so. I had it near me all day long, but I could not bear to see him play with it. I did not feel jealous of anything else, but when I used to see him kiss her, I got a sick feeling at my heart. He always called me his little girl and his little sunshine when we were alone, and at last it seemed to me as if he were the only real thing in the world; all the other people seemed like dreams. I liked so to go and put his room neat; it was so nice to touch the brushes he used every morning and to fold up his clothes and put them away, and it was so nice to touch his great-coat when I passed through the hall. One day I picked up a torn likeness of his on the floor, and I put it in my mother's locket by mine, and that was nice, too.

"One afternoon, when all the others were out on the beach and I was left at home to get tea ready, he came in. I was kneeling on the pantry dresser, filling a glass pot with jam, when I looked round and saw him standing behind me. He came up and lifted me down in his arms and carried me into the dining-room. Then he sat down with me in the great armchair and held me very close to him, and asked me if I loved him, utterly, better than anything else in the world. When I said yes, he put his face down close to mine and said very softly. 'Then you must come away with me, far away, to another land where you and I can be alone with each other till we die, and we will make each other happy, so happy.' He told me he loved nothing in the world but me; and when I looked up at him it seemed as though his eyelids were wet. I lay quite still for a minute and then I tried to jump up and run away, but he did not let me go.

"'How can you leave your wife and your little child?' I asked him, and then I crept close to him again and told him that I loved him. I don't know what else I said; I don't think I even knew then.

"But after that day I loved him with another kind of love, not like the love I loved him with before; and I could not bear to be in the same room with him when there were other people, because it seemed as though they must see in my face how much I loved him. And every day he begged me to go away with him, but I always said, 'No, no, no.' It would have been wrong of me to go, but I did not care about that, I was so wicked; I could not bear that he should be selfish and leave his wife and his little child. If he had asked me to do anything I would have done it, I would not have cared; but I did not like him to be wicked.

"So many weeks went on and sometimes I used to get miserable and ask him to go away. Then he used to hold me in his arms and kiss me, and I forgot everything. You see, I was working, working all the day and at night I was tired, so tired. Sometimes when I was with the children on the beach in the morning I was so sleepy that I went to sleep sitting on the sand.

"At last one day they all went away to see a great show in the next town. They went for two or three days, and I was left to take care of the house. It seemed so dreadful to have to think of being there alone for two whole days and never seeing him once. I cried, and in the afternoon I fell asleep on the sofa wrapped in his great-coat, and did not wake till next morning. Then I put the house in order and got a great heap of his stockings to darn. When I went to bed that night I was not very tired.

"I lay thinking and thinking, and I cannot tell how it was, I seemed to see so suddenly all at once how wicked I had been, and how wicked I had made him. It was just like being in hell to think of it all. I felt as if I should go mad, and at last I got up and lit the candle and sat down and wrote to him. I don't know just what I wrote, but I know that I told him I had been very wicked; it had been all one great lie; I had tried to look and act as though I did not care for him, and I had made him do wrong. I told him I would never speak to him again or touch his hand, and that I would go away, but I would always love him. I must have said something more, for I wrote many sheets, but I don't know what it was. Perhaps it was the same thing over and over.

"It seemed to me as though the morning would never come and I would go mad before it came. He had called me his little angel and his sunshine and I had been like a devil to him, making him sin, and now it was done and could never be undone.

"The next day they came. I thought he had got tired of me, for when he came into the dining-room where I was standing he hardly said good-day to me or looked at me. He took the letter from my hand and we never were together again. I told my aunt that evening that I was going away. She was very angry and said I was mad and very ungrateful, but that she would be glad when I was gone. Then I went into the nursery and wrote to the teacher of the school I had been to, and asked her if she would let me come and teach the little ones. I would not want money if only she would let me come at once. When I had done I sat thinking and it seemed to me as though I must go and tell his wife everything; it was sin, nothing else mattered, and it seemed as though if we told everything that it would be less. So I got up, but when I got to the door of her room I thought how angry he would be and so I went back. By and by, I went again; but now the light was out, and when I stood close by the door I could hear her breathing and his. I listened for a little time and then I went back again to my room. The next morning when I looked out at the window I saw him walking on the road that led to the beach, and I never saw him any more. I got an answer from my old teacher and I started that day, but I did not stay with her long. Perhaps I was very foolish, but it seemed to me as though, if I worked very hard all my life for other people and at work I did not like, it might make it right for him a little bit. I was very foolish, but I could not help thinking it would be of use, a little use. I always hated so to see blood and people that were in pain; so I got them to let me help in a great hospital, and I learnt to be a nurse. I used to feel faint at first, and as though I wanted to run away, when I saw anything dreadful, but I used to think it was helping, and then I felt strong. I never heard of him any more, I thought he was tired of me before I went away, and that he would soon forget me. I thought so for twelve years and I never heard his name. But the other night I was sitting up with another old nurse. She was telling about a gentleman with whom she had gone out to South Africa. I was stirring the gruel before the fire and I did not listen to what she said till I heard a name; it was his name. Then I asked her to tell me all she could about him. She told me that he had some disease and the doctors said he must take a long voyage; but it did him no good. At last when they got to a little town in Africa they saw that he was dying. He did not like his wife to come near him or do anything for him, and all the day and all the night he lay groaning. At last one night just before the light came they saw that he was going. He lay quite still, but at last he opened his eyes and looked all round the room.

"Come to me, come to me," he said.

"They asked him if he wanted his wife, but he said, 'No, no; my darling, my little sunshine, once, just once, darling.' He did not say anything more. And so now I am going to him," said the grey woman, very quietly.

When Undine turned to put the locket in her hand, tears were in her own eyes; but on the woman's face was only that strange smile, sadder than any tears.

The voyage was almost ended. That night they would be in Table Bay.

Undine sat with her companion on the deck.

"Do you stay here or go on to Algoa Bay?" [1] she asked her.

"I must stay here," the woman answered. "I must earn money to take me on. I never worked for money before."

"It is not very hard to live without it," said Undine.

"No, I never wanted it till now," said the woman, "and a lady whom I had taken care of paid my passage and my dog's. I don't know what made her so kind to me."

[1] Port Elizabeth.

A little while after, Undine got up and went down to their cabin. She got her little bag from under her pillow and took out her purse. It was not heavy; there were only ten pounds in it, the price of a brooch her grandmother had left her. She counted out five and quickly pulled out the small black portmanteau that contained the woman's work and slipped them into it; then she went up on deck again.

The woman was gone, and she sat there by herself watching the captain's pretty sister as she walked up and down with her hand on the arm of the handsome boy-man. He was not chatting with the other ladies this morning, nor playing with the children, but he carried her great white hat in his hand and looked down at the little black head beside him.

XV.
IN AN OX WAGGON

"GOLD! What is Gold?" So we ask scornfully in the days of our ignorance. "Gold! What is Gold?" We ask it derisively.

King Gold sits on his throne and laughs secure, for well he knows that sooner or later, if he withhold his cold light, the proud knee will bend and the stubborn hands will rise and the old prayer of humanity will come from the derisive lips:

"Oh, Gold, thou art King and Lord; if not the God, yet a God forever, in whose hands lie health oftentimes, and joy oftentimes, and the desire of the heart and of the eyes. Pour down upon us the light of thy countenance we beseech thee, O Lord!"

But the God of Gold is growing old and deaf now, like the other gods, and he often lets our prayers rise and die unanswered.

"Gold! What is Gold?"

Undine had asked it and laughed her glad mocking laugh in the frosty lane years before. She had thought it with a bitter heart and envy, as she looked in at the broken window of the wicked woman who had her baby. She had asked it of herself, when two months before she had thrown it from her and made up her mind to wander free over the world and enjoy life and learn. And she was wandering free and learning, but the enjoyment was still yet on the hills before. Yet she had not bowed her knee to King Gold—only thought that a purse heavier, a little heavier, were an improvement.

She was walking through the streets of Port Elizabeth, her head bent down to preserve her eyes from the rain of sand and fine stones that fell on the flat roofs with a sound as dismal and disheartening as the fall of sand on a coffin lid.

She had sat in the hotel till she thought it was better to go out and face it than sit there listening to its dreary music. Moreover, no work or any other good thing would find her while she sat there, and her money was surely taking wing at the rate of twelve-and-sixpence a day; so she went out into the street to escape the tap-tapping and to seek her fortune.

Africa, as it appeared in that desolate and sand-smitten seaport, was not the Africa of her memory. The old Africa with its great grass and karoo flats and rough rock-crowned mountains, unridden and un-man-defiled old Africa, was little like the sand-smothered town in which she stood, which might have been in any country in Europe but for the ragged niggers slouching about the streets and the dark, dirty, half-clothed fish-boys who dragged their wares along with tails draggling in the sand.

One thing was certain, here she would not stay; though how to get away remained as yet an unsolved problem. One of her pounds was already gone, and four pounds take one nowhere in a country where all locomotion is at the expenses of muscle and sinew. She was attracted, like all others who were near enough to feel its influence, by the great magnet that draws to itself all who are good-for-nothing vagabonds, wanderers, or homeless—the Diamond Fields. [1] Three hundred miles of bush flat and karoo are not to be bridged over by four pounds, however. Cobb and Co., as it tore past her as she laboured up the street, made thicker, if it were possible, the thick cloud of dust around her; but it was not for beggars with four pounds to enter its red swollen body or perch on its crowded roof. Presently she stopped to take breath in front of a large store, before which was standing an ox waggon with a long span of red oxen. She stood resting and considering what was next to be done.

[1] Kimberley. The distance is 485 miles. Cobb & Co. was the line of horsedrawn coaches.

Why should a woman not break through conventional restraints that enervate her mind and dwarf her body, and enjoy a wild, free, true life, as a man may?—wander the green world over by the help of hands and feet, and lead a free rough life in bondage to no man?—forget the old morbid loves and longings?—live and enjoy and learn as much as may before the silence comes?

So she had asked herself on the first morning of her freedom, the morning after her husband's death, as she lay back in the velvet armchair of her boudoir while the maid stood behind her combing out her hair.

Now she had broken through conventional restraints and was free—free to feel that a woman is a poor thing carrying in herself the bands that bind her. Now she was free, but how to extract enjoyment from the present state of things was more than she could accomplish at that instant; and how long would she be able to maintain herself without getting under some one's thumb?

If she had been a man she might have thrown off her jacket and set to work instantly, carrying the endless iron buckets and coils of rope and wire with which the waggon beside which she stood was being laden. She might have made enough in half an hour to pay for a bed at one of the lower hotels, might have wandered about the town, seen something of life, and enjoyed herself in a manner. As it was, being only a woman and a fine little lady with the scent not yet out of her hair nor the softness rubbed from her hands, she stood there in the street, feeling very weak, bodily, after her illness, and mentally, after her long life of servitude and dependence—very weak and very heartsick.

Two men passed her carrying a large packing-case, and even through the dust that descended before them her eyes could distinguish the "New Rush Diamond Fields" [1] that was painted in great black letters on its lid. She stood still a moment to consider, and then stepped up to the back of the waggon, on the back of which a small tent was fixed. Between a gap in the closed sails a woman's kappie [2] was visible. Undine raised one corner of the flap and looked in.

The part of the waggon occupied by the tent was not more than six feet square, and was one great bed covered by a vel-kombaars [3] on which were seated the owner of the kappie and two fat children. The former held in her arms a great baby whose clothes she pulled quickly down to hide its not over-delicate feet. It was a shrewd, bright face that was concealed by the kappie, the face of a woman of about thirty-two, which would not have been without its claims to beauty had it not been for the marvellous display of stumps made visible whenever her thin sharp lips moved. She was dressed in a black-and-white print, as was the fat and dirty baby at her breast. The two children were busy wrangling over a brown paper of sweets which their father had just thrown in for them, but they stopped as soon as the strange face presented itself under the sail.

[1] The Kimberley mine of "the Diamond Fields" was, on discovery in 1871, called "Colesberg Koppie," then "New Rush," before the town was officially named Kimberley in 1873.

[2]Kappie—sunbonnet.

[3]Skin rug.

"Is this waggon going to the Diamond Fields?" inquired Undine, while the woman, not best pleased at being found in her waggon trim by a stranger, was busy pulling down her sleeves. She answered in the affirmative graciously enough, but stared curiously at the intruder and wondered what could bring a lady to the back of her waggon on such a day with such a question.

"Do you know what the owner of the waggon would charge for taking a passenger to the Fields?" Undine asked again, with no hope that the contents of her purse would be sufficient, but thinking hurriedly that her shawl and one or two good clothes might bring her something.

"The waggon belongs to my husband," answered the woman, "and I'm sure he can't take anyone. You see, there is me and the three children, and the tent is small, and I could not undertake to care for anyone else. I would rather try and get some one to help me."

"I would do all I could to assist you," said Undine, "and I have very little luggage. If you could make it convenient to take me I would pay four pounds and should not mind doing anything."

The woman looked at her *very* shrewdly now. There was nothing visible except a pretty pale face and a little black velvet hat, but they were scrutinized closely. She could not quite make up her mind, so resolved to solve this difficulty as she did many others by finding what view her husband took of the matter. She poked her head out in front, between the tent and a great box, and hailed him.

Mr. Snappercaps, a huge, sluggish English Africander, with mild light eyes and a red beard, approached, and she proceeded to inform him of the offer.

"You don't mean to take her, do you? You don't know what sort of a character she may be," said Mr. Snappercaps. "If she's dressed up it does not say much for her that she's knocking about by herself and wants to go to the Fields. Is she married?"

"I suppose she can mind the children just as well if she's married or unmarried," said Mrs. Snappercaps, "but you never think *I* need any help."

"I don't expect it's much help you'll get from her, but do as you like," he said, and walked off to his work. His wife drew her head in, and, it being evident that he was decidedly opposed to her accepting the offer, all hesitation on the subject was at once put an end to.

After plying her with half a dozen questions, Mrs. Snappercaps informed her that, if she would have her box there and be ready to start in fifteen minutes, she might come.

The tone and manner in which this information was conveyed contrasted somewhat sharply with that of ten minutes before; but when first the little black hat made its appearance she could not tell that its owner was not possessed of a phaeton and a score of silk dresses; now she was wiser, and acted accordingly.

In the middle of the afternoon a day or two after, the great buck waggon, with its long span of red oxen and heavy freight of wires and buckets, was creeping slowly along the sandy road. It was a sweltering day, and the small oven-like tent at the back of the waggon was buzzing and alive with little black flies of every shape and a pair of droning blue-bottles.

The oxen, reluctant as they were to lift their weary feet only to put them down again on the burning road, and leisurely as they ploughed up the heavy sand with the great waggon wheels, yet raised a cloud of the finest dust which, covering hands and face and clothes with a thick red coat, seemed to enter the very windpipe. Undine was seated at the extreme edge of the waggon, Mrs. Snappercaps having declared that under any other state of affairs she could not possibly find room to extend herself. She lay now with her arms and legs stretched out, her head on one pillow and another on her face to keep off the dust. Very fast asleep she was, if judged by the periodical snorts that at regular intervals proceeded from beneath it; but in truth very wide awake, with a small cylindrical curve made in the pillow straight from her eyes to the little black hat, now fast changing to a reddish brown.

Ferdinando Shakespeare and Algernon Sidney were fast asleep, the former with the piece of fat mutton still between his lips which he had been engaged in consuming when overpowered by the heat and the motion of the waggon. It attracted to his countenance a score of black flies and one of the blue-bottles, making it, if possible, a more interesting scene of animal activity than that of Master Algernon Sidney, whose infant charms were totally concealed by a coating of syrup, coffee, sand and flies.

The baby, otherwise Master John Wesley, was not asleep, however, but awake and endeavouring with furious kicks and struggles to precipitate himself into the road, or at the best on to the "trap." [1] It seemed hardly impossible that he would ultimately succeed, for he was fat and powerful and there was not much strength in the "bits of paws" that held him—"bits of paws" being Mrs. Snappercaps' designation for those useful appendages in the object of her scrutiny.

[1] (Pronounced "trop.") "Trap": the little movable stepladder at the back.

The baby was dirty, astonishingly dirty, several days of ox-waggon dirt having accumulated on him. Mrs. Snappercaps saw this, and saw that some one else hated dirt, was always washing her hands and trying to rub the grease spots off her clothes; and so, by way of bringing down the things that are mighty and do exalt themselves exceedingly, Mrs. Snappercaps ordained that no ablution should be performed on the person of Master John Wesley, and, moreover, that except when absolutely necessary, he should never be out of the "bits of paws" for a moment.

Now also Mrs. Snappercaps was desirous of ascertaining whether her employee would, when thinking herself unobserved, maintain that serene urbanity of manner which irritated and exasperated her yet more than her constant ablutions and her good English. Would she still keep her leg curved in that most awkward posture, to prevent it from touching Ferdinando Shakespeare's face? Would she yet do her best to keep the baby from bumping its head against the bottle bag, though it was clearly to be seen that she loathed it to the tips of her fingers?

To discover all this Mrs. Snappercaps snored and breathed hard and looked out from under the pillow, only to see that, as far as any desired result was concerned, she might as well have saved herself the trouble. Ferdinando Shakespeare's face was not pressed nor the baby allowed to knock its head.

She was just about to throw off the pillow and declare that she didn't know when she had had such a sound sleep, when Mr. Snappercaps, who was engaged in putting a new lash to his whip, dropped behind the waggon.

He was a great, good-hearted fellow, though he *was* fond of a glass of brandy and water when in pleasant company; so, when he looked up and saw the pale little woman endeavouring to manage his great baby and sitting on the very edge of the waggon and looking worn out and weary, his good nature and his ignorance led him up to the back of the waggon, and he said, "Expect you're pretty near done up; not used to riding in an ox waggon and minding babies."

These were the first words he had ever addressed to her, and, his conversational resources being exhausted by them and his whip being needed, he stepped out in front to try it on the backs of his oxen.

Mrs. Snappercaps threw the pillow off her face, sat up and rubbed her eyes. John W. had screamed himself stiff by this time, so she took him and, having pacified him, proceeded to loosen the comb-and-brush bag and, putting its not very delicate contents into the "bits of paws," remarked that there was nothing so wretched as having nothing to do and that Undine had better clean them. "It's miserable to have nothing to do," said Mrs. Snappercaps, asserting a fact the truth of which she had had ample opportunity for verifying during the last few days, during which the sum of her own labours had been to eat, sleep, and slap the children. Truly, Mrs. Snappercaps had underestimated her own ability and womanliness when she imagined she might fail to extract her bread-and-meals' worth of labour from her passenger. Not that she was a hard woman, or a cruel one. Mrs. Snappercaps was looked upon among her female acquaintances as an exceptionally kind-hearted and generous woman, better than the run of themselves, and no doubt they were right. She shut her eyes and ran away screaming if she heard they were going to kill a sheep; and she used to call Mr. Snappercaps a cruel beast when he lashed his sticking [1] oxen—except she were very anxious to get on, when she sat still in the waggon and thought he did not cut half deep enough.

No, she was not a hard woman, only a woman, and she envied her white-handed soft-voiced little dependent as one feminine thing envies another. She was the daughter of a Lower Albany farmer who had sent her to a Grahamstown boarding-school, where Miss Sarah Jane had taught her to play the piano and make slippers and caps and use long dictionary words without the slightest idea of their meaning, and long words that are not found in any dictionary and whose meaning was known only to herself.

[1] When the waggon "sticks fast" (in mud or deep sand, for instance), it is said to be "sticking."

When she went home she was regarded by her elder sisters with mingled awe and envy and by her mother with unfeigned admiration. She reigned supreme, and only in her own mind was there a dim perception that, after all the money that had been expended on her, she was not quite the lady, not quite the genuine article.

Her mother never let her make bread or salt the meat, her sisters ironed her petticoats, and her father gave her an extra pound whenever they went into town, yet she ended by marrying Will Snappercaps, who rode transport and was the son of a neighbour. When she met in the street any of her old schoolfellows who had since married attorneys or merchants, they always looked up into the sky, onto the ground, or at the houses, at anything but the particular spot of earth on which she stood. They were out of her reach, that upper ten who talked good English, dressed in taste, and went to balls; she could never retaliate on them. But now, good fortune had put into her hands one of the order, soft-voiced, white-handed, and refined as any of them, and for many stiff bows and for many clear cuts Mrs. Snappercaps had to indemnify herself. Her heart rejoiced as the heart of a homeopathic quack might do who held under his thumb a licensed practitioner. Mrs. Snappercaps' faith in the efficacy of vicarious atonement was not stronger than in other uncultivated minds, so she did not allow her joy to express itself clearly in her own mind, but it was there all the time as she sat on that sweltering afternoon watching the "bits of paws" at their comb-cleaning. She was certain, she remarked inwardly, that there was something wrong about her; there always was about people who were so agreeable and never got out of temper, never got savage with the flies, never were ruffled or put out by the jolts or the grouty [2] coffee or any of the innumerable evils attendant on an ox-waggon journey. And then, to be sure, as her husband had remarked, would a woman who was good for anything be knocking about in that way by herself? No, there was no doubt of it, she was a bad character, a very bad character; and her own—Mrs. Snappercaps'—great goodness of heart had prompted her to do a very foolish thing in taking her. If she were not a sinner, where did she come by that diamond ring? If she had friends of the right sort, rich enough to give it her, would they not have looked after her? And a nice story this was about her husband being dead and her having no relations. Mrs. Snappercaps was not a child and she was not born yesterday; no, not she!

"You had better leave the combs alone," she said; "you don't seem to understand it; you sprang a tooth again without cleaning it. If a thing is not well done I would rather it wasn't done at all." With which remark, the combs being now fully cleaned,

[2] Grouty: full of coarsely ground coffee grains.

Mrs. Snappercaps seized them and the brushes and with great energy put them into the bag and hung them up; while Undine, her hands empty for the first time that day, sat watching the deep oscillating track of the waggon wheels in the red sand.

After a time Mrs. Snappercaps found the heat and closeness becoming something really unbearable, and she was about to direct Undine to loosen the front clap by way of producing a current of air, when that individual proceeded on her own responsibility to roll it up. Mrs. Snappercaps instantly discovered that her neck was stiff, that she had neuralgia in all the teeth on one side of her head, both of which complaints would be infinitely aggravated by such a proceeding; so the clap was carefully fastened down again, and Mrs. Snappercaps endured suffocation for the rest of the afternoon with a martyr's fortitude.

But even Mrs. Snappercaps must sometimes really sleep, and so it came to pass that night that she and her three children were snoring in chorus, while Mr. Snappercaps plodded along at the side of his oxen, calling out to them every now and then drowsily as they stepped on steadily in the cool night air.

Up above the still stars glittered and gave out just light enough to make visible the great round clumps of bush through which they passed.

Undine crouched down in her corner at the back of the waggon and listened to the rink, tink of the tin coffee pot and mug that were tied to the roof and the tom, tom of the great iron kettle and gridiron that were fastened on the trap, and the creak, creak of the waggon. She could rest her head on the wooden blackboard and look out and feel herself again a little child, Socrates curled close in her arms. Frank's clear light-hearted whistle came from the front box, her mother's voice sang the evening hymn as they rode home in the starlight from the town, and the loves and passions of her womanhood looked strange and unreal to her in the creaking waggon, under the light of her childhood's stars—the still, unchanging stars that shine on unaltered while our poor little systems go to ruin and desolation—the silent stars that can hold so many memories, which but for them would be forgotten, that we sometimes dread to look up at their white, faraway lights, for fear of hearing whispers and feeling the touch of fingers that can bring only coldness now.

Yes, the old faiths and the old loves, they are written up there; and when we have put them from us and buried them deep, the night sky gives them all back to us.

About eleven the waggon stopped, and Mrs. Snappercaps, by no means in the best of humours after being roused from her slumbers, allowed Undine and Mr. Snappercaps to spread a skin counterpane at the side of the waggon and make as comfortable a seat as might be with half a dozen pillows against the hind wheel. Here she bestowed herself and her baby, while Undine took out of the back box the coffee, bread and ribs of mutton that were to form their repast.

Mr. Snappercaps, worn out with his day's work, flung himself down at full length on that part of the counterpane which his wife had not appropriated, and in five seconds was sound asleep. Undine, when all was finished, sauntered off to a little distance among the bushes, where she could have a good view of the waggon as it showed in the light of the blazing fire.

It looked picturesque enough, the great red waggon with its little white tent and rows of iron buckets that glittered in the firelight. A little further on the tired oxen were dimly visible, lying down just where the yokes had been taken off their necks, too weary to look for food. Even Mrs. Snappercaps, as she sat in her spotted print and white kappie hushing her baby, added to the scene; and her husband also, lying close to the fire with his hat drawn down and his head resting on his crossed shirt-sleeved arms. Among the bushes, a little to the right, the driver and leader had made their fire.

The driver, a great heavy Basuto, lay in his master's fashion on the ground; the leader, a sprightly little Hottentot, sat watching the meat on the roaster with his wicked little black eyes. He had a more than usually apish appearance as he sat there with his knees drawn up to his chin.

After some time, when the meat was ready and the coffee made, Undine returned to the waggon.

"I thought you were inside," said Mrs. Snappercaps.

"No," said Undine, "I was walking about."

"Walking about?" said Mrs. Snappercaps. "What on earth for?"

"It looks so nice at a little distance, the waggon and the fire," said Undine.

Mrs. Snappercaps gave her long flexible lips a little screw.

"I should think you had seen enough of ox waggons and fires by this time," she said, and looked upon this proceeding as an additional proof of the badness of her employee's character; though why she did so she could not very easily have explained to herself. She could hardly fancy that Undine had made love to the green bushes, or galavanted with the dry stumps even in the dark. But Mrs. Snappercaps was unable to assign any reason for her walking off in the dark, and the story about the beauty of the waggon was on the face of it a lie; and, as there must incontrovertibly have been *some* reason, she felt sincerely persuaded it must have been a bad one.

Undine's wandering about in the dark proved her a bad woman; and that being proved, one did her no injustice in suspecting her of evil, even though there might be no harm in her wandering about.

Mrs. Snappercaps' logic was conclusive, so she gave the coffee-pot an energetic shake as she poured out Undine's basin, by way of winning her disapproval. She could hardly drink her own cup when she saw with what apparent unconsciousness and exasperating indifference the contents of the basin were drunk, grounds and all. "All put on. What a hypocrite! That's the worst part of her," thought Mrs. Snappercaps, as with her stumps she tried to masticate a piece of tough mutton. "It's worse than her immorality; I could get over that. Thinks she looks beautiful now, with her head on her hand, staring into the fire, and her hair flying about like a mad thing's."

Whether she thought so or not, great good Mr. Snappercaps, as he sat drinking his coffee, thought she looked tired and sad, and felt sorry for her, as he did for his Hottentot leader when he thought he was overworked.

When he had finished he rolled himself up in his blanket under the waggon.

"There's no use to tie the oxen," he said to his driver. "They are too tired to stray tonight."

The morning came and brought woe to him who had trusted to the weariness of his oxen's legs, and double woe to him who hoped to recover them through those of his Hottentot.

The oxen had vanished and Jan was sent to look for them. He had followed on their spoor [1] for a little distance, when it suddenly came to his recollection that he had not had his sleep out. Accordingly, he ensconced himself snugly under a large stone, and in three minutes was wandering amid quids of tobacco as large as himself and brandy the very fumes of which made him merry.

From these visions he did not return till the sun, now inclining to the west, had burnt him out of his hole, when he rose and instantly retraced his steps. He appeared before the waggon with a limp and an air of extreme dejection. He had searched up hill and down kloof, but had seen no trace of them, and he rubbed his weary feet with his right hand as he spoke.

Mr. Snappercaps saw there was nothing for it but to give him a good feed and himself to set off on the search.

"The poor devil of a Hottentot must be tired," he remarked.

Mrs. Snappercaps smiled a mingled smile of pity and contempt. She was not a child, and she was not born yesterday, and she was up to Hottentots at least.

Mr. Snappercaps returned late that night after a fruitless search; and neither on that day nor on the next nor on several after that was there any sign of the oxen. It was weary work, waiting there day after day. Sunday morning came. It was six days since they had decamped—six days of endurance of half the plagues of Egypt: six days of flies; six days of water red as blood, alive with monstrosities of every shape; six days of being devoured by red ants if one sought for shade under the bushes; six days passed in the care and company of three wretched, screaming, sun-oppressed children.

[1] Spoor—footprints.

They had wellnigh exhausted everyone's patience and had made Mrs. Snappercaps very desirous of improving others, and very virtuous. Her desire to improve others was made manifest by the copious corrections she administered to the Masters Ferdinando Shakespeare and Algernon Sidney; her virtue, by the petty but constant mortification of the flesh which she caused to be felt by the immoral person whom chance had placed in her hands.

On this Sunday morning Mrs. Snappercaps woke early and poked her head softly out at the back of the waggon to take, unperceived, a survey of her antagonist's proceedings. That individual, in happy unconsciousness, sat on the trap just below her, reading a small shabby book.

"A Bible, no doubt," soliloquized Mrs. Snappercaps, as she drew her head softly back into the waggon. "I could get over anything else, but her pretending to be religious—it's too much."

She prepared a nice little homily to be delivered at breakfast-time on the duty of serving God in secret and unseen; and when she had finished lacing her boots, she poked her head cautiously out again.

On a second and closer inspection the book appeared to be no Bible, but, judging from its long words and dry look, she concluded it to be a volume of sermons. It was not so good as if it had been the Bible, but still, if judiciously modified, the homily might still be delivered with great effect.

At this moment Mr. Snappercaps, who had been to the top of the mountain to see if any signs of the men or oxen were visible, returned.

"Having a read?" he said, wishing to say something kindly but not exactly knowing how.

"Yes," said Undine, smiling and closing her book.

"No going to church today," he said again. "I don't mind it. I'm used to it. But I expect it won't seem like Sunday to you without."

Undine made no answer, so, wishing to be very agreeable, he continued: "What church do *you* belong to? Now *I* like the Methodists."

"I belong to no church," said Undine as she climbed off the trap and, slipping the unfortunate book, cause of many sorrows, into her pocket, proceeded to make the fire.

Now, making a fire seemed a particularly easy and pleasant occupation when watching a nimble little nigger throw a dozen sticks on one another and in half a minute produce a blaze big enough to roast a lamb by; but when once the sticks were in her own hands it seemed a very different matter. Surely they must be wet or of the wrong kind; for after she had expended a whole box of matches, two Grahamstown *Journals*, and all her breath in trying to blow them into flame, they remained as obstinately cold as though there were no combustibility about them.

Undine, having blown herself red and dizzy, was about to give up in despair when Mr. Snappercaps' good nature brought him to the rescue. He handled the sticks with as much science as his own Hottentot could have shown, and in no time produced a roaring blaze.

Mrs. Snappercaps from her spy point in the waggon saw all that passed and, perceiving a weak point in the enemy, she proceeded to place her artillery accordingly.

Presently the baby cried. Undine climbed up into the waggon and took him, but he was not easily pacified. "Of course he cries, and he will cry till you take the hard thing out of your pocket," said Mrs. Snappercaps; "it hurts his leg." Undine took the book out; Mrs. Snappercaps took it up.

"'Spencer's *First Principles.*' Who wrote these sermons?" asked Mrs. Snappercaps.

"Spencer," said Undine.

"Spencer, of course; I know that," said Mrs. Snappercaps, perceiving for the first time that Spencer was the name of the author and not of the book. "Of course I know his name's Spencer, but who is he? What is he? What does he believe?"

"I shall be glad to lend you the book," said Undine, "if you care to read it."

"Not unless I know who he was," said Mrs. Snappercaps, combing the hair down over her eyes. "What church does he belong to?"

"None," said Undine.

"None! No church!" cried Mrs. Snappercaps. "What church do you belong to?"

"To no church," said Undine, quietly.

"To no church, *no* church! But of course you don't mean to say you never go to chapel anywhere."

"It's a long time since I last went," said Undine.

"Why, surely you're not a Roman Catholic, are you?" asked Mrs. Snappercaps, putting down the comb and brush and dividing the hair that hung over her face with both hands.

"No," said Undine, and prepared to follow Ferdinando Shakespeare, who had just descended from the waggon. But her interlocutor scented a rat and was not to be thus eluded. "You must be *something*; everybody is *something*," continued Mrs. Snappercaps, fixing her dark eyes on her antagonist to make her words more impressive. "You *must* be something; nobody's *nothing*. You aren't a Unitrinitarian nor anything of *that* sort, are you?"

Undine very gravely disclaimed all knowledge of or participation in the errors of so deluded and extraordinary a body as the Unitrinitarians; but Mrs. Snappercaps was not satisfied.

"Well, what are you, then?" she asked. "You are not an atheist, or a deatheist, like Shakespeare or Votter or that wicked Bishop Colso who lives at Delagoa Bay, are you? You believe the Bible, don't you?"

"Ferdinando will be getting into the fire," said Undine, quietly slipping down onto the trap, and showing her astonished catechiser that there really were limits to what she would endure in return for her bread and meat.

At night, a corner not big enough for a rat to crouch in; grouty coffee; meat which John Wesley had mauled; work to which the amen was never said:—all these she accepted with smiling indifference; but Mrs. Snappercaps had spoken with a woman's own shrewdness when she remarked that it was those very agreeable quiet people who have the devil's will and spirit in them in spite of all their softness.

"There is no need to rush away in a rage," she continued, speaking very rapidly and her lips becoming very moist. Undine, who stood leaning against the trap with the baby in her arms, might have edged in some answer, but Mrs. Snappercaps' speech was as voluble as it was energetic and carried all before it.

"Of course you'll try to get away, of course you don't like to speak about it, when you know it's true. If it wasn't true, wouldn't you be glad to disown it, wouldn't you be glad to disclaim it, when charged with it? If that book you've got in your pocket was not some monotheistical nonsense, would you read it alone on the sly, in secret when there was no eye to see you? Oh! no! no! I wonder you are not afraid to say such dreadful, terrible things lest the God you don't believe in should strike you dead. I wonder that you weren't afraid, when the waggon went over the bridge, that God would break it down and let you tumble into the water. I wonder you weren't. If it wasn't—if it wasn't that I want to act like a Christian by you, I would not let my oxen take you one step further. How do *I* know how you may divert my poor innocent little children. Give me the baby!" said Mrs. Snappercaps. Undine gave it, with all the more alacrity as Algernon Sidney had just fallen over the pole, to the great damage of his skin and nose.

At breakfast Mrs. Snappercaps maintained a rigid silence; she ate with a purpose and drank copiously and with energy, and her husband clearly perceived that evil was approaching. He picked his chop and drank his coffee in silent uneasiness, though in what direction the storm would burst he could form no conjecture.

Breakfast being ended, Mrs. Snappercaps climbed into the waggon, and after some trouble produced from one of the lowest boxes a great red bible and a copy of Wesley's hymns with great shining clasps. Armed with these weapons, she again descended, and took her seat on a camp-stool that stood against the back wheel on the shady side of the waggon. Her husband, having already assumed his favourite posture, lay at full length on the ground, with his head resting on his arms.

"Mr. Snappercaps, do you intend to listen?" said his wife.

"Listen to what?" asked Mr. Snappercaps, looking up sleepily.

"To the word of God," responded Mrs. Snappercaps. When the question was converted into these terms it was impossible to reply in the negative, so he picked himself up and, leaning back against the front wheel, pulled his hat low over his eyes and wondered what on earth this new turn of affairs portended. Six years he had been married, and never yet had she used such instruments for administering to him the reward of his numerous transgressions; but today he felt a vague yet strong conviction that the books were to become the instruments of his correction for some as yet unknown dereliction from the path of duty. To Undine, who sat on the ground nursing the baby, she said, "*You*, no doubt, will not wish to remain; you may go. I compel no one to stay," she continued. "The worship and the love of God flow from the inner mind, from the outer soul—it must be free—it must be like the rays of heaven. I compel *no one* to stay."

"If you have no objection, I shall remain," said Undine, who felt no inclination to leave the shade of the waggon and march off into the broiling sun with Master John Wesley in her arms.

Mrs. Snappercaps now seized Masters Algernon Sidney and Ferdinando Shakespeare, and seating them with great force very flat on the ground on each side of her proceeded to loosen the clasps of her Wesley's hymns. Having given out in the most approved style the whole of Hymn 1, she proceeded to sing it with great energy. Mr. Snappercaps pulled the hat yet lower over his eyes and reckoned out for the hundred and fiftieth time how much he was losing by this delay with the oxen. Nor were the rest of the audience very attentive. Ferdinando Shakespeare was engaged in counting his fingers, Algernon Sidney in catching the ants that ran up his legs, while Undine sat wondering for how long a time John Wesley might be counted upon to remain quiet. That young gentleman sat motionless, with a finger hooked in his mouth, staring with wide-open eyes and rapt attention at the marvellous display of maternal stumps made visible on Mrs. Snappercaps' upper and lower jaws during her vocal effort.

The last verse having at last been reached, Mrs. Snappercaps put the hymn-book down on the ground exactly in front of her with great precision, and proceeded to open the red book. From its pages she made a careful and apt selection of passages applicable, she deemed, to the case of at least one of her hearers. These she read with much emphasis and many a long and ominous pause; denunciations against Pharisees, hypocrites and unbelievers she delivered with equal fervour and point. Having brought this part of the proceeding to a termination, she went on to part two of the programme. This consisted in reading the eleventh and twelfth chapters of the second book of Samuel, wherein is recorded how the amorous King of Israel walked on his roof at evening tide and beheld the limbs of the beautiful wife of Uriah the Hittite; how for love of them he caused the faithful soldier to meet his death before the walls at Rabbah; how the wife of Uriah the Hittite, when she heard that her husband was dead, mourned for him many days, and when the days of her mourning were ended went to the arms of the king.

Mrs. Snappercaps had just reached this point in the very appropriate narrative she had selected, when John Wesley, no longer entertained by the dental display, made the most emphatic demonstrations of disapproval and obliged his nurse to carry him off.

Mrs. Snappercaps now turned one eye on her husband, otherwise King David, and beheld him, much to her wrath, either pretending to be or really fast asleep. Preferring to act upon the assumption that he was pretending, she addressed him thus, but in a tone loud enough to awaken him, however far gone in the land of dreams:

"Thank you, Mr. Snappercaps, thank you, but I'm not quite such a child as you fancy me, no, not by a long, long way."

Mr. Snappercaps opened his eyes.

"No, I'm not a child! I was not born yesterday! You are no more sleeping than I am, Mr. Snappercaps; but I wonder, yes, I *do* wonder that you can act as you do. I wonder you can act so. You can sit there still, you can listen, when even that vile, lowly, venomous outcast felt it; she could not sit still and hear it; she had to get up and go away; but you, you have no more heart than a stone, than a Kaffir, than an adamantine. When David heard the voice of the Prophet *he* repented, but you, you have no faith, no pity, no affection. Ho-o-o! Ho-o-o! Ho-o-o!"

This latter sound was as the whistling of the wind through a keyhole, produced by drawing her lips into the smallest possible circle and moving her head to and fro.

It was her way when she reached a climax and language failed her, and Mr. Snappercaps was accustomed to it; but waking suddenly he felt confused, and looked out over the still Sunday landscape, the clear blue sky, the hazy brown hills clothed with clumps of dark green bush, looked out and wondered whether he were still asleep, whether Sarah Jane had taken leave of her senses, or whether he had.

"Oh, it's very nice to put on that innocent look," said Sarah Jane. "Very nice, so nice; but it won't do with me, no it won't. You think I've not seen it, do you? I've never heard you call my baby heavy, have I? I never saw you go down on your knees to blow the fire for her. I was asleep, fast asleep, of course, in the waggon. Oh yes—no, don't speak, don't try and deny it; it's no use, William, it's *no* use. It's not once, it's not twice; it's four times: it's *four* times that I've seen you with these eyes turn the chops over to find a raw one because she said she liked them raw. I saw it once"—Mrs. Snappercaps' tone was now low and subdued—"I saw it once, and I kept still. I said, 'I'll see if he does it again, and you did it again, and you did it *again*. No, don't speak; I don't wish you to take more guilt upon your guilty soul. That puff-adder, [1] that ringhals [2] has caused you to do sins enough without adding any more to them. Oh, William! William! how can you? How can you? How can you?"

"I don't know what you are talking about, Sarah Jane. You've gone mad," said her husband, staring stupidly at her.

"That's right, Mr. Snappercaps; say I'm mad, send me to Roben Island,[3] slaughter me, murder me, as David did Uriah. There'll be no one to trouble you then. But you shan't, no, you shan't; for the sake of my children I mean to live." So saying, she raised the Masters Ferdinando and Algernon from the ground, with each arm and with as much energy as she had seated them.

[1] A snake.

[2] A snake, one of the cobras.

[3] Where lunatics used to be kept.

"The man who stabs my body I can forgive," said Mrs. Snappercaps; "but the man who runs a sword into your *soul*—no-o-o! no-o-o!"

"Oh, damn it all, Sarah Jane!" said Mr. Snappercaps, rising, "what confounded nonsense you do talk!"

"Curse and swear, Mr. Snappercaps, curse and swear; that's right. They cursed the prophets and apostles, but it didn't hurt them. You can't deny what I've said; you know it's true; you love her, you know you do!"

"Oh, hang it! Damn it! Confound it all!" said Mr. Snappercaps. "I wish the woman would go to blazes, to the devil."

"There is no need to wish that," responded Mrs. Snappercaps; "every step that your oxen take they are bringing her nearer to him. What do you think she's going to the Fields for, if it's not to go to him?

"Oh, don't try and defend yourself any more, William," seeing he was about to speak; "don't, don't."

"Look here, Sarah Jane," said her husband as he turned to go away, "if you give me any more of this nonsense I'll put the woman down at the first hotel we come to.

"No, you won't," said Mrs. Snappercaps, who had no intention of losing her drudge, and he well knew it. "No, you won't. Vile as she is, I'll act to her as a Christian should. I've said I would take her to the Fields, and I shall take her there."

"Didn't know Christians took folks to the devil," said Mr. Snappercaps under his breath, as he walked off in the direction of the muddy kloof [1] from which they got their water, to seek for a sleeping-place under some brush.

It was near evening, and as he had not returned, Mrs. Snappercaps, after dozing all day in the wagon, descended to resume her old seat on the camp stool, and took her baby.

Undine, now her arms were free, sat with the children at the side of the road, making houses in the sand for them.

As mischance would have it, Master Ferdinando Shakespeare bethought him at this moment of getting a mug of water from the iron bucket that stood under the waggon, the better to moisten their sand. Stumbling over the disselboom [2] with the mug in his hand, its contents were deposited on his person, drenching his begrimed white pinafore.

[1] Ravine.

[2] Pole of the waggon.

"That is what comes of playing on a Sunday," said his mother. "You wicked little boys! Leave that sand alone."

"It was my fault; I began the play," said Undine.

"Well, I wish you would take his pinafore and wring it out; and if you have his, it would not be more trouble to take Algernon Sidney's and the baby's and give them a rub," said Mrs. Snappercaps, loosening the pinafore as she spoke.

Undine rolled them up with a piece of soap, and was just starting off in the direction of the kloof when Mrs. Snappercaps, speaking in a high shrill voice, detained her.

"Oh yes, do go to him, go at once. I don't wish to hinder you, not at all. Go to him! Go! Go!"

"Go to whom?" asked Undine, looking round in blank astonishment, for she had been out of earshot when the little encounter of the morning took place, and imagined that Mr. Snappercaps had gone in search of his oxen.

"Oh, you *sweet* little thing!" said Mrs. Snappercaps. "*You* don't know that he is over at the kloof, do you? You never sit with your head stuck on your hand staring at the fire, just to try and look sentimental and make him feel sorry for you. *You* never do, do you? You would not do such a thing! And you never pretended you could not make a fire on purpose to get him to come and help you! And you don't get up early," continued Mrs. Snappercaps, speaking very rapidly, with the solitary canine, the only complete tooth she boasted, looking very strangely like a fang; "you don't get up in the grey dawn and sit on the trap and try and look melancholy till he comes to talk with you. You would not think of doing such a thing! I'm glad to see you don't deny it; you can't," said Mrs. Snappercaps, rocking herself and her baby energetically to and fro.

The true state of affairs now dawned on Undine, who stood irresolute with the soap and pinafores in her hand, half inclined to laugh, half to enter a protest.

It ended in her doing neither, but asking very quietly whether Mrs. Snappercaps could tell her in which kloof she would find the little fountain the driver had discovered that morning.

This cool manner of receiving her attack brought yellow spots to the corners of Mrs. Snappercaps' mouth. Her only reply was a passionate and often repeated injunction to go to him, go to him, go, go, at once.

In direct opposition to these kindly instructions, Undine walked off through the bush in the direction of a small kloof where, instead of the great clumps of elephants-food [1] and coonie with which the hills were covered, a thin line of forest trees showed, at least sometimes, the presence of water.

[1] Elephants-food and coonie are hardy shrubs.

The sun was almost setting; his rays made the great round clumps cast long oval shadows, and the busy red and black ants were hurrying home with their last load of sticks. Undine killed many of them as she walked on quickly, and her heart was not very light as she passed in and out among the bushes. She had worked till she felt as though she had no head left, and no soul, and the golden glory of the sky and the still beauty of the bush said nothing to her. In her ears rang the yells of a baby; with its weight her arms ached, and her whole body too, from head to foot, for want of rest. She was tired; she was wretched; she was finding out that there are aches other than those of the heart, and weariness unutterable that is not of the spirit. May a man's soul be tapped out through his muscle? Are there things more enervating and destructive to its life than being the idle plaything of a rich man? Is it crueler pain to be pricked by a woman's pins than lashed by a great affliction? When we labour like brutes, do our hearts become like theirs, till to eat and have rest becomes all our ambition?

The busy ants as they hurried home had no answer for her question, nor the still green bushes. Only one feathery outstretched arm of wild asparagus caught at her dress as she passed by and tore it, because she would not stay to loosen it, but hurried on angrily, petulantly. She was tired, she was wretched, she was disappointed.

To rush the world over seeking for happiness is a fool's work. Is it also a fool's to look for a life which, however hard and rough, shall be high and noble, a life worth living?

From being the useless plaything of a man, from dressing and eating and lounging on sofas, to nursing another woman's children, to making another woman's bed! Will life's changes be always so, shall we never get any higher? Oh, the things of life are very little, and the soul is great.

She walked on till, just as the sun set, she reached the little kloof and, forcing her way through the rocks and trees, came to the bed of the mountain torrent. She clambered down its steep bank and leaped on to the smooth white sand that lined its bottom. Then she paused to take breath and leaned against one of the great dark boulders that lay about on every hand. Long years ago the rushing torrent had torn them down from their home on the mountain-side, but they lay very quiet and unmovable now on their bed of white sand. Over one of them, a little higher up in the bed of the torrent, a tiny stream of water trickled. The drops as they fell down slowly on the face of the flat stones below had the soft silver sound of far-away evening bells, and everything else was very silent. The silver band of water as it crept through the sand made no sound, and the long low tremulous bank of maiden-hair fern, though it heaved and swayed to and fro in the stillness, made no sound. High on the western bank of the stream against the white dreamy evening sky, the branches of the oliven [1] trees were visible, with pale, quivering, up-pointed leaves. All the dark trees around lay glittering and motionless, but the air stirred those pale green upward-pointing leaves till they shook against the still white night sky; and on Undine, as she stood looking up at it, a great hush came and a great joy; for heaven is not a long way off, nor the beautiful for which we thirst. She dropped the pinafores she held in her hand and knelt down on the smooth white sand, and when she rose, just above the treetops the first star was shining.

She washed out the pinafores and then walked back with them to the wagon.

Mrs. Snappercaps wondered that she sang so softly to the baby as she put it to sleep and sat half smiling in the firelight with only the remnants of their supper before her.

"She's a fool and out of her senses," said Mrs. Snappercaps as she leaned back against the wheel, munching the last biscuit.

Aye, and a fool sees more than a wise man, sometimes.

[1] Oliven—wild olive.

XVI.
NEW RUSH

EVERY grace must come to an end, so philosophises the hungry child; and even the dominion of a Mrs. Snappercaps has a limit and a termination. She and her little soul and her little tortures may shut out all the great varied world for a little time; she may seem to engulf everything for a little time, till all above, around, below is Mrs. Snappercaps and her babies; but land must be gained at last, if it be only the land of death.

For Mr. Snappercaps that land might be the only one in which his poor good old soul should find refuge; but Undine's deliverance came near at hand when the white tents of Du Toit's Pan [1] came in sight, gathered like a flock of white birds round their monster sandheap.

[1] Du Toit's Pan—now a suburb of Kimberley.

The next evening, free and emancipated, she stood before a store in New Rush, where Mr. Snappercaps had just unloaded his wires and buckets. She felt very strong and very free as she stood there, with her box at her side and two shillings in her pocket, and watched the wagon roll slowly up the street and out of sight.

It was glorious to be alone again. Alone, though the street was so thronged with the streaming crowd of niggers and diggers returning home from the work that they kicked up the red sand into a lurid cloud over their heads—stark-naked savages from the interior, with their bent spindle legs and their big-jawed foreheadless monkey-faces, who, though they were going home to fire and meals, could hardly get out of their habitual crawl—colonial niggers half dressed, not half civilized, and with some hundred per cent more of evil in their black countenances than in those of their wilder brethren—great muscular fellows, almost taller and stronger than their masters, the white diggers, who formed a thin sprinkling in the crowd and who, in spite of the thick dust that enveloped them, might be distinguished by their more quick and energetic movements.

Undine stood watching the crowd as it rolled past, till the sound of some one closing the window just behind her made her look round. A very swell nigger with a real gold chain and a black cloth suit was putting up the bars.

He was a gentleman who made his living principally at night, but he found it useful to have some ostensible employment which might serve to account for his gold chain and black cloth, if ever he found himself in the close hand of the law.

She asked whether she might leave her box there till the morning.

"No," was the prompt rejoinder, "not if you don't give me a shilling."

She gave it, for it was impossible to carry it with her or yet to leave it there in the street. She saw it safely deposited in the store, and then walked off in search of a bed of some kind, nothing doubting but that her shilling would gain her a resting-place, if it were only a little square of hard ground in the corner of a tent.

She went to a greasy-looking yellow canvas house with some kind of sign over it, in front of which half a dozen men were lounging. In the house there was only one woman, very gaudily dressed and very florid, whose eyes Undine imagined saw right through her pocket and purse and beheld the one poor shilling that lay there in solitude. She wished herself out in the street again, but it was too late now.

"Can I get a bed here for tonight?" she asked.

"She's a bad one," thought the woman, who, being one herself, ought certainly to have judged rightly.

"You can get a bed for four and six," she said; and Undine with her shilling made a very speedy exit.

Out in the street once more, she plodded on through the wilderness of canvas, past round tents, square tents, torn tents, and whole tents; past canvas houses and wooden houses and iron houses, and non-descripts. There were places enough and people enough, but just no place for her. The fresh night breeze as it crept among the tents struck her chill and made her feel cold and heavy to her heart. She was now in the poorest and most wretched part of the camp which lay around the Circus, and was walking on slowly when an empty scotchcart, coming home from the Kop [1] and tearing down the street in the gathering darkness, caused her to step quickly out of its road and almost into a small open tent.

It was hardly dark yet but there was a candle alight in it, and at a great packing-case a dark bright-eyed Malay woman stood ironing white shirts. On another case close at her side, a heap of articles, still waiting to be done, lay piled. There was little else in the room except a torn red curtain covered with lions, which marked off the sleeping-place. On the floor sprawled the woman's brood, forming a motley forest of dusky arms and legs. She was so engrossed in her work that she did not notice the intruder's presence till she had wished her good evening, then she looked up quickly and curiously.

[1] Colesberg Koppie, now the Kimberley Diamond Mine.

"Could you tell me where I could get lodgings for tonight?" inquired Undine when her salutation had been returned.

"No, not in this part of the Camp," said the woman; then eyeing her sharply, "Have yer been long in New Rush?"

"No," replied Undine. "I arrived this evening." A pause followed, then Undine said:

"Perhaps you would be so kind as to tell me where I might be able to get work. I should be very much obliged to you if you could."

"Work?" said the woman. "There's work enough if there were only hands to do it. What sort of work do yer want?"

"Ironing—any kind of work," said Undine. "I don't care what."

The woman looked at the great pile of ironing on the case beside her. She must get it done that night though she stood over it till morning. So she said:

"If yer can iron, yer can come in and help me get these things done and stay here tonight, but I can't give yer a bed; we've only one and that's only sacks."

So Undine stepped into the tent, to pass her first night at New Rush in ironing gentlemen's pocket handkerchiefs and nightshirts, leaving the other shirts for the more experienced iron of Mrs. Snods, which glided over them with marvellous rapidity and ease, leaving no singe or crease in its track. By-and-by the noise and squalling of the children ceased as one by one they fell asleep on the ground or crept off to the sacks; only the eldest, whose occupation it was to carry the irons in and out, remained awake. He was an over-worked, under-grown boy of about nine years, with a very solemn face and a pair of squinting bead-like eyes that were always trying to see each other across his nose. He wore a narrow-brimmed crownless hat, from the top of which his curly black hair rose in a great bunch; the tattered remains of a red tancord jacket and trousers covered his body; on his feet he carried a solitary boot, whose sole was loose and, at every step, flapped solemnly as he passed in and out with the irons. When not so occupied he stood bolt upright before the packing-case, with his hands clasped in front of him, slowly twirling his thumbs, always in the same direction and always very regularly.

About twelve the last shirt was finished, and Undine, half asleep, crept into one of the great packing-cases and slept soundly till morning. When she awoke she found the woman already busy putting fresh clothes into starch, and Tommy just starting off with last night's work. It was agreed that Undine was to remain there that day, and in consideration of her assistance was to get food and a bed in the packing-case that night. Before setting to work, however, she started off in search of her box. It was a real New Rush morning. The fresh air seemed thrilling with a life that even in the close man-defiled camp it could not be robbed of; it crept among the tents and houses and brought back for the moment the roses to the sunburnt sallow faces of the dirty children, and made Undine feel brave and able to face anything. She was almost sorry when, after wandering about for a little while, she discovered the store at which her box had been left. Before it stood a digger examining some picks that had been placed outside and a couple of naked niggers who were gazing affectionately at a row of guns. In the doorway leaned the swell nigger with his legs crossed, playing with his watch chain.

"I've come for the box I left here yesterday evening," said Undine. The nigger pointed with his thumb over his shoulder.

"There it is," he said.

Undine went in and saw it standing against the counter.

"Is there anyone here I could get to carry it?" she asked. "It's not very heavy."

"No," said the nigger.

"Can't you? It's not very far," she said, holding out the shilling.

He took it without making any reply, and spreading out his white handkerchief upon his shoulder to prevent the nap from rubbing off his coat, he raised the trunk.

Undine led the way; he followed close behind; but they had not gone very far when the sound of his loudly creaking boots suddenly ceased, and looking round she was astonished to behold her box depos- deposited ited in the middle of the street, and the tall black form of the nigger disappearing round the corner.

"This is not the place; you have made a mistake," she said.

The nigger was not a man of many words, so he merely screwed up one eye very tight and opened the other very wide, and walked off. Undine went back to her box and stood by it, looking at the passers by, but none were available for her purpose. There were troops of niggers going to work at the Kop, [1] and sharp little diamond-buyers going to look for the worm, [2] and busy diggers in a desperate hurry, with their sleeves rolled up above their elbows. To none of them could she apply. At last a good stupid-looking Kaffir made his appearance. He had no bucket or pick and seemed to have nothing to do, and though he stared stupidly at her English and broken Dutch, he soon comprehended the meaning of the scarf she held out to him; and the trunk was shouldered once more, Undine taking care to walk behind him. When she reached the tent Tommy had just returned with three loaves of bread, and the solitary knife of which the establishment boasted not being forthcoming, Undine opened her box and produced a handsome silver-mounted penknife. The bright black eyes of the Malay woman marked it eagerly, and marked also the rich red shawl that covered the contents of the box. She watched the knife as it cut the bread and watched it as it went back into the box, and then began ironing again. Presently she called to Tommy to come out with her to the back of the tent and help her chop some wood. Tommy went, but there was no sound of chopping, nor, when they came in a few moments after, was there any wood to be seen.

[1] Kop: an abbreviation for "Colesberg Koppie" (the Mine).

[2] Presumably the "worm" that the "early birds" were out to "catch."

Undine, who was busy ironing, never noticed this; something in one of the children's faces had reminded her of what lay in a little English grave far over the water.

The woman began ironing, too, but presently she stopped and, leaning both elbows on the table and fixing her bright eyes on her companion's face, she said:

"I've been thinking that perhaps yer'd like rather to get work on yer own account; if yer *would*, why, I knows a Mr. MacCuligan who pays well, he does, and he's not over-particular neither. I would not give him up, but, yer see, I've got more work than I can manage, as 'tis. You see, everybody knows me, that's the thing; they know that I'm a *honest* woman, would not touch a button. It's the character as brings the work. If nobody knows yer, why, yer won't get a shirt to iron," said the woman, still fixing her bright eyes on Undine's face.

Undine wondered, if that were the case, how anyone ever came to be known, but she answered that, until she got irons and a place of her own and knew something of ironing, it was useless for her to think of taking work.

"Oh, yer could use some of my irons; I've got a lot yer see; and wood and such like yer could pay for, yer know, and Mr. MacCuligan *he* don't care how his shirts are neither."

Somehow Undine did not take vastly to this idea of doing Mr. MacCuligan's ironing, but she felt touched by the woman's kindness; she could not pain her by refusing to take advantage of it.

It was very hard to be a stranger at the Fields, the woman said; she had known what it was; but when once a person got known, why, there was more work than they had hands for.

"It's an awful paying thing, ironing is," said the woman, "awful paying. It's as good as having a claim in New Rush Kop, it is"; and when she saw Undine cast a glance round the empty tattered tent she added quickly:

"To yer it would be, of course, I mean. I've got so many brats, what I makes goes."

After a little more conversation it was decided that Undine, with Tommy for a guide, should set off to Mr. MacCuligan's to fetch the ironing.

"It's a long way," said the woman, "and perhaps yer'll think it round about, but the ways in this Fields *is* round about. Tommy, he knows the way to Mr. MacCuligan's well, he does. Don't yer, Tommy?"

Tommy nodded his head very confidently and was soon pattering along the road in front of Undine, the flying sole of his boot flapping up and down at every step.

They turned in the direction of the West End, and Undine, as she trudged behind him, tried to be profoundly philosophical and to place before herself very clearly her own advanced ideas on the subject of labour.

How superficial were the general ideas on the subject. Is not all work, if it be earnestly done, noble and ennobling? Is not all labour worship, be it only scraping a carrot or ironing a shirt? No longer would she be bound by prejudice, but, leading a life based on reason, she would enjoy the greatness of the man who labours.

They had now reached the West End, that most desolate wilderness of gravel-heaps [1] and tents, the tents for the most part not arranged with any attempt at order but forming acute and obtuse angles of every degree. They with their gravel-heaps are pervaded by a melancholy air of decayed greatness. To Undine it seemed a more desolate spot than the most barren plain of the Karoo as they wandered in and out among the gravel-heaps on which the blazing sun was now pouring down dazzling light—blue gravel-heaps and yellow gravel-heaps, new gravelheaps beside tents, old gravel-heaps, where once, in better days, tents had been. Up them and down them, over them and round them, before them and behind them, their course was like that of the wind which goeth to the south, and turneth to the north, and whirleth about continually.

[1] The "débris" heaps—the residue after the diamonds have been washed and sifted from the diamondiferous "earth" in which they occur.

"Are you sure this is the right road?" she inquired of her dilapidated little guide, who was trotting on steadily before her.

"It's the way," he answered confidently, turning his head but not his body, and with both eyes still fixed most solemnly on his nose; "it's the way." So Undine plodded on.

"Why, I thought we passed this tent with the barrel before it a little while ago! Are we not almost at Mr. MacCuligan's yet?" she asked again after a little time.

"It's the way," said Tommy, shaking his head confidently three or four times, but not even looking round; and soon they found themselves in the Circular Road.

The Road was lively and busy enough, and the glare of the sun on the white road was almost blinding. A scotchcart drawn by a wretched mule and containing a huge barrel of water rattled past them. It leaked, and some ragged little savages, one white and the rest black, were clinging to the cart with their mouths wide open and upturned to catch the drops as they fell.

"Where can I get a drink of water?" inquired Undine of her guide, the bright drops making her more thirsty than ever.

"You can buy some at the well," was Tommy's answer.

Buy some! Undine walked on and tried to forget she was thirsty, and wondered what the charm of these strange Fields might be that drew all to them.

"If we're not near Mr. MacCuligan's yet," said Undine, "I think I shall turn back. I can't go on any more." She was growing dizzy from the fierce heat of the sun, and the white tents seemed to throb before her, and the burning sand into which they sank ankle-deep at each step blistered her feet.

"It's the way, but yer don't get there if yer don't keep on," said Tommy, looking back over his shoulder but never pausing for an instant.

Undine, fixing her eyes on the flapping sole of his shoe, followed on.

They were in the best part of the Camp now, where tents were scarce and pretty little canvas houses with verandas and reed fences lined the road on every side.

Before one of these Tommy stopped.

"There's Mr. MacCuligan's," he said, "and I'll run round to the back and see if he's in."

While Undine stood waiting for his return, she leaned against the reed fence of the house that stood at her right and looked over into the enclosure. There was a new canvas house with a pretty veranda, at the ends of which hung great Venetian blinds to keep off the sun and wind. On the veranda were some green garden benches and two large cane armchairs. In one of them sat a lady, a delicate milk-white thing dressed in pale blue, with rippling gold hair that was simply gathered into a knot at the back of her small head. Undine looked at her breathlessly. Women as beautiful, more beautiful, she had often seen, but none had ever looked to her as that woman did, contrasted with the coarse clay she had looked at for so many weeks, and contrasted with the boiling, toiling, sandy, grimy world around them. The lady's white slender hands were crossed softly over the gamboge cover of the novel that lay in her lap, and she leaned back with closed eyes, looking like some fairy queen whom a strange chance had transported into the land of dust and diamonds. Undine leaned long against the fence, watching her till she slowly opened her eyes and looked up. They were straight-out-looking, cloudless baby-blue eyes; there was not much expression in them when they fixed themselves on the head and battered hat that showed themselves over her fence; but Undine limped away quickly and looked down at her own "bits of paws," already brown and rough, and at her own dust-begrimed garments, and felt a little ashamed of them. What are fine clothes, and a fine skin? Well, nothing, just nothing, when you come to reason about them, and just everything when you come to look at them.

Undine limped away as quickly as might be to the back of Mr. MacCuligan's compound, but when there she was astonished to find no opening by which Tommy could have gained an entrance to make his inquiries, and no Tommy was to be seen. The fence was very high, but, mounting on a gravel heap that lay against it, she was able to look over. A coolie was squatting in the shade, cleaning a pair of boots. Undine inquired whether he had seen anything of her guide and whether the compound were Mr. MacCuligan's. To both these questions the coolie replied by shaking his head and staring. Did he know where Mr. MacCuligan lived? The coolie shook his head again. Didn't live in that part of the Camp. Didn't know him if he did.

Undine dropped down on the ground in the shade of the high fence and held her throbbing head between her hands. She tried to think, but before she knew she had dropped into a heavy sleep.

When she awoke it was almost evening and the cool breeze was blowing in her face. She felt better after her sleep, though her feet were still blistered and her legs trembled a little. She made her way back into the street, and after not many inquiries found herself once more in the neighbourhood of the Circus, and was soon in sight of the iron [1] canteen, that she knew stood next the tent she was in search of.

When she stood before it, Undine raised her hand to her forehead, for surely the terrible heat of the day had touched her reason. She looked and looked again. There was the iron canteen on this side; there was the shoemaker's tent on the other; but the tent she looked for and the box she came for were nowhere to be seen. A good-natured man who stood at the door of the canteen noticed her bewilderment and called out: "If you're looking for the Malay woman who used to take in ironing, she's shifted early this morning. If she's got work of yours there's not much chance of your seeing it again, I'm afraid. She was a bad lot," said the man, stepping back into his house to serve a customer.

It took her a moment fairly to understand her situation, and then she soon persuaded herself that it was a most fortunate occurrence that had befallen her and freed her from her possessions. Were they not more trouble than they were worth? And had not experience taught her a lesson which, as that bitter dame teaches nothing for nothing, left her nothing to complain of?

She began slowly to retrace her steps, thinking the while that she clearly perceived where her mistake had been. She had allowed her pride to keep her from her own class, from the white-handed, silver-voiced people of refinement and polish—that was the only reason why she had fared so ill.

[1] Corrugated iron.

With that cool veranda and its milk-white blossom in her eye, she pressed on through the now crowded and busy evening streets till she came in sight of it once more.

Just as she had sat there in the morning, the lady sat there now, only that she had now a pure white dress, and in place of the gamboge-covered book she held now a small china cup. A few rays of the setting sun had found their way under the veranda and played on the rippling hair till it glittered like burnished gold.

When Undine's dusty figure and battered hat appeared before her, she raised her clear blue baby-eyes from her teacup and looked at her—looked very straight, and said: "What do you want? Work? Yes, I have plenty of work."

Undine's eyes followed her tall graceful figure as it moved into the house.

She returned in a moment with a small child's garment in her hand and held it out.

"You can take this first," she said. "If it is well made I will give you two shillings for making it—if it is well made," she said in a clear measured voice, and, without giving the dusty little figure before her a second glance, sank down into her chair and resumed her teacup.

Undine hesitated and spoke again, for work, without needle or thimble or cotton to do it with, would be small help.

"I will give you needles and cotton, if you wish it," the lady said, "but not a thimble. I never do that; and sixpence must be taken off for the needle and cotton."

The little reed gate closed behind Undine, and soon she was again threading her way through the crowded streets—crowded with home-goers. They were all going to a place of their own; even the naked Mahoras [1] had a pot of mielie [2] pap and a skin waiting for them; but she wandered on till she found herself at the entrance of the Kop [3] they had just deserted. She sat down to rest on the side of one of the mountains of gravel [4] between which the road passed, and, when the camp below was aglow with evening lights, and the noise and stir in its tents and streets became louder and stronger, she rose up and walked into the Kop in the bright moonlight. It was like entering the city of the dead in the land of the living, so quiet it was, so well did the high-piled gravel heaps keep out all sound of the seething noisy world around. Not a sound, not a movement. She walked to the edge of the reef and looked down into the crater. [1] The thousand wires that crossed it, glistening in the moonlight, formed a weird, sheeny, mistlike veil over the black depths beneath. Very dark, very deep it lay all round the edge, but, high towering into the bright moonlight, rose the unworked centre. She crouched down at the foot of the staging and sat looking at it. In the magic of the moonlight it was a giant castle, a castle of the olden knightly days; you might swear, as you gazed on it, that you saw the shadows of its castellated battlements, and the endless turrets that overcrowned it: a giant castle, lulled to sleep and bound in silence for a thousand years by the word of some enchanter. You might gaze until you almost saw the ivy clinging to its yellow crumbling walls, till you almost saw the figures of brave knights and lovely ladies, whom the death-like sleep had overtaken as they wandered on the castle terraces, till the motionless horse and the small arched window and the mighty dragon resting in the gateway were all visible.

[1] Natives.

[2] Pap of ground maize.

[3] The Kop was the actual site of the mine.

[4] Débris.

Undine, as she crouched beneath the staging, looking at that silent moonlight wonder world, forgot she was hungry and forgot she was weary, and, when she grew drowsy, dropped asleep on the ground with her head resting on her work.

[1]The mine was then worked by surface haulage. This immense circular hole is now claimed to be the largest hole ever sunk into the earth by man. The diamonds are found on a huge perpendicular pipe, not in the reef surrounding it.

The next morning the turning of the wheel [1] overhead aroused her. It was hardly light, but the Kop wakes early, and there were many men at work already among the staging. None of them seemed to notice her, and she got up feeling a little stiff and a little cold. There was nothing of beauty about the scene before her now; *that* had gone with the moonlight. It was nothing now but a great oval hole in the ground where worshippers of King Gold burrow and scrape and scratch, all in his service.

Very dull, and very prosaic now—unless indeed one had happened to be so high mounted above earth that all things fell into perspective, when even Colesberg Kop with its grovelling and grasping might, like niggers and blue-bottle flies and rouge pots, have a charm, a beauty of its own.

But Undine was not high mounted nor was her soul inclined to soar that morning; rather to grovel very pitiably. She was cold, she was stiff, she was hungry, and she held the creed of the hungry—that ideas are a delusion and sentiments a snare, that the way of the world is the wise way and leads to bread and butter, and that all ways which lead elsewhere are inventions of the devil and must be forsaken. She made her way into Main Street, and as she turned the corner she saw a great naked nigger devouring a huge lump of mielie-meal pap which he held in both hands as he passed down the street on his way to work. She thought him the happiest soul she had passed that morning as she walked on looking for a place where she might sit down and work.

[1] A haulage wheel on the rim of the mine.

No such presented itself till she found herself free of tents and houses on the long low grassy ridge that separated New Rush from Du Toit's Pan. There she sat down, screened by the low scraggy bushes, and began to work.

She stitched as one stitches who stitches for bread, but the calico was stiff, and without a thimble the needle hardly went through, and it made long stitches and little ones, and worked a small hole in her finger which stained the work with little drops of blood. Yet she worked away, without pausing, for an hour, then she sat still for a moment and lay down upon the ground.

It was so strong and drawing, that earth; she stretched out both her hands and clung to it as she used when a little child, as we can cling only when we are weary and heartsick and lonely, as we must cling to something if it be only a tree stump or a stone, feeling as if we were not then so forsaken.

It was a bright warm morning, but she was cold from hunger, and underneath the ground it must be warm, so warm. The earth, the dear old earth that has been mother to us all and must cover us all again sooner or later—it would be so easy to drop asleep upon it, so much better than to go on living with nothing worth living for.

"I will die," she thought. "Why should I go on like a fool, labouring and striving to keep a life that is worthless? I will lie still and die."

She turned her face round and looked at the grass on which she lay. Mingled with it were tiny blue and red bells and a bright creeper with yellow flowers. The sunshine came through the low bushes and danced on their golden faces, and up above the bushes she could see the clear blue sky.

It is not *all dark*, it is not *all* evil in this life; while the sky hangs overhead and the many-tinted earth lies at our feet, there will always be what is beautiful, always be what makes life worth the battle; and her heart grew strong again. Very empty life may be, very useless, but worth having while there is sunshine.

Hour after hour Undine sat there stitching, and the work became more stained and the stitches bigger and her hands trembled more. At last by mid-day it was finished. She rolled it up and sought her way back to the canvas house with its cool veranda and green Venetian blinds. The lady was inside and opened the door, looking as fresh and fleecy-white as she had done the day before. She took the work from Undine and examined it carefully.

"I don't take such work," she said, raising her round baby-blue eyes to Undine's face. "You must take it back and unpick it carefully and wash it, or if you wish you can leave it here; but of course I can't pay you for it. It is for a bazaar and should have been kept very clean."

They were so pitiless, those baby-blue eyes.

Undine felt the tears starting to her own; so without giving any answer she turned round quickly and went out again to the hot sandy street.

As bad as a beggar! Crying for sixpence! Faugh! She hated herself.

She had undertaken to do the work, she had done it badly, she had got what she deserved. Besides, was it not for a bazaar that was to pay for a church? There should be no stains or long stitches in work intended for such a purpose. She was in fault, no one else.

"Old clothes bought here," was written in large letters on a piece of battered cardboard that hung at the door of a little wooden house. Undine noticed it and went in. She had nothing to sell but a fine white handkerchief, for which the woman gave her sixpence, which at the next shop she exchanged for a drink of water and a small piece of bread, such a small piece. When she sat down on the shady side of some gravel heaps that lay behind the houses, she held it in her hand and sat looking at it for a long time before she began to eat. She had felt so hungry in the morning, she could have made friends with the naked Kaffir for the sake of his mielie-meal pap; and now she sat there with the lump of bread in her hands and could hardly eat it. Slowly breaking off little bits of crust here and there, she got through half, and with the remainder still in her hand laid her head drowsily on the gravel and for half an hour lay there almost sleeping, but hearing always the rumbling of the carts as they passed in the street. When she aroused herself she felt gnawingly hungry and very glad of the bread, which she still ate very slowly to make it go the farther.

Not far from her, crouching on the ground with his head between his paws, was a great brown dog; surely the leanest and lankest that walked New Rush. While she had slept he had crouched there, watching the piece of bread in her hand, and now with half-closed eyes he looked at it still.

Undine looked at it too and then at him, and then took another bite, and then looked at him again, and then at the bread in her lap; and feeling sure that if she waited it would not be there much longer, she took it up and threw it from her straight into the hungry jaws that were opened wide to receive it.

Almost without a gulp it was gone, and, resuming his old posture, the dog waited for more, but none came.

Picking up the crumbs that lay in her lap, she rose to go. The dog sprang up too, and, sidling nearer to her, proceeded to perform around her a grotesque dance, at every step of which the sharp bones threatened to protrude through the brown skin.

When she walked away he tried to follow her, but she drove him from her again and again. "Go away," she said. "Go away. Do not follow me. If you do I shall learn to love you, and I am tired; I have had pain enough."

The afternoon light was beginning to grow old and yellow when Undine, passing among the tents at the North Side, was attracted by a small figure seated on the ground between two tents. 'Twas a child of it might be twelve years. She was leaning back against an old box, with her naked feet stretched out in front of her, and the afternoon sun looked full into her face and on the great shock of red hair that hung around it. Everyone else Undine had passed had seemed so hard at work and so engrossed, even the little children in their play and the women in their talk; but here sat some one alone and doing nothing except gazing down at the half of an old iron three-legged pot which she held in her lap.

Undine came near her.

"What have you got there?" she asked, softly.

The girl raised her head quickly and looked up. It was a broad freckled face with very little forehead, and that little wrinkled and knit in every direction, with a great heavy mouth and a pair of clear grey eyes.

Before she answered Undine she fixed them on her, and then said in a low, sullen tone, "Looking at my plant."

Undine stooped down and saw, surely enough, growing in the broken pot, the tiniest of rose slips not half an inch high and crowned with two tiny green leaves.

"Do you like flowers?" Undine asked.

"Yes."

For a moment the sullen look vanished and a smile that parted the heavy lips showed a set of dazzling white teeth; then it settled down on the child's face again and she looked at her pot.

"It's the first flower I have seen growing here," said Undine, touching it softly with her finger.

"A gentleman threw it away one day. It had a withered rose on it then; but I put a white bottle over it, and I hold it in the sun all day, and now it's growing, you see." She touched its little leaves softly and caressingly with her finger as she spoke.

"Don't you get very tired of sitting still with it all day?" asked Undine.

A very black look came over the child's face as she answered shortly, "I can't walk; my back's hurt."

"And so you sit here alone all day nursing your flower."

"Mostly, but sometimes the woman who stops with father don't always go out. I wish she always did. When mother was here she always stayed in, but she's dead," said the child. There was infinite satisfaction in the tone in which the last three words were uttered.

"Have you been long unable to walk?" said Undine, laying her hand softly on the red head.

"Since she beat me the night before she died." She spoke more sullenly than ever and twitched her little brown toes backwards and forwards.

"What do you do to try and get better?"

"Nothing," said the child. "One of those gentlemen that go about with the little black bags and the sugar pills, he stopped and talked to me one day and he gave me something to rub with, but I can't rub it and there is no one can."

"Can't I rub it for you?"

The child looked up half suspiciously, then her eyes brightened a little.

"It's in the tent, and Mary Jones would be angry if anyone went in when she's gone out. Do you live far from here?"

"I don't live anywhere," said Undine. "I am looking for work."

The child scrutinized her from head to foot, with the shrewd suspicious old woman's look that the faces of Field children so soon learn to wear. Then she said:

"What kind of work?"

"Anything—ironing." She would have added, "Needlework," but a short experience had made her very wise, and she knew that a man's dog is an animal more enviable than a woman's friend if so be the one is mistress and the other maid. Needlework must be done for women, ironing might be for men, so she decided in favour of the ironing.

Her red-headed little companion meditated for a time, then she said, "Mary Jones has lots of ironing in the tent, and she always drinks too much to do it. If you stay till she comes I think she'll let you get some.

So Undine sat down on the ground beside her and waited.

XVII.
LITTLE IRONS

SIX months after, Undine stood in her own little tent, sorting and piling into heaps the ironing she had just finished.

'Twas a New Rush winter's morning; in the blue sky there was not a cloud, and if it was cold and numbing in the inside of tents and on the shady side of gravel-heaps, out in the sunshine it was warm and genial.

She was hurrying to get out into it, and truly to impartial eyes there was nothing very alluring in the interior of the little tent. 'Twas a small place, six feet by eight, and held three packing-cases. The largest was a table, covered over with shirts. The second was a bed; it had low sides which lay flat on the ground and served to keep off the wind which at night blew in chill under the skirting. The smallest had a kind of tick; it was a desk and general repository. It did not lock, but that mattered less, as its only contents were paper scribbled over and clothes that would not have paid a Kaffir the time it took to steal them. It was an empty place, and cheerless it would have looked to other eyes; but to Undine not a yellow water stain in the canvas nor a mark in the cracked poles, nor a knot in the rough cases but had its own story, and a pleasant familiar face showed itself in each of them. Even the old black bottle stood in the corner made home, more home. She might have changed it now for a candlestick, but so many pleasant thoughts hung round its old black neck that the bottle kept its ground.

Placing on a tray one of the piles of ironing, and putting on the huge white kappie which had replaced the battered silk hat and very much added to the respectability of the ironing woman, she went out into the sunshine, buttoning down the door after her.

The tent stood in a quiet corner of the Camp on the outskirts of the North End. The only very near neighbours were a family of Dutch Boers who camped on the right. On all other sides it was surrounded by low gravel-heaps, [1] among which the tent nestled like a white bird in a yellow nest, as Undine said when describing it to her little broken-backed friend.

She went to visit her this morning before taking her work to its destination, and found her basking in the warmth at the back of the tent, a veritable Diogenes, with only her head and shoulders sticking out of the great tub in which she had ensconced herself.

[1] Débris.

In answer to her visitor's look of inquiry, she said, "The ground's so wet I can't lie on it, and in here it's so nice. I can rock from side to side. Just see!" And she put the tub in motion, leaning heavily first on one elbow and then on the other.

"And the rose?"

"Oh, it"s all right, but it seems as though spring would never come," said the girl, touching with her thick little forefinger the still leafless and brown slip that stood in the side of the old three-legged pot.

"You only stayed such a little while yesterday, you must not go soon today," she said; and Undine put down her tray and sat down on the ground beside her.

"I can"t stay very long today," she said. "I must try and find the owner of those shirts. Three months ago they were brought me, and no one has ever called for them; I am afraid the person to whom they belong must be poor and need them, they are so fine and so old and worn."

"He's waited so long, he won't mind waiting a little longer," said the girl, resting her head in her companion's lap and looking up into her face with her clear grey eyes.

"Tell me what you wrote about last night," she said.

Undine's hand rested on the same great shock of wild red hair, and the broad freckled face that looked up at hers was the same that six months before she had seen for the first time; yet it resembled that face only as a face awake resembles the same face asleep. It was like a dark room into which the sunshine had looked.

"I did not write anything," said Undine, as she passed her finger tenderly along the lines in the low forehead; "I was so tired I went to sleep with the pen in my hand, and when I woke the candle had quite burnt out."

"And have you not anything to tell me?"

"No. I have been so busy all the morning."

"And can't you think while you work?"

"Sometimes, not often; but yesterday evening, when I was putting the collars into starch, a little story came to me that seemed beautiful then, though it does not now. Shall I tell it to you?"

The child nodded; and Undine, running her fingers through and through her coarse hair, began:

"A mother was lying on her bed, dying, and at her side was a very little baby. The people who stood round her thought she knew nothing, saw nothing; and truly she saw none of them. She felt only the touch of the little baby's fingers upon her breast, but she saw what no one else could see—in the far end of the room were two, drawing balls from a box which had no bottom; and Death's balls were the pure white and Life's were the blood red.

"Death was very tall and calm and his face was smooth and white, like a face cut out of marble; his eyelids were half closed and in the eyes beneath them lay the shadows of wonderful dreams. Round him was a mantle of many cold grey tints, and his wings were folded close against his side.

"A ball was drawn, and it was Death's white ball; so the mother knew that she must go to him; but when they were going to draw again, she prayed and said:

"'Stay! stay! O Death; give Life my child!' For she feared him, he was so still and cold, and they were strange wonderful dreams that wandered beneath his eyelids.

"And Life said, 'Let the mother see what we have to give it, and she shall decide who is to have the child.'

"And Death bowed his head slowly.

"Now Life was very beautiful; her hair was like the yellow glory of the sunset, and her limbs were strong and soft and round, and her breast was as white as an open lily. Her cheeks were red, so red that the tear traces could hardly be seen on them, and her white dazzling wings were always quivering and expanded, yet they never raised her or took her from the earth. She was very lovely, and the bright robe she wore was of spotless tender green, the colour of the first shoots on the white-thorn tree; only here and there, where it turned up a little, the lining showed it was red and had clots on as though it had been dipped in blood. She was very beautiful; but when the mother looked at her forehead, knit with thought and pain, and at her large wide-open eyes through which the light and darkness chased each other endlessly, she feared her also.

"Life spoke first, and her voice was like the singing of the birds in spring-time, and the murmuring of the crowd in a great city, and the weeping of a lonely woman at a graveside, all strangely blended.

"'Look in my eyes,' she said, 'and see what I have to give'; and the mother looked.

"In the streets of a great city rolled the carriage of a rich man, and the mud from its wheels sprang up into the faces of two who were poor and hungry and stood at the corner of the street talking.

"'Whose carriage is that?' asked the one.

"'The man who rides in it is the richest and most fortunate man in all this city,' answered the other. 'From his boyhood upwards all that his hand has touched has turned to gold. Misfortune has never crossed him. His very dogs live longer than another's and die easier deaths. We were friends once in our youth, but now he counts his gold by millions, and I have nothing but a starving wife.'

"'And why do you not go to him for help?'

"'Because how should he pity me who has never known want, and how should he remember me who has entertained lords and princes?' But still when they parted the poor man turned his steps towards the house of the great.

"'If I had but half that one of his horses eats I would be happy,' he thought.

"The fortunate man was walking in his garden. He was very fat, and the only walk he ever took was up and down its gravel paths. The air was rich with the scent of the flowers, and the light of the afternoon sun made the drops of the leaping fountain sparkle more brightly than the diamond on his finger. A small bird was bathing itself in the water.

"'Now,' said the rich man, 'if it were not too much trouble, and the shot worth more than the fruit it eats, I would kill that bird.'

"Then he thought of the grand dinner he was to give the next day, and how his beautiful daughter was to marry one of the great lords who would be there.

"Then he thought how they all envied him his grand old mansion and his priceless horses; then he looked up and saw the poor man standing between him and the sun. He did not know him, for it is very hard to remember people who are so shabby, and so he asked him who he was. The poor man told his story, and when he had finished went back out of that beautiful garden sorry that he had entered it.

"Then the rich man walked up and down again and basked in the sunshine. It was a man's own fault if he had trouble and was poor and friendless, for the world was a good world. There was no help for him but in the grave, the poor man had said, and the fortunate man thought, as he walked up and down, what a very great fool he must be. It was such a nice pleasant world this, with its great red sun warming one on a chilly afternoon all for nothing, and ripening one's fruit and vegetables and asking for no pay. It was such a nice pleasant world this, with such a nice pleasant sea, over which pleasant ships could bring pleasant wines and turtles from other pleasant lands. He moistened his lips when he thought of his old, old wines; and then he thought of another disagreeable dark place that the man had spoken of, where there were great cobwebs which were not round old bottles and living things that were not gay horses. That was the place he did not like to think of; it made the sweat stand in great drops on his red neck. Life had been so good to him; she had given him all the sweet and kept back all the bitter; she had brought no tear to his eye since he had been old enough to tell a sixpence from a penny; it would be hard to leave her now, when all men envied him. So he pulled out his watch with its setting of jewels and wondered when the dinner hour would come, and tried to forget that other hour. And at last the dinner hour came, with its guests and its laughter and its wine. And at last that other hour came also—the only hour of which we are all sure; and the fortunate man, who had never suffered and never wept and never pitied, went to the place he feared where the living things and cobwebs were. Nobody missed him, nobody wanted him back again—not his pretty daughter, for she had all his money.

"Now, when the mother saw all this, she would have given the child to Death, for she said, 'It were as well he had died a baby.'

"But Life prevented her: 'I have other things to give,' she said.

"And the mother looked. It was a garden again, a wild neglected garden where the flowers and creepers grew rank and free in each other's arms, and beauty was not measured out. At the root of a great tree, almost enfolded and hidden by the shrubs that grew around it, stood a man. His face was young and one to be pitied by the old and wise, for it was very glad and full of hope. In his arms, pressed close to him, was a woman, and not one of the flowers had a face so fair as hers; but, deep in her eyes, crept a look like the look which crept in the eyes of the serpent in that First Garden long ago. They were sweet long kisses; and the words she spoke to him were sweet, the sweet old words of love and faith which women speak to men; and he believed her.

"His heart grew very strong and great through the mighty love that came to him, and their life path lay before him in a mist of light and beauty. Truly God's world was good, and the life He gave great and beautiful, and only the pure and true of heart were worthy of it. So he thought; and looked in the eyes of the woman he loved, and pressed his lips to hers, and drew her closer to him, for he never saw the serpent's look that glided in them.

"But the day came, at last, when he did see it—when she looked into his face and laughed, and he knew that when he pressed the woman he loved to his heart it was only the grey old father of lies he had held. Now, life being for him that woman and that woman being evil, he became evil too. For the sake of what he had once loved, he deceived all women, and drank and cursed, and gained gold by evil, and spent it in sin; and men said that, wherever he passed, you might trace him by the ruin and evil he left behind. Yet they envied him, for the women loved him, and where other men would have starved he made gold. He might eat of the fruit of the earth and satisfy himself: its gold, its wine, or its women—they were all free to him who had no conscience to restrain and no faith in a higher power.

"The woman he had once loved was told of him—how the devil befriended his own, how he sinned and came to no evil, and enjoyed life as other men could not.

"Then she said, softly: 'It was well that I deceived him, very well'; but in her inmost heart she feared to meet him, and when she knew that he was dead the world seemed larger to her and her breath came lighter.

"'I have that to give,' said Life.

"'And I have sleep,' said Death.

"And the mother would have given the child to him, but Life said: 'I have yet other things to give'; and again she looked.

"There was a street with great and noble houses, and out at the door of one of them came a young man. His shoulders were bent and, as he walked, his eyes were fixed upon the ground; only once he looked up at the great houses at his side and saw the faces of two soft women looking out of a large window. Then he clenched the fingers of the hand that hung at his side till the nails went into the flesh, and clenched his teeth and swore under his breath a bitter oath.

"'Twas a strange presumptuous oath for a man to swear who wore brown threadbare clothes out at elbow and boots that were split and who lived in a garret; for he swore that the day should come when those rich men should ask him to their tables and he would refuse to come, when those white proud women whom he cursed in his bitterness should covet a smile or a word from him, when the world should know him and call him great. This he swore and went home to his garret.

"It was a dreary empty place where the sunlight never entered and where dry bread was eaten and where nothing pleasant ever came except only a young girl with hard work-worn hands. She was the landlord's daughter, and she crept in every day to rub the dust off the rotten table and turn the straw mattress and carry out the ashes, if there were any. In the long evening, when to save light he would sit there thinking in the dark, she would sit there too, close beside him with her hard little hand in his, just as she had done when he came there three years before. She had been a child then; she was a woman now; but it made no difference to her.

"One evening she did not come, and he sat there alone, thinking, thinking. The room was very quiet, but there was a great war raging in the man's heart. At last he brought his hand down on the table and swore between his clenched teeth, as he had sworn that day before the rich men's houses.

"'She will not help me in my work,' he said; 'she and her children will be a weight on me, dragging me down. If I stay here it will conquer me. I must leave her, I must leave her, for she cannot help me.'

"So in the grey dawn of the winter morning he stood in the door of his room, ready to leave it for the last time. She was labouring up the stairs with a great heap of coals in her arms.

"'These are for you,' she said, her breath coming quick with pleasure: 'the lodger belowstairs gave them to me. See, how many!'

"There were burning drops under his eyelids, but he let her pass into the room; then he said, 'I am going away.'

"She looked up into his face, for his voice sounded strange, but it was too dark to see him.

"'Will you stay long?' she asked.

"Then he told her he was going away forever, that he would never come again; and he shut the door behind him very quickly for fear he might turn back. Quickly he shut it, but it was not quick enough, for he heard the coals fall on the floor, and a low short cry that followed him out into the street and on and on into the long years that followed.

"Years came, years went; his hair grew whiter; his shoulders stooped lower yet; and alone and in bitterness he laboured on.

"'Oh, you rich and noble,' he said, 'you who think no more of me than of the dogs in your kennels; when you vanish and your names are as forgotten as theirs I shall live on, my name shall be immortal!' And then he pressed his lips together and worked on.

"And at last it came. The world called him great; it wrote of him in its papers; men talked of him on the street, and women in their houses. The children learned to lisp his name; rich men asked him to their dinners; noblewomen came to visit him, only that they might say that they had seen him.

"He was very great, and his fame was very great, and his riches were very great; but he was old with work and his life was done.

"'Put me in my great chair beside the fire,' he said to his servants, 'and leave me. You say I am dying—why should you stay for that? You cannot help me.' So they went out and left him.

"Nodding, dozing in the firelight, he looked up and saw before him, sitting in a velvet armchair, an old man with cap of crimson and a silver silken tassel that was shaking in the firelight. 'Twas the phantom of himself who sat there, nodding in the golden firelight.

"'You have been fortunate,' said the phantom; you have succeeded as few men in the world succeed. You are very rich, and all men pray for riches.'

'I never cared for gold,' said the great man. 'Of what use is it to me, alone? Once—'

"He had grown a little deaf of late, and now he could hear less; there was often a low short cry ringing in his ears.

"'Fools pray for gold,' he said, 'not wise men.'

"The phantom nodded. 'In your youth,' he said, 'you swore you would be great and that the high and noble should receive you into their houses, fair women should covet your notice and proud men your visits. You have gained all that; surely you are blessed. It is true you have paid something for it—a little—some pleasure, the rest of a few thou- thousand sand nights, the woman you loved—but what is that! Many pay all that and die in a garret, or on a dung-heap. You are blessed!'

"'If that were all, then better never have been born,' said the great man, bitterly. 'They write of me in their papers; I never read their praises now. My house is better—why should I go to theirs! Fair women come to see me—what are fair women to me! They only disturb me with their childish chatter; and sometimes, if they have blue eyes—Ha! if that were all, better to have died a baby.'

"The phantom leaned his hands upon his knees and leered across the firelight.

"'What *has* it been for then? All this battling, all this striving, all this heartache? Surely it has not been for nothing?'

"'No,' said the great man; 'it has not been for nothing. The man who looks for happiness in this life is a fool. I live for the future. *I* would be immortal. Immortal!'

"The phantom leaned back in his armchair and laughed till the silvered tassel of his red cap trembled again in the firelight!

"'Immortal! I thought you were a great man, yet you juggle with this word immortal, like the rest of your kind. What do *you* mean by it now? That your name shall live after you are dead? Well, if that is all you seek, you shall have it. They will give you a grand funeral, and write of you in papers bordered deep with black, and for a few days, a very few, everyone will speak of you. But there will be no woman to wear one flower the less in her hair, and no man to drink one glass less of wine, because you died that morning. You are a great man, a very great man, so perhaps they will raise a statue of you, and for a few hundred years, now and then, some one will speak of you, oftenest in praise at first, oftenest in blame at last; for to men of the new ideas and the new light the great men of old look very small. Immortal! Ha! Ha! Who are you? What are you?' laughed the phantom. 'A paltry two thousand years has dimmed the radiance of her redeemers and prophets; how long do you think earth will remember you?'

"The phantom laughed again and looked into the fire: 'That coal that is burning there: Five million years ago or so it was a great tree growing in the green old forests. Perhaps *it* thought *it* was to be immortalised—immortalised into coal. And so it was, for five million years; but in five minutes it will be ashes now. In five million years where will you be?—Immortal—Ha! Ha! Ha!' laughed the phantom. 'Fool! Fool! Fool!'

"With his hands clasped over his face and his head bowed down to his knees, the old man sat.

"'Oh, my life,' he cried, 'my life! I have given it, I have given it, and I have gained nothing.'

"Three days later the great man died, and the noble and the great followed him to his grave, and they wrote of him in their papers. They said, 'Weep, weep, for a great man is dead; weep, weep!' But for all that, no one wept. Only one half-starved man who lived alone in the garret where he laboured and toiled, he wept for envy, for he said, 'Why should he have all the good, I all the evil?'

"Then Life dropped her lids for a moment.

"'And I have rest,' said Death.

"And the mother would have given him her child, but Life said: 'Look again, once more;' and the mother looked for the last time.

"It was four o'clock in the morning, and beside a table, with his forehead resting in his two hands, a man was sitting. The candle was almost burnt out, and soon it would be time for him to go out to his day's work; for all day he stood behind a counter, selling yards of print and muslin to the ladies that came in.

"The other clerks called him fool; if they had known how his nights were spent they would have called him so more often. When their day's work was over they went out to amuse themselves, but he only shut himself up in his room and walked up and down and prayed and wrote himself half mad before the morning came.

"It was well there was no living thing to see him but the little brown mouse that looked out of its hole and wished it could have nibbled at the candle. But the candle stood safe and did nothing but devour the bits of paper scribbled over with songs that were always being put to her. She had just devoured two great blue pages, on which was much of such hot talk as comes from young pens at four o'clock in the morning.

"She would get no more, however, for the pen was lying under the table, and the man looked very disconsolate as he sat beside it.

"If he had written anything just now, it would have been: 'Yes, I'm a great fool, as they say. Let us eat and drink, for tomorrow we die. Let us do as the sheep do; they only are wise. Beauty is an angel that no man ever caught; truth is a deception that changes to falsehood while you finger it. We are shadows among shadows. Why be so in earnest? Why make oneself so hot about it all? Why strive and pray and make so great a bluster? Life isn't worth it. Something, nothing, here, gone; let us make the best of it, wear the nicest clothes, eat the nicest meat, and love the easiest love, and believe what comes to hand; tread on, steady and safe, step by step, in the narrow sandy path our fathers cleared from stones and bushes long ago. If this cannot be, why, curse life and die—it is the best thing left.'

"So he thought then, for he was weary, and threw himself down on his bed. Perhaps he slept, but his eyes were heavy and red the next morning as he stood behind the counter, selling ribbons and prints.

"So this poor clerk went on, month after month, praying and writing all night and measuring off dresses by the yard all day; but at last it happened that one of his dreams took a human shape, and a pair of clear still eyes looked into his life and made him richer than the great princes of the Golden Isles, whose houses and whose shoes are covered with jewels. It was true, as men speak, that the eyes belonged not to him but to a woman who was nothing to him—a woman who was high above him and who would surely be carried, some day, to another man's home. Yet when he was beside her she spoke to him kindly, and in her face he found the beauty in her mind, the truth he dreamed of. He knew that she was his though she did not love him, for he loved her, and no one could ever take her from him, not she herself.

"He heard at last that she was going to be married, and then he left the town and went far, far away, and for a little time there was a heavy aching at his heart all day as he stood behind the counter or sat alone in his silent room. But at last the aching went, and there was only gladness left. He had not her body, it was true, but her beautiful soul was living somewhere and it was true and real, and the earth was never again quite empty for him.

"The years passed on, and they still called him a fool, for he made no money. He never stayed long enough in any place, but wandered on from town to town and land to land, just when the longing seized him. Sometimes a child's face, or a reach of sea beach, or the charm of snow-crowned mountains made him pause a little, but having got all they had to give, he wandered on again.

"He made no money and no friends, this poor fool of a clerk. Only sometimes, when pain or sorrow would draw people to him, they would enter his life for a little time; but when they were comforted they would go out of it again, and he would go on with his wanderings and sing his songs and smile and love the beautiful green old earth.

"Sometimes his songs were sad, but oftener they were glad, for it did not take much to make him happy—a little stream of sunlight breaking in through the goods within the window, or the shadows which the trees cast as he passed below them on his way to work or to lie on the grass on Sunday morning and watch the rippling in the pool of water; that was enough to make life sweet to him—so sweet that, when the death he had once longed for came to him, he was almost sorry to leave it. Yet it seemed so pleasant to think of lying deep in the soft old earth he loved, and he was glad he had lived. There was not one night of sleepless agony, nor one hour of bitterness he would have missed, even if he might. It was all good, looked at from the end. Life lay very beautiful behind, and death was not terrible, only very strange.

"He died young and they buried him in the earth he loved; but there was not a tear shed over him. For why? What had he done all his life? Sold a few yards of print and ribbon, cast up a few accounts, suffered a little agony, prayed a little, doubted a little, comforted a few people who were sad; and for the rest lived much as the birds live, singing and loving and revelling in the sunshine.

"'I have that to give,' said Life.

"And the mother said: 'Take my child. Your best is bitter sweet, but it is sweet.'

"So Death took the mother and Life the child."

When Undine had finished her story they sat quiet for a little time. Then the girl said, "It's because such beautiful stories come to you that you are never miserable and are always smiling. I like this story."

"I like them too," said Undine, "when they come to me as I am at my work. They seem so beautiful, they make the blood run all through my body with little throbs; but when I try to write or tell them I wonder what I liked in them. But I must be going now, Diogenes, or Mr. William Brown will be without a shirt and dying of the cold." And Undine got up and put her tray upon her arm.

"Diogenes—what does that mean?"

"Why, Diogenes was a man who lived in a tub, as you are doing today; and I call you Diogenes be- because cause I like to call my friends by names that no one else has for them."

"Am I your friend?" A strangely bright look came into the little freckled face that looked up at her out of the tub.

Undine answered, "Yes, my only little friend."

She was turning to go when Diogenes stopped her:

"Do you really think people do nothing but dream after they are dead? You said Death's eyes were full of dreams."

"No, I don't think so," said Undine, trying to balance the tray on her head and finally returning it to her arms. "The stories come to me just as they like. I never think about them."

"I'm sorry," said Diogenes, still resting her folded arms on the ground and looking up. "Last night I dreamt my rose bush had a great white rose and you had it in your hair, and you and I were walking over little sandhills. The air was so cool and it was dark as though there was going to be a great storm; I was looking up into your face, and you were looking straight out before you, and your eyes were so strange. And at last we came to the sea, and you said you were going over it. It was a sad dream, but I liked it, and when I woke up father was drunk and they were all quarrelling and I wished I had never woken up any more. It's so nice to dream."

"Yes, dreams are nice. Good-bye." And the little ironing woman trudged off with her shirts, leaving Diogenes with enough food for reverie, conjecture and enjoyment for the rest of the day.

The owner of the shirts, she had been told by the Kaffir who brought them, lived near the Circus; that his name was W. Brown the shirts themselves told her; but to discover his whereabouts seemed a hopeless task.

Most people answered her shortly enough. One old woman, in answer to her questions, began the long story of one Bill Brown, who might be the Bill Brown she was in search of, who had lived at Graaff Rienet, who had set out for the Fields, but who, as turned out in the sequel, had died before reaching them.

He could hardly be the owner of the shirt, nor yet the widow Brown to whose tent some well-disposed digger sent her. Undine was giving up the quest when a Kaffir woman, hearing her question, directed her to a small tent the top of which was just visible behind its larger compeers.

Making her way between the tents over broken bottles, empty tins and rubbish of all kinds, Undine soon found herself before it, and a glance through its open door convinced her that she had found the right place at last.

'Twas a tent of about the size of her own, but its interior presented an infinitely more comfortless ap- appearance pearance, though it was furnished with a wooden stretcher, two camp stools and a huge padlocked sea-chest.

The gravel that covered the floor was trodden into mounds and heaps of all sizes. More laths of the wooden stretcher hung down broken than were left to support the red sand-coloured bedding that lay on it. On the sea-chest that stood in the middle of the tent was such a multifarious and miscellaneous collection of articles as surely never sea-chest bore before. There were tins and bottles of every description, the latter crowned with the remains of half burnt candles; there were old newspapers and shoe blacking, books and a pepper caster, pens and cigar ends, a paint box and a broken looking-glass, a microscope and combs, hair brushes, tooth brushes, boot brushes, nail brushes and a papier-mache desk on which was a silver-clasped album across which lay the broken head of a pick; these with an infinitude of other smaller and larger articles covered it. On the ground at its side lay an empty meal sack, the last of whose contents had evidently been used to compose the great leadeny-looking roaster-cake that was standing beside a tin mug of water on the sea-chest; the look of the roaster-cake was not inviting, except it were to throw at the head of an enemy, yet some one had evidently tried to put it to some other use, for there were small pieces chipped off every here and there.

Close beside the sea-chest, on one of the camp stools leaning against the central pole, with his head hanging on his breast, sat a man. He was in digger trim, with his shirt sleeves rolled up above his elbows, perhaps to hide their frayed and worn condition, certainly not for work, for the long arms they left uncovered seemed hardly strong enough to raise themselves, still less to handle sieve or pick. His eyes were closed, but a very light tap at the door-post caused him to raise his head and look up heavily at the white-clad figure that stood in his doorway.

If he were Mr. Brown, she said, she had brought his shirts.

A slight flush came into his face.

"I don't want them; you had better take them and keep them as payment," he said; then he drooped back into his old posture.

He was greatly changed, but, when he looked up, Undine at once recognised him as the passenger who, on that first morning on board the steamer had seemed the only glad thing in harmony with the fresh breezy water and the sweeping sea-birds.

He was in harmony with his surroundings now also, for the broken tins and bottles and the old stretcher did not look more hopelessly down-and-out and good-for-nothing than their master.

Undine looked at his wasted arms, at the empty meal sack, and the leaden roaster-cake, and listened to his hollow cough, and wondered where the long- whiskered captain and his brilliant sister might be. Perhaps they were only of the sunflower species whom only fools think to find growing in the shade.

She watched him in silence for a minute, then she stepped lightly into the tent and, putting her tray down on the floor, came and stood beside him. It was not till she had spoken twice and touched him softly on the shoulder that he seemed to hear her.

"You are very ill," she said. "Have you much pain?"

"No," he answered, heavily, without raising his head or opening his eyes.

"Have you been ill long?"

"Yes—no—I don't know;" and a long hollow cough followed.

"Would you not feel a little better if you tried to lie down? It must be very hard to sit up here," she said, gently.

"I would, but it's such a long way."

He raised his head again and looked with his heavy eyes across the three feet that separated him from his stretcher as a man might to a land of promise across an ocean.

Undine shook out the pillows and smoothed the blanket, and putting his hand on her shoulder helped him to reach it.

He did not thank her, but dropped down on it with a weary sigh. He had bonny light curls like some one she had cared for long ago, and he had broken boots and stockings so old that the red flesh showed through. She hardly knew which drew her to him most, the curls or the boots, for there is something achingly pitiable in broken boots.

When a man who has called himself a gentleman falls to that, he can fall no lower.

XVIII.
LITTLE IRONS AND A DIGGER

DIOGENES' little red head peeped out of her tub and she rolled herself from side to side and felt sadly disconsolate. Her rose bush was full of tender leaves, her back was not bad and the weather was glorious, but for three whole weeks she had had no story, and for three whole weeks her daily visitor had come only to go. She felt aggrieved and greatly wronged.

"I wish he had stopped in England; it would have been a great deal nicer for *him*," she soliloquised, her little forehead all gathered up into knots and puckers.

"England's such a nice country, they say, and there's nothing nice in this land. I wonder why he came."

Just at that moment Undine arrived.

"Is he better?" inquired Diogenes, evidently with great interest, and her lips seemed to grow yet heavier when she had received her answer.

"I don't believe he tries to get better," she said in an aggrieved tone. "Don't you get tired to keep running up here all day?"

"Not tired, but I am going to look for some Kaffir men to carry his tent down next to mine; then I will be able to take care of him and iron too. How is your back this morning?"

"Well," said Diogenes, sullenly.

"I'm glad," said Undine. "I'll come back again when I have got the Kaffirs. Good-bye." And she was gone.

"I wish *he* was gone," said Diogenes. "It is not a bit nice any more. Heigh-ho!" And she traced with her finger on the ground the B's and C's Undine had taught her to make.

As Undine had thought, it was a change for the better which brought the second tent into her little nest among the gravel-heaps. While one pair of hands and four irons had to skim over shirts enough in the twenty-four hours to pay for doctor, eggs, milk, medicine, and sufficient bread to keep the hands themselves going, they could ill afford to be long at rest. Now she could go on ironing all day without interruption, peeping in at his tent every time she passed to change an iron at the fire, which was built between three round stones at the back of the tent.

The doctor did not give much hope of his recovery. He was completely broken down, said the doctor, with hard work and bad living. All day he lay there as helpless as a little child, never speaking but when his mind wandered. Then he would often fancy himself talking with the mine-captain and begging him not to give up yet, to keep on a little longer, to advance a little more money. Luck must turn soon. Or sometimes he was walking on the deck with the captain's pretty sister, and he would be whispering on softly for hours.

When Undine heard him she sometimes wondered whether it would not almost have been best to let him die alone, with his bit of roaster-cake in his solitary tent. He did not look much like winning the heart of any woman as he lay there moaning, with even his bonny curls cut off.

At last he grew better, and then it was hard to find time for the inevitable ironing. Let him seem ever so fast asleep, his eyes were sure to open if she rose to leave him. If she had nothing else to do for him, he liked her to sit beside him and talk.

One day she looked in at the door with a furiously red face and in one hand a hot iron that she had just been to fetch at the fire.

"Put that iron away", he said, feebly, "till it gets cool. My eyes ache with them. They are always in your hands. I want you to answer me a question I can't answer for myself."

"Well?" said Undine, pushing back her cap a little and leaning over to one side to balance the iron she held in the other. "What is it? I don't think the irons have absorbed quite all my intellect yet."

"As the spades and picks did mine. Tell me how it is that I am quite contented to lie here and be fed and nursed by you, and don't feel as though I ought even to thank you, when I would die sooner than take a broken sixpence from my own flesh and blood? How is it? I'm too weak to think."

"You must be weak if you can't think *that* out," she said, twisting one arm round the tent-post to keep her steady, and looking, he thought, almost beautiful in spite of her redness. "Don't you know there are things we have to be more grateful for than being nursed and fed? You've given me something to take care of, and so, though you don't think it, you feel you have done more for me than I for you. As for getting help from our relations," said Undine, resting her head against the pole, "they are just the last people to go to unless one likes getting a pain in one's pride bones. One always has a lurking suspicion they are doing it from principle or necessity or something equally disagreeable; and that's why their money hurts. But my irons are getting cold," she said, turning to go.

"Don't you ever get tired of them?" he asked. "It's so burning hot today."

"Oh no, I never get tired, and it's not so hot today—as it might be. I get to like it."

She walked off, but the iron she was using must have been a very heavy one, for when she was taking it back to the fire she stumbled two or three times as though she would have fallen.

"What a very uneven little path this is," she said to herself, thereby greatly maligning the very smooth little path over the gravel that led from the door of her tent to the fireplace. Perhaps it was by way of smoothing it that she knelt down by the water barrel and damped the crown of her head and lay there for half an hour looking very white. Anyhow, she did not say any more about the path being uneven after that.

A few days later, Undine paid her daily visit to Diogenes, who as usual lay in her tub with her rose bush before her. The discerning eyes of that small individual perceived something unusual and amiss in the face of her friend, and when Undine sat down beside the tub and leaned her hand against it, she said,

"Are you very tired today?"

"No, not at all."

"You don't look happy. I wish I knew what was the matter; I wish you need never be tired or sad"; and Diogenes took Undine's rough little hand and rubbed it softly up and down with her chin. It was her way of showing sympathy; and it showed it more effectually than any words could have done—so effectually that it ended in making Undine cry. She pressed her face against the tub, and Diogenes fancied she heard a sob.

"Oh dear! what is it?" said Diogenes, looking up, terribly troubled at the sound. "I did not know you could be *so* miserable. I thought you saw such beautiful things, you were always happy. I'm sure it's all that man's fault"; and Diogenes' clear grey eyes filled with wrathful but partly sympathetic tears.

"No, it is not; only I am weak and faint, and I want money."

If her rose bush had stirred its tender leaves and said it wanted high-heeled boots and a fashionable bonnet, it would not have astonished Diogenes more.

"Thou shalt not love money; thou shalt not desire it; thou shalt despise it; it is the child of the devil, and his eldest born." This was the little bit of ethical teaching which was sure to lift up its head in the wildest of Undine's fairy stories, and the effect on Diogenes had been so great that she often seriously debated in her own mind whether, seeing a pound lying at her feet, there would not be a certain amount of degradation in stooping to pick it up. To look up, therefore, and see her instructor's face wet with tears because she wanted money, wanted money, so puzzled Diogenes that she remained quiet for a few minutes.

Then she began to use her very practical little brains, and quickly came to certain conclusions.

"Can't you get money enough to pay the doctor?" she asked, looking up softly from under her great shock of red hair.

"No, I can get that. I want much money, almost a hundred pounds. If I can't get that I don't want any, I don't want anything."

Diogenes drew a long breath. She felt sure that disagreeable *he* was at the bottom of it all, but she would ask no more questions. She was rubbing her chin softly up and down Undine's hand when it touched the ring upon it—Aunt Margaret's ring.

"If you were to sell this, perhaps you would get much money; diamonds are so dear and it is so beautiful."

Undine lifted her head quickly and looked down at it. She had as little thought of it as a thing to be parted with as the hand which wore it. The one link between her and the old days. She had worn it till it seemed to have grown a part of herself. Her baby friend had touched it, pleased with its flash and gleam. It had whispered to her that truth and love were possibilities when she had sat toying with it in the great, gayly filled, empty rooms of her husband's house. It had shone on a soft hand that had so often rested tenderly on her head. It had been the sign of a great love, faithful even unto death. She moved it softly round her finger two or three times; then she drew it off.

Why sacrifice the living to the dead, the present to the past? The past is a fruitless dream, the present only is living and demands all things.

"Are you going to sell it?" asked Diogenes.

"Yes, at once," said Undine, rising quickly, "and I will come back soon."

"I know she liked that ring, and now she has got to sell it," said Diogenes to herself as soon as Undine was out of hearing. "It's all his fault, I know it is. Perhaps she wants to send him to England. She said yesterday he was worse and would never get better if he couldn't go. I do wonder why he did not stay there," said Diogenes, in her anger pulling so vigorously at one leaf of her rose that it came off. "*I* don't go about everywhere making everybody miserable." Lost in the contemplation of her own virtue in abstaining from a crime which by no possibility she could have committed, and finding immense satisfaction in so doing, Diogenes lay still in her tub and waited for Undine's return.

She was long gone, but when she did make her appearance, it was so radiantly, joyfully, that Diogenes felt ashamed of her tears. If she had not liked parting with her ring, there was no sign of it in her face. She had got as much as she wanted, almost more; now he would know that he could go to England, and the hope would make him well.

"I knew it was for him," muttered Diogenes under her breath; but Undine was too glad to hear it, too glad to sit down, and soon fluttered off. She hardly felt the sandy road she plodded in, but only the little roll of notes tight-clasped in her hand, the little roll that meant hope and strength and life for him and, it might be, more than life—gladness in place of long years of weary loneliness. Even if he got well and, staying at New Rush till he had money, at last went home to find the woman who had charmed away his soul given to another, would he not curse the hand that had kept him from a quiet sleep in the New Rush graveyard?

It might be that, going home even now, he might find the bright eyes had fooled him; but Undine put the thought from her and enjoyed the sunshine of the moment.

He should never know from whom it came; it should be burdened with no debt of gratitude. Generally the work is heart-sickening, that of trying to bring joy and good to our heart's own, work in which failures are in number as gravel bort, [1] and the successes as diamonds. But for once Undine found success. The mysterious little parcel which the post brought him seemed to work in him all the wonders of the old life waters.

There were no more refusals to eat; no more weary days of stupor and relapse coming when he had wearied himself out with calculation as to the length of time it would take him to get strong and then to earn money enough for the long journey.

[1] "Bort"—diamond dust; i.e., the "dust" infinitely outnumbering the "diamonds."

When the days grew warmer, he was strong enough to sit outside, among rugs and cushions on the shady side of the tent; sometimes to use his pencils; sometimes to watch Undine through the tent door as she stood smoothing away at her packing-case.

Pleasant days they were, flying all too quickly, for one at least, who worked and enjoyed the present and put the future from her.

At last the time came when they were only hours that could be counted before his departure. He was still so weak that it took him a long time to get from one tent to the other, but he was to leave by the next morning's coach. The last evening came. He lay on his stretcher, and Undine sat at its foot on the skirting in the doorway, trying to make the most of the daylight. She was darning the best of his old stockings, and he all the while chatted on eagerly of the future, in spirits unnaturally high, springing quickly from one subject to another.

"You are such a genius, Little Irons, in spite of your big kappie and your shirts. The world shall know of you some day, and I shall be so proud of the Little Irons who came to help me when all the world would have left me to drop out of life like a dog." Then he speculated as to where the money could have come from, then on his own course for the future; then talked of those first dreadful days of labour and failure, of the time it would take him to reach The Bay, [1] and at last talked himself to sleep. Then she stood up and put the stockings she had mended into his bag, and moved softly about the tent collecting pencils and various trifles that still lay about.

She had just packed the last of them when a coolie,[2] late out, passed the tent with his tray of wares upon his head. There were still two oranges left on it, so she told him to wait, and went into her tent to the broken ink pot where she kept her money. There was only one shilling in it, so one of the oranges had to go; the other she put in the pocket of the coat he was to wear tomorrow, which lay on the box at his side. There was no more money left in the ink pot, but what did it matter? There would be nobody to care for after tomorrow. What did anything matter? She went to her own tent and sat down in the doorway and tried to eat her supper; but eating did not answer; so presently she sat still with her head leaning against the door-post.

Across the road were the children of the Dutchwoman, shouting and tumbling over one another in their play. They had done so every night for the last six months, but did that night seem just like every other night to them?

[1] Port Elizabeth.

[2] Indian.

He did not wake to eat his supper, and slept on straight till morning. Just at daybreak she stepped softly into his tent to wake him. The cart they had ordered to take him to the hotel would be there soon. He was scarcely ready, and Undine was still busy cutting up his tobacco when she caught the sound of the approaching wheels. He did not hear them till they were just before the tent; then he rose quickly and pressed the cut tobcacco into his pouch while the driver carried out his luggage. Then he turned to wish her good-bye. The grey light was just turning into white, and gusts of cold early wind blew in through the rolled up door.

"Good-bye, my friend, my dear Little Irons," he said, warmly yet very gladly, and he stooped down to kiss her; but it was such a cold, trembling little face he touched that something smote his heart.

"I've been a great bother to you, dear Little Irons," he said, resting his right hand tenderly on her shoulder. "You will have rest when I am gone and go back to your happy, quiet old life; and I shall never forget you, never. How could I?"

She stood on tiptoe and wound a scarf round his neck.

"Don't take it off till the sun gets warm," she said.

"Oh, I'll take good care of myself," he answered as he passed out of the door. Then he turned round to say good-bye once more. "Good-bye, but not for very long; I feel sure we shall soon meet again," he said, as he took her hand in his.

He climbed up at the back of the cart, and a moment after only the faint rumbling of the wheels broke the stillness. Undine stood in the tent door.

"Meet again! meet again!" Poor human hearts that must still their aching with such vain words. Meet again! Who ever met again? The child we love goes from us and comes back to us a man, and all others praise the change; but we, even while we run our fingers through his curls, we hunger for the little child that sat upon our knee.

We part with the friend of our childhood, and we say, "We part only for today; through life we shall often meet again," and it may be we clasp hands often in the years that come and talk of the old days; but we know, though we never say it, that the two who parted have never met again, that the sea of time has run up between us, and we cannot touch. Who can part, forever; only when we come so close that nothing separates us can we meet again, only when what binds us is not my need of you or your need of me nor any chance circumstance, but a deep ingrained likeness of nature that cannot pass away.

"We shall meet again some day," said Undine as she stood in the tent door, comforting herself with this great lie.

A little after the sun had risen, she hurried along the path in the direction of the Toit's Pan Road, and stopped when she came to the last of the enclosures that lined it on either side. The coach would have to pass there, and she must see it; so she stood there waiting while the quickly moving passenger carts from Toit's Pan passed and repassed her, breaking the stillness of the quiet morning.

At last, after long waiting, it came with its great red tent, with its blowing bugle, with its eight prancing horses, with its crowded roof; and inside, just as it tore past her, she saw him. It was only a glimpse, but that was enough, for he looked bright and glad. He was speaking to the passenger who sat next him and laughing and peeling the orange he had found in his pocket. A piece of peel he threw out fell at the roadside, and she picked it up after the coach had passed.

"It is all right. He is happy, very happy," she said, and turned to go back to her tent. "He is happy, very happy," she kept on repeating to herself when she got back to the tent. Remnants of the tobacco she had been cutting still lay on the old sea-chest, the boots he had worn yesterday still lay beside it, and the half drunk cup of chocolate was hardly cold. She looked in at the door for a minute, and then went to her own tent.

Her own little tent, which she had said was so full and rich to her, which was so empty and silent now. She walked up and down, not daring to sit down and rest. Well had she said to that hungry dog on that day long ago: "Go away, and do not follow me. If you follow me I shall love you and I, I have had pain enough."

At last she sat down by the old packing-case and drew out the old papers, and the pens that had been unused so long. She took up the newspaper and scribbled all over the edges one of those stories in which the heart of Diogenes delighted. Its keynote was the very safe and comforting reflection that all love dies sooner or later; only that which has no existence, which the young dream of, lasts forever. It comforted her greatly that morning. After a few months she would be happy without him and almost forget this boy whom she had loved with a more yearning tenderness than her own little child.

"I will forget, I will forget everything, and live only in the present; then, soon, there will be no reason to forget, for this little love will fade away like the yearning for my monkey and the madness that looks so grotesque, and unreal now and which nothing could ever again bring back—nothing."

The margins of the newspaper were full to overflowing and she was already crossing it over in every direction, when a shadow fell across the sunlight that streamed in through the tent door.

Some coolie bringing the milk he was accustomed to sell there, she thought, as she looked up to see the figure of a man with his back turned to the entrance. The opening was so low that his head was not visible, but an elegant little black cane moved slowly backwards and forwards, and there was that in the cut of the black cloth coat and the hang of the trousers that carried her back from New Rush to that first meeting before the picture in Blair House. Soon the figure turned and Undine hardly knew what she expected to see, but it was only the very ugly face of a very black nigger that stuck itself in at the doorway.

"Have you done the shirts a girl brought here yesterday?" he asked in very good English and in a very leisurely and self-possessed manner. Evidently he had taken some Englishman, probably his master, as the model upon which to form himself. Undine brought him the shirts, which the swell nigger took with the extreme tips of his fingers, as though it were greatly derogatory to his dignity and he only submitted to a most painful necessity. Touching gracefully his woolless upper lip with the hand in which he held the cane, he said:

"If you want more work, I dare say you could get it if you come to our place—Mr. Albert Blair's."

The nigger rolled out the name very full and with evident satisfaction, at the same time holding out a five-shilling piece to Undine with an air that clearly evinced how greatly he scorned the performing of so trivial an action. He thought the ironing- woman was certainly half daft, or it might be drunk, for she stood in the tent door staring at him and never holding out her hand to receive the money. He was on the point of informing her of his opinion in very plain language when she said, "You can keep the money for yourself."

There was no doubt now as to the ironing-woman's daftness or drunkenness, for who gives five shillings for nothing? But the nigger no longer felt himself under the painful necessity of informing her of the fact, and, great as his scorn for the five-shilling piece had appeared to be, it quickly found its way into his waistcoat pocket. In reply to a question from Undine he proceeded to inform her where his master's house might be found, and wrapping up the shirts in a newspaper he had brought for the purpose, and tucking them under his arm, he walked off switching his black cane.

Near evening Undine too went out, but in an opposite direction, and forgetting today even to button down her tent door. There was not a shilling in the bottle nor a whole slice of bread in the box, yet she was not going to look for work now. She was going to Diogenes, but the walk seemed a weary long one; it had never seemed so long before. Her legs ached, her head ached, and sometimes she grew dizzy.

Diogenes was not in her tub today. She was greatly excited and the tub seemed to confine her. She was leaning against it and almost started to her feet when Undine appeared round the tent's corner.

"I've been so tired of waiting for you all these two days. I thought you would never come. Stoop down before the tub and shut your eyes tight and then look in and see what I've got for you," cried Diogenes, giving two gentle claps with her hands, for once a perfect child in her delight. Undine did as she was told and looked in, to see the tiny rose bush adorned with one deep-bosomed red rosebud.

"Isn't it beautiful? Isn't it beautiful?" said Diogenes, enthusiastically clasping her hands. "Pick it; it's for you. No—you must not pick it. I will—and fasten it in your hair just like it was in my dream. Oh, how beautiful!"

Undine put the iron pot down in Diogenes' lap, but Diogenes' fingers were so tremulous with gladness that she almost uprooted the rose bush before the flower was severed from the stem. "Now," she said, putting the old pot down at one side, "lay down your head and I will put it in."

Undine sat down beside her and put her head in Diogenes' lap, and the child did and undid the hair half a score of times before the flower was fixed to her satisfaction.

"Now turn round and look at me," she said, when all was done. But it was such a weary face that looked up at hers that Diogenes' face fell also.

"I had quite forgotten he went away this morn- morning ing, and you must be sorry, you've taken care of him so long," said Diogenes, who, in truth, for the last forty-eight hours had been gloriously oblivious of every existence save that of her wonderful rosebud.

Diogenes did not know what to say; so she resorted to dumb sympathy, which she did understand, and drew Undine's face very close to her and smoothed it with the palms of her little hands.

After a long quiet she said, "I love you better than anything, better even than my rose bush." It was only a child's way of comforting, those few words of love and that smoothing her cheek with her little hands. A child's way, yet by it she paid back more than all the good that had been brought to her.

"It is nice to lie here and rest, but I must go," said Undine, when the last rays of the sun were shining on the little green leaves of the rose bush, which stood just beyond the end of the tent where it could catch them.

"You are sick, too," said Diogenes, noticing how she leaned her hand against the tub to help herself in rising.

"Not sick, only tired. I have not been so tired for many years. I want to sleep for a long, long time. I shall be better then."

She smiled as she looked down into the earnest eyes that were fixed on her.

"Come again soon, very soon," said Diogenes, as Undine was going out of sight.

She did not answer, but turned round for a moment and looked back at her, still smiling. The rose had fallen out of her hair and she held it in her hand.

"You look just like you did in my dream," Diogenes said; but Undine did not hear her, for she had turned to go.

It may be that in the years to come Diogenes shall grow into a great, coarse, red woman as her mother was before her—the mother of many children, the wife of many husbands whom she may drop as easily as she does every hour the words that are not choice.

It may be—but there will come hours when the one pure and tender memory of her childhood will come back to her, and her children will wonder why she speaks so softly and the men why she has no oath to throw back at them. They would wonder if they knew it was only the picture of that summer evening at New Rush and the little slight figure standing at the tent corner with the red rosebud in its hand, and its great white kappie, and the yellow evening sunlight streaming over it from behind.

As Undine had said, she was tired, very tired; but instead of going home she turned slowly to that part of the camp to which her little squint-eyed guide had once conducted her.

She stopped when she came to the reed fence that encircled the home of the baby-faced golden-haired lady. She was on the veranda again this evening, but she was not alone now. Over her chair was leaning a man, whose head was bent so low over hers that the black beard mingled with the golden ripples on her forehead. They spoke very soft and low, and they did not notice Undine, for their backs were to her and their talk was very interesting. But a little boy, who sat behind them playing, now lifted his blue eyes to look at the woman on the other side of the hedge and caught sight of the bright rose she held. He slipped down from the veranda and stood before her.

"Give," he said, and held out imperiously one small hand.

Undine dropped the rose into it and turned to go back to her tent.

"You must come," whispered the dark-whiskered gentleman as he stooped low over the golden head. "Come if it is for only one short half hour. *You* may allow yourself to be robbed of all pleasure, but others must not be quite forgotten, you know; even if our claim to be considered is not *very* strong."

The lady smiled very softly and smoothed out the fringe on her sleeve with her little pink finger.

"Surely you have done enough in coming to such a place as this. You need not renounce the world *altogether*; you are too young to do penance yet"; and the gentleman's breath was warm on her cheek. Then she lifted her baby face up to his, and her eyes were just as they had been when she looked down at Undine, placid, smiling; there was no harm in them.

"I've been out two nights this week," she said, "and people might think it strange, you know. The doctor said he was much worse today, and he would be so angry if they told him."

It might have ended in her not going to the ball that night, but at that moment the child passed them with the bright flower in its hand.

"What a lovely flower!" said the mother, and she held out her hand for it; but the child clasped it tightly in his fist and held it close against his little breast.

It was only a moment's work for the gentleman to unclasp the little fingers and put the flower into the mother's hand. The child did not cry; he only pressed his little thin arched lips together and drooped the lids over the blue eyes with which he looked at them. He was only a baby: there was no sin in taking it. "You see the very gods have condescended to interfere in my behalf," whispered the gentleman. "This rose means that you are to go and wear it here tonight."

He lay it very softly on her breast and whispered words, so softly that only the ear in which they were spoken could catch them; and when the mother rose to go into the house she said, "Well just for one hour, just for one, you know."

And so she went to the ball that night and danced, the loveliest of all the women there, with that bright flower at her heart; and all praised her and looked at her.

And that night, alone, when the nigger who had been left to watch him had gone out to spend the five shillings, Albert Blair died.

XIX.
ALBERT BLAIR

"Vat jou goed en trek, Ferreira, Vat jou goed en trek; Swaar dra, swaar dra..." [1] whistled the swell nigger next morning as he walked, switching his cane, in the direction of Undine's tent.

Generally she rose early, but this morning she was sleeping late and so heavily that he had to knock two or three times at the tent pole before she came to unbutton the sail.

"Do you want any needlework?" asked the nigger, touching his hat quite respectfully, for, even with a salary of six pounds a month, five shillings are not to be despised.

Undine said she wanted no work.

The nigger looked disappointed. He had hoped she would take the work, and show as great an objection to accepting payment for black skirts as for ironing shirts.

[1] "Take your things and go, Ferreira, Take your things and go; Heavy to carry, heavy to carry..." These words are from the Afrikaans folk-song (lied) "*Jannie met die hoepelbeen, Ferreira*" (Johnny with the bandy leg, Ferreira)—perhaps the best known folk-song in South Africa. Ferreira is a not uncommon Afrikaner surname.

"You see, my master died last night, and Mrs. Blair wants her mourning quickly. Don't you think, if I was to bring some stuff now, you would be able to do it for her?"

There was no doubt today about the ironing-woman's daftness. She took no notice of his question, but said, after a pause, "What did your master die of?"

"Well, you see," replied the nigger, resting his hand on the head of his cane and leaning elegantly forward, "I don't just rightly know. He came here just to have a look at everything, and he took ill, something wrong inside, and the doctors they won't let him travel; and this six months he's been lying here, and they've been saying he was going to die, but he never did till last night."

Having got so far, the nigger turned round and looked across the road to see what it might be the ironing-woman saw that made her eyes look so strange. He could see nothing but just a blade or two of grass which had not yet been trodden down and which were heavy with the morning dew; so he looked at her again.

"When are they going to bury him?"

"Tomorrow morning. They've put him in a house in the yard; for Mrs. Blair she's frightened of ghosts."

There was nothing to be gained by wasting more words over her just now, so the nigger resumed his "Swaar dra, swaar dra," and, without touching his hat, turned away and walked jauntily whistling down the road.

Undine stood in the doorway and looked after him. There were sparrows hopping about at the tent-side, picking up crumbs and insects; and diggers passed with their sleeves rolled up above their elbows, walking briskly, whistling, some of them, for the morning air was fresh and made them feel that life, though it might mean small finds and hard work, was a pleasant thing and worth the having. Some of her children die every day, and Nature might go about forever in deep weeds and mourning if she took the trouble to lament for them; so she goes on smiling, though the best loved and the dearest have just gone—smiling, smiling, when our hearts are breaking. Why should the sky be clouded and the birds fly home hungry, because in one small tent a man lay stiff and white? Men whom women's hearts had yearned over died just so every week, and the world rocked on the same.

Undine slept heavily all day, a heavy sleep but troubled by many dreams; and when she woke the sun had long set. She went out to the barrel that stood at the back of the tent, and drained the last drop of water into the mug. She was thirsty, parched with thirst, but she felt no hunger. The slice of bread, very dry now, still lay upon the box unfinished.

She sat down on the side of her bed and held her head between her hands and tried to think, but her brain seemed very numb. After about an hour she stood up and went out, taking the road by which she had come yesterday evening. It was very dark, but she knew her way well.

The Compound was very quiet tonight. There was no one on the veranda, no light in the house. Only in the little tent at the back there was a light visible, and presently two men came out. The night was still and, though they spoke low, she could hear every word that passed:

"Put the candle and matches down, Jack, just there inside the door and button it down tight," said the first man. "I wonder they like leaving it alone like this without a soul in the place. Dogs might get in."

"No fear of that while this dog lies here," said the second. "If I was not with you, I expect you'd rather be pretty near anywhere than here; he'd think no more of tearing you than of growling, if you tried to go in there alone; he don't half like it as it is, for all that I've had the feeding of the beggar for the last six months. Down, Prince, down!"

The men passed close to where Undine stood.

"I tell you what, Jack," said the first, "that coffin was damned heavy. My shoulders ache."

"Charge it all in the bill," said the second with a laugh:

"Ten little nigger boys Fiddling over wine; One got so jolly drunk, And then there were nine, nine, nine."

Then they went out at the gate, and the Compound was silent once more.

By and by Undine went round and opened the gate and walked in.

"Prince, Prince, old boy," she called softly; for Prince had risen to his feet and uttered a low growl at the sound of approaching footsteps. "Prince, have you quite forgotten me?"

The dog did not leave his post, but when she came close to him he laid his head against her knee.

"Prince, Prince! Oh, Prince!"

He seemed to understand her, for he uttered a long low growl, and they crouched down together at the entrance. Is *he* listening for the sound of his master's breathing in the quiet tent? Or is it only *one* who remembers how they two waited and listened, long ago?

Only the heavy breathing of the dog and the quick low breath of the woman break the stillness and are heard loud and clear in the quiet night; but in the tent, in the tent, there is deadly stillness.

It was near midnight now, and in the street passenger-carts rumbled past, bearing home Toit's Pan visitors from the fast-closing houses of amusement.

Now she stood up and loosened the lower buttons that fastened down the canvas door. Stooping low, she went in, and the dog followed her, lying down close to the doorway and uttering a low short howl. Then it was quite silent in the tent, and very dark. Feeling her way along its side, her fingers touched at last the cold back of a chair, but that was not what she looked for; then the edge of a small table; then something lower than the table, long and narrow but with nothing inside. She felt that it was empty, so she moved on softly. Her hand was on the iron bedpost, then on the smooth sheet, and then on something cold—O, God—how cold!

She took the sheet down off his face, and the cheek of the living woman was pressed close to the cold face of the dead man. In his ear she whispered the wild words of love that to the living she would never utter—wild passionate words, the outpourings of a life's crushed-out love, the breaking forth of a fiercely suppressed passion. And the dead man lies so still; he does not send her from him; he does not silence her; he understands her now; he loves her now. She will see his face once more before it goes, and then she will creep close to him, and lie there, and never leave him.

In its place near the door she found the glass candlestick and matches, and when she had struck a light she came and stood with it in her hand at the bed's foot till her eyes had grown accustomed to it; then she looked up.

It was a calm white face that lay there above the sternly folded arms—a calm white face with the old smile, half scornful, half defiant, on the delicate arched lips.

The old face! What use to cry aloud to it! Mad, mad, and fool! Was there room in those sternly folded arms for her! He had lived alone and self-sufficient; he had died alone. There was no room for her now.

With a cry, as of one whose last hope has passed away, she let the light fall upon the floor, and the glass broke into a thousand fragments. But she stayed at the bed's foot till the grey light glimmered through the canvas. Then she crept out and left him.

A few hours afterwards, when all New Rush was astir again, the young wife came in to see her husband for the last time. She had never looked so lovely as that day in her flowing crape, with the great tears of fear in her baby eyes when they told her to stoop down and kiss him.

"I cannot, I cannot," she cried; "I am so afraid." And as she turned to go out, the trailing crape rolled the broken glass upon the floor.

That was all that told of last night's watch.

XX.
ALONE WITH THE STARS

WATER! Water!

She had slept again all day, and now that she awoke it was dark, and she was parched with thirst and there was no water—none in the barrel, none in the jug; her tongue clave to the roof of her mouth and her veins seemed scorched by liquid fire. She shook the barrel fiercely in her anger and tried to draw the tap out with her teeth. There must be some water in it, if only one could get it; it seemed to her some cruel living thing withholding life from her; and when she found she could do nothing she ran round and round the tent in the vain hope of growing cool. In her delirium it seemed that behind her a whole host of small hideous beings followed, howling—old women with long canine teeth that touched their breasts, old men with hunchbacks and little twinkling eyes which they closed tight and then opened suddenly: before, behind, they followed her; at every side they pressed her; and her thirst grew greater, till her tongue refused to move and keep them off by words.

"Water, water, water!" was all she could murmur. And at last, as if in answer to her cry, water came. The great clouds that had made the night so dark burst, and the great torrent poured down on the earth. In an instant the heavy canvas sails were drenched, and she knelt down eagerly, holding them in both hands and sucking them. Then she lay down and let the rain fall on her till the fever left her and a great shivering seized her.

She went into her tent and climbed into the box, but her hands seemed powerless to undo her wet clothes, so she drew the blanket over her and lay there till morning.

"Mother," said the children of the Dutchwoman opposite—"mother, perhaps some wicked man has been to kill the Englishwoman in the little tent. Three days the sail is hanging loose, but we never see her coming out or doing ironing. We think she must be dead."

"Nonsense!" said the mother. "Don't you have anything to do with her; she's a bad woman."

"How do you know that?" asked her husband, who sat at the door, smoking his pipe.

"Because I asked her the other day if the man who lived with her was her husband, and she said no. And I asked her if he was any relation of hers, and she said no. So she must be bad," said the wife.

Nevertheless, when her work was done, curiosity led the dame over to the Englishwoman's tent. She looked in at the door and at first thought there was nothing but the three packing-cases in the tent; then, in the farthest of these, which lay bottom downwards, she noticed the purple blanket move, and went up to it.

"You are very sick," said the Dutchwoman in English, better than Boers generally speak.

Undine opened her eyes, but did not answer.

"You are very sick," repeated the Dutchwoman. "What is your name?"

"Undine, Undine Bock," said Undine, slowly, as though puzzled to remember what it really was, and going back to the old name of her childhood.

"Great heavens!" said the Dutchwoman. "Do you remember me—Sannie Muller?"

"Yes," said Undine; but her eyes had closed again.

"Can I do anything for you?" Sannie asked with some real kindness in her voice, as the memory came to her of the little schoolmate who, in company with her monkey, had been first and foremost in all evil and forever in disgrace.

"No, thank you," said Undine.

But the woman remained sitting by her till it grew dark; then she lit a candle and stood at her side, saying as she did so: "I will come again during the night and see you."

"Mother," asked the little child who had been waiting for her in the road, as she trotted along at her side, "is the Englishwoman very sick?"

"Yes," said the mother. "She will be dead in the morning."

The Dutchwoman had worked hard all day, and when once she fell asleep she did not awake.

But the little tent had another visitor that night.

Not long after the Dutchwoman left, a great, rough curly head pushed itself in at the door, sniffed for a moment, and then four black paws carried it up to the side of the box. Undine was roused by a soft warm touch on her hand and when she opened her eyes the rough old face was close above hers, looking down at her. Her mind was too confused and dull for his presence there to cause her even the vaguest wonder. She only moved her fingers feebly and called his name, "Prince, Prince."

He stepped over the low side of the packing-case and lay down across her feet, with his head turned to one side so that he could watch her as he lay there.

A very quiet sleep followed, and Undine did not know when the candle dropped into the bottle, or when Prince moved higher up so that his head rested on her breast. She knew nothing till she woke at one o'clock. Then she raised herself a little on her elbow, looked round, and fell back heavily again on her pillow.

The racking pain, the fever, the dull confusion of brain, all had vanished. Free from pain, calm and clear as she had never felt before, she lay there, yet cold, strangely cold. What did it mean, this strange feeling? She lay wondering, thinking, with her hands folded on the dog's black head. Then the truth came to her suddenly.

Death—only that, nothing more. What she had longed and prayed for; what she had looked for in the muddy pool; what she had sighed for in days of emptiness—it had come at last.

Again she raised herself and again fell back heavily upon the pillow. "Not death, not death!" she said, "not death!—anything else—death is too horrible and I, I am so young, so young to die!"

What was the use of crying out! She only grew stiffer and colder and her breath came slow and heavy in the closed tent. She would leave it and go out into the starlight, she would be braver there. The great horror that was upon her gave her strength, and she pushed the dog from her and crept slowly over the side of the low box. There she lay long, and then again, inch by inch, crawling on hands and knees, she reached the doorway. The skirting that crossed it, three inches high, was hard to pass, and again she lay still; but when she turned her head and caught sight of clear starlight outside, she crept on once more. Still on her hands and knees, and falling sometimes with her face into the dust, she gained at last one of the low gravel-heaps [1] and lay down on its side.

[1] Débris.

She looked up at the old stars that she had looked up to and loved from her childhood as other men love their friends of flesh and blood—the dear old stars that had shed their light on the thatched roofs and stone walls of the old farm on the Karoo; that had looked in at the window of the little whitewashed room and on the leaves of the small brown Testament and the little child who cried and prayed there; the same and yet, tonight, looking so strange and new to her. Over the tumult and agony that reigned within, they spoke a great peace, and she lay still and watched them.

'Twas one of the gorgeous nights when the sky, shooting light from a million points, overwhelms and silences us; and the little circle of our life, that has seemed to fill all creation, sinks to its proper size—a shadow, a breath of wind that, being or not being, matters not.

High over her head was one great blue star that gave a steady and unflickering light. At this she looked with dark wide-open eyes till it seemed to speak to her as clearly as the priest speaks who stands at the bedside of the dying with bread and wine, reproof and blessing, whereby he hopes to help the soul in its last struggles among the waters.

"Is death so horrible and ghastly to you?" said the star, "so ghastly that even the pain and suffering and despair that are in life grow beautiful in your eyes? I am only your brother," said the star, "a few million years older than you, and I know nothing; but I have seen some things—a few.

I have seen the sun pour forth his light and heat as a great heart pours its life-blood for others. I have seen it fall on a world dead and silent, and awake it; till in place of death there was life, and for silence sound and ceaseless change. I have seen a world find birth through that light, even those strange and tiny creatures [1] who deep at the floor of the sea have formed their graves and a new land; the waves have rolled back from it and the land that is built from their skeletons has become tree and grass and a million forms of life; on these other creatures have lived; and these again have died that others might have life; and at last man has come, to bring one of whom from the shapeless germ in which he lies plants innumerable die, and his very next of kin are sacrified that he may grow and be. I have looked long and carefully," said the star, "and I have seen that the thing which you call death is the father of all life and beauty. Till life goes, till blood flows, no higher life can come. There is nothing added to Nature, nothing taken from her. She has only so much in her hand, and with that she must do all things. Would she build better, she must pull down first; would she raise a new world, an old must sink; would she double a flower, the seed of the single must go; and to make a man a million million forms have been and are not.

[1] Coral.

"Without death there is no change, without change no life; without the shedding of blood no good thing.

"If what you fear in the death that is upon you is not change but a fearful endless silence and annihilation, then take comfort," said the star; "I have been young and now am old; I have seen great ebbs and great flows, and myriad never-ending changes; but such death as you dream of I have nowhere seen. Nature is too poor to lose, too poor to let rest; her work is not yet done; she has other things to make.

"Mark you well, I know nothing," said the star; "and what you are, or I am, or the gravel is on which you lie, I cannot tell, and what we mean I cannot tell; only that which I have seen I speak of.

"The stump now burning at your side, it was a great brown lifeless stump an hour or two ago, now a lurid glowing mass shooting out flames and heat, cracking and changing every moment. It will be a small heap of ashes soon, but the light and heat were in it before the match touched it, and I know they are not lost, only doing other work in other forms.

"I have been young and now am old," said the star; "yet if I should say I have seen death as you fear it, I should lie. Change I have seen and desolation, but no death. Take comfort."

And she was comforted and looked upwards with her arms folded and almost a smile on her lips.

For, as in our hours of sin and weakness, we weep because the great ever-changing, many-waved current on which we find ourselves will flow on just the same when our small wave has spent itself, so, in our moments of sight and strength, a joy, calm and mighty, comes to us when we see that the great current will flow on uninjured, unchanged by our loss, in its deathless progress.

She lay still and was comforted. And what if the star never spoke, and only her own thoughts were thrown back to her! If it be to a bedside with priest, wafer, and book, or to a gravel-heap under the stars, that peace and strength come, are they not the children of the soul, and no outcome of wafer, priest, or star? Though blessed be all three if they can call them forth in the hour of that battle the last and strongest.

She rested till it seemed as though a mist were creeping over the brilliant night sky, and then as though the smoke from the fire passed before her eyes. She raised her hands slowly as though to wave it from her; but it grew darker, and one by one the stars vanished. Then she knew that it was the shadow of death that lay between her and them.

Slowly she turned away her head, and even in that darkness could see lying between the two great stones the stump, now coal from end to end with blood-red cracks upon its surface.

The cold was growing greater, so she crept a little nearer the coal and lay with her face to it.

Was it because the glowing light, seen through the mist, brought back a night of long ago, that she heard in the dim delicious confusion the voice that had called her so tenderly under the red lamplight in the little hall?

"My little girl, my own little girl—Undine," it said over and over, and the soft tears of gladness filled her eyes, and in delicious dreamy darkness it seemed as though his arms were close around her.

Presently the moon rose and looked over the ridge of the tent into the little yard among the gravel-heaps. The glowing stump had burnt out and gone to ashes between the great round stones.

Before them, in her little purple print, with her feet crossed and her head resting on one arm, lay Undine.

Her white kappie lay near her and cast a grotesque shadow, like a man's face with long nose and chin; and the light glistened on her soft brown hair.

There was nothing else to be seen in the little yard.

THE END

www.ingramcontent.com/pod-product-compliance
Lightning Source LLC
LaVergne TN
LVHW041103080826
845145LV00007B/1676

9781473322431